NOT EVERY GIRL

BY JANE MCGARRY

Not Every Girl
by Jane McGarry
Published by JM Books

This is a work of fiction. Names, places, characters, and events are fictitious in every regard. Any similarities to actual events and persons, living or dead, are purely coincidental. Any trademarks, service marks, product names, or named features are assumed to be the property of their respective owners, and are used only for reference. There is no implied endorsement if any of these terms are used. Except for review purposes, the reproduction of this book in whole or part, electronically or mechanically, constitutes a copyright violation.

NOT EVERY GIRL
Copyright © 2022 JANE MCGARRY
ISBN 978-1-7365884-3-7
Cover Art Designed by FirdaGraphic

To D and R who inspire me every day.

1

My mother is going to be angry at me. Again.

Granted, it is unwise to take my eyes off Lydia even for a moment. Now, I will be subject to yet another reprimand, one where my training with the squires is the culprit. Mother never misses an opportunity to blame that for everything wrong with my life.

A brisk breeze whips strands of hair into my eyes and mouth. I brush them away impatiently along with the dust kicked up from the dry road. It swirls around my feet like a swarm of angry bees, a reflection of my ill-tempered mood. The thought of Puck's amusement does little to improve my irritation. After all, he was with me when I lost my sister, but he is not out here traipsing toward the city walls. No. He is at the lesson. The one I am now missing. He knows my sparring days are numbered, knows how the frustration eats away at me. A little sympathy would have been nice.

Taking orders from a miniature monarch all morning was maddening. I was about ready to tell her exactly where she could stick her crown. Luckily for me, Lydia is merely a pretend princess with a circlet of daisies, not jewels. She is four, a precocious four as my father always points out. All about her is bright and fair, from her coloring to her charismatic personality. Lydia enchants anyone she meets in an instant, her winning attributes magnifying all that is plain and ordinary about me. In her young mind, if she grows up and marries a prince, she is guaranteed a euphoric, problem-free existence.

The past few hours were a perfect example of her royal charade. First she had romped through the wildflowers, a host of windblown seeds dancing around her like a troupe of little fairies. Curtseying to imaginary guests was next, her face half hidden behind her substitute fan, a large hydrangea leaf, before she grandly settled on a fallen log, a radiant blossom on its gnarled hull, to hold court. At last, when my backside was sufficiently numb from the hard ground, it was my turn to issue a command to head home. On the way, we ran into Puck, who distracted me with those wooden swords. Footwork sequences and parries soon had my full attention. One second of not watching my sister and off she went.

I scan ahead for any sign of Lydia, but there is just one figure on the dusty road. Lettie, the widow of an old dairy farmer, shuffles toward me. At the sight of me, her face breaks into a semi-toothless grin. The folds of skin around her cheeks and neck hang so loosely on her jaw, they appear ready to slip off altogether. She is hunched with age, her right leg dragging behind like an afterthought.

"Ah, the second beautiful Davenport girl to cross my path," she says in a raspy, thin voice. Word has always been she smokes her husband's pipe at night, a theory bolstered by her chronic, hacking cough and not-so-faint tobacco aroma.

"Oh good. You've seen Lydia."

"Just a flat minute ago. Running toward our city's walls. Chasing a black cat." She points behind with a bony finger, misshapen with time to a crooked hook. It is a marvel her filmy eyes can discern anything at all.

"Now hurry and catch her. I sense she is heading for big trouble," Lettie says.

Yes, she excels at that.

A smaller path converges with mine on the right. My sister Ellen hurries along it in my direction. Her brown hair bounces on her slight shoulders with each purposeful step. Puck must have sent her to help, one point in his favor at least. Ellen is the family member I relate to the most. Unlike my other sisters, she has more thoughts in her head than boys and love. She is a voracious reader, so her head is filled with more important topics. I stop, wait for her to catch up, and explain the situation. She falls in next to me without a word. Lydia's antics are nothing new.

The sun plays peek-a-boo with the puffy clouds, our shadows melting in and out of view. Soon we come through the main gate of Adelina, but there's no sign of my wayward sister. A gatekeeper leans back on a chair against the wall. Squat and round in the bright red watchman's livery, he resembles a giant apple. A bald head with a grizzled face is punctuated by a round, red nose. His eyelids flutter like lethargic wings in an effort to remain open. Not exactly the level of attentiveness you would like to see in someone who is tasked with the security of Stewartsland's largest city.

"Excuse me, have you seen a small girl with blond curls and a crown of flowers?"

He is so unresponsive at first I wonder if he is deaf. Then, slowly he lowers the front legs of the chair down to the ground and rubs his chin. "I can't say for sure, but I think she may have run off over there." He nods toward the left.

"You *think* she *may* have? Isn't your job to know all this gate's comings and goings to keep our city safe?" I huff.

Ellen grabs my arm, pulls me away before the nature of my remarks settles into his thick head.

"Shush," she whispers. "Don't let your big mouth start one of your fights. Finding Lydia is enough trouble. Concentrate on that."

She is right of course. Ellen is by far the smartest in our family and smarter than most adults I know as well. Though she is five years younger than I, she is far more level-headed. My tendency to act and speak without thinking is legendary—a habit I have not managed to outgrow in my almost seventeen years. Better to heed Ellen's advice.

I peek over my shoulder to check the guard, hoping he is not offended enough to bother with us further. He already reclines on the chair to his former position, unfazed by the whole encounter. After a few deep breaths to clear my head, I decide on the two most likely possibilities for Lydia's whereabouts.

"Ellen, go to the city square by the markets and check around by the palace entrance."

This is a place that Lydia holds in particular awe. She could spend hours watching the merchants hawk their wares; enjoying how the colorful fabrics and exotic smells radiate amid the bustling crowd. Then there are the people who go in and out of the main palace entry. Lydia speculates reverently on their business, imagining all sorts of importance and intrigue.

Meanwhile, I head off to search around the back of the castle. One of Lydia's other favorite pastimes is climbing trees and trying to peer over the wall into the royal gardens. Mind you, the gardens abutting the castle walls are at the far end of the property and are rarely, if ever, occupied. And the trees aren't tall enough to see over anyway. But, every once in a while, the faint tinkle of music or the chatter of people farther into the grounds can be heard. This hint of royal life always sends Lydia into raptures and provides her much fodder for her make-believe games.

And she is not the only one in our family entranced by the royals. My two older sisters, Jayne and Anne, are equally infatuated, particularly with two of them. We were lucky enough to have had until recently, not one, but two eligible princes in our kingdom of Stewartsland: Prince Harold, the heir to the throne, and Prince Liam—jokingly referred to as "the spare to the throne." About a year ago, King William announced it was time for Prince Harold to take a bride.

Oh, the frenzy this unleashed. Hopeful ladies jockeyed for position in an attempt to win Prince Harold's favor, during which time Prince Liam was forgotten. He should be getting his due now though, after the announcement of Prince Harold's betrothal. Of course, this news left a trail of broken hearts and bruised egos throughout the young females of the court. However, after a short regrouping, I feel sure they will settle for the consolation prize—or should I say consolation prince.

In the meadow earlier, I teased Lydia about Prince Harold no longer being available.

"That's all right, Livy, I can marry Prince Liam instead. He is much more handsomer anyway. Don't you think?"

"It's just *handsome*, not *handsomer*, and I guess it depends upon your taste in men." I shrugged.

Our princes are, in fact, quite opposite in looks. Prince Harold is fair like his mother, Queen Helen; Prince Liam has the darker coloring of King William. In my opinion, though, their differences extended far beyond their appearances. In fact, fair and dark also describes their personalities from what I have seen.

Shrill cries of a crow rouse me from my musings. I shake off all other thoughts and focus on finding my sister.

It is a fair walk to get to the back of the castle. The walls of the city wrap around in this general direction as well. A dense swath of unused terrain fills in the space between the two barriers. Birds flit among the many trees, blurs of brown and grey. Untamed clumps of bushes encroach on the overgrown path. My toes catch on hidden rocks and trip up my footing. I move next to the castle wall, use it to steady myself. In this forsaken place, the grey stone, though imposing in height, is in relative disrepair.

I mentioned this once to my father, who is the King's Master of Arms, because I found it to be somewhat lax where security is concerned. He agreed, but after many years of peace, precautions routinely performed in wartime are now neglected. According to him, the King would have to request the wall be repaired, and to this point he had not. I believed my father's position entitled him to initiate the repairs if he saw fit.

We had a lengthy discussion, each expressing a differing point of view. Finally, my father mused that perhaps repairing the walls would be a good job for the squires to tackle. Whether he was serious or not, I do not know, because I quickly dropped the subject. The last thing I needed was my class angry at me for getting them stuck with such an awful assignment.

Up ahead I hear Lydia shriek with delight. "Here kitty...c'mere kitty."

Wonderful.

My little sister has a penchant for collecting stray animals. Her menagerie includes several cats, a duck, a frog, a goat, and most recently a new family of field mice, although their odds are pretty slim given all the cats. Now she has her eye on this particular cat to join the group.

I round a corner and spot her on her hands and knees, daisies still in place. She crawls toward a fat, black cat. The animal faces Lydia, his back arched, ears flat to his head. Every forward move Lydia makes causes him to skittishly recoil until he is flush against the castle wall. With nowhere left to go, he hisses, baring his sharp teeth. Lydia freezes in her tracks.

Time to interrupt this impasse.

"Lydia, get over here this instant! Mother is going to have both our heads if we don't get home now!"

Startled by my voice, she jumps, and the cat, spooked by Lydia's sudden movement, runs through a small opening carved out between some fallen stones at the wall's base.

"Livy, you fool! You scared Midnight." She lunges toward the spot where the cat disappeared.

Midnight? Fabulous, she already named him. Now I will have to bring her home in a hysterical fit over this blasted cat. Why does she always get into this type of trouble on my watch? I advance on her, prepared for the tantrum sure to ensue. But, to my utter disbelief, she lies on her belly in an attempt to squeeze herself through the hole. My mouth just starts to form the shout, *"No!"* when, with a small thrust, she vanishes under the wall.

Uh-oh!

This is not good. I pray no one is near this garden today. All I need is for the King to find out that my sister is loose on his grounds, especially since he is, in essence, my father's master.

I race over and crouch down by the hole. The mortar has separated from the stones, falling away piece by piece over time, no doubt dug out by some industrious creature. The cavity this has formed causes the stones above to sag down like wet clothes on a line. Eventually, when the gap widens, the upper part of the wall will collapse from lack of support. At the moment, however, there is a breach just big enough for a small animal to fit through or, unluckily for me, a four-year-old girl.

Kneeling down, I bend my head to the opening. From my vantage point, only scattered rocks and grass are visible on the other side. No Lydia or cat in sight. Perhaps she will come back on her own accord. Minutes pass, the seconds ticking by loudly in my head. There is an unusual hush over everything, as if the world holds its breath in anticipation with me. Hopefully, the silence indicates there is no one anywhere in this general vicinity to discover Lydia before I can rein her in.

Finally, I am left with no choice but to call for her.

"Lydia," I rasp in a harsh whisper, "get back here *this* minute!"

No reply.

I push on the stones around the edges of the hole; some more crumble off and I toss them impatiently aside. The space is bigger, but it is questionable whether I can fit through it or not. Goodness knows, I don't want to have to find out.

"LY-DI-A!" I cough, choking on the chalk-like powder my excavation has unearthed.

Still no reply.

How far into the gardens could she possibly have wandered?

This is a frightening thought. Once inside, Lydia could find all sorts of ways to cause the maximum amount of trouble. She is apt to chase the blasted cat all the way up to the King's throne, for goodness sake. Or she could realize where she is, forget the cat, and start to explore. Lydia would love nothing more than to play princess in a real castle.

Suddenly, a commotion of running feet and the familiar sound of clinking armor rings in my ears. Lydia's frightened voice carries across the air. It cries one single word and my blood freezes in my veins.

"Help!"

All my anger evaporates. My sole objective is to get to her. I lie on my stomach, stick my arms through the hole and wrench through to my waist, before my hips get stuck. In an effort to break free, I wriggle them back and forth. Jagged rocks gouge into my sides like a hundred daggers. With the ground as leverage, I dig my elbows into the dirt and pull with all my might. The stones around my body give way with a puff of dust as I burst through. Behind me, the wall buckles, then collapses with a loud crash. I spring onto my hands and knees frantic to locate Lydia. Her little legs stand a few feet in front of me. When I make a move in her direction, the tip of a sword touches my neck.

"Slowly, my lady, get up slowly," commands the person attached to the weapon. Both his size and voice are imposing. They leave no room for debate.

Cautiously, I rise and see Lydia, my tiny sweet Lydia, encircled by several enormous palace guards, their swords pointed at her.

"Lower your weapons. She is a child!" I order.

"And are you the person responsible for her?"

"Yes, I am her older sister." I still have not dared to look him in the eye.

"Uh-huh. And with the wisdom of your years, you thought it would be a good idea to trespass in the royal gardens?"

His voice is harsh and I sense not particularly open to explanations. By his tone and the fact no one else has spoken, it is easy to identify him as the leader of this unit—a group that must not see a lot of conflict and is overeager for some action right about now.

"We didn't mean to trespass. She was chasing a cat and…"

"A cat?" he interrupts, incredulous.

In my head, I realize how ridiculous the whole story will sound. But I blurt out the account because—well, that's what I do when I am nervous. Some might call it my trademark.

"Yes, a cat. She's four. She saw a cute cat. She chased it. It went under the wall so she followed. Is this so difficult to believe?" My tone is snottier than I intend. But there is another feeling starting to bubble up in my chest— annoyance. How can these men be so hostile toward two unarmed girls? I cannot imagine two less threatening figures.

I take a deep breath and steal a glance at Lydia. She trembles, her small eyes brimming with tears.

"Well, we take trespassing seriously, whatever the reason for it. We will have to see what the jailer says about all of this," the guard sneers, a hint of glee in his tone.

"The jailer? Over a four-year-old and a cat?"

Lydia begins to wail outright.

"Please," I beg, "let me at least go over and comfort her. She's terrified."

"Well, she should be," he states matter-of-factly. "You have both broken the law."

Is he serious about pursuing this course? Surely there are more important jobs to occupy his time and attention. And besides, the jailer wouldn't possibly lock us up. Right? He has real criminals who committed real crimes to take care of, not this petty nonsense.

Lydia weeps louder and I take a step toward her. The guard grabs my arm, wrenching me back. "Stay where you are, Miss, if you know what is good for you!"

"Let go of me this instant!" I yank my arm away.

"That's it." He picks me up like a sack of potatoes and throws me over his shoulder. "Get her," he motions to another guard, who scoops up Lydia.

I can't believe any of this is happening. My mind is racing with a thousand different thoughts. What should I do? How can I get out of this without my parents finding out? Where exactly is the jailer? We are an eruption of flailing limbs and indignant screams as they carry us away.

Without warning, a figure steps out from behind some high bushes to our right.

"I thank you, Lieutenant," a confident, smooth voice says, "for your dutiful service in this matter. However, I think I can handle things from here."

In an instant, all the guards fall to a knee while my sister and I are dropped rather unceremoniously at the figure's feet. Sprawled out in the grass, I peer up, curious to see who has come to our rescue.

There stands Prince Liam, a sly smile on his face, and propped in the crook of his arm, being stroked by his royal hand, is that blasted cat.

For a moment everyone is silent—the guards with indecision, Lydia and I with astonishment, and Prince Liam…well, I am not sure, but his smirk indicates he rather enjoys everyone's reactions.

"Sire," says the leader, with little hesitation, "we do not know who these intruders are. I would not want to expose you to unnecessary danger."

I keep my head down to prevent anyone from seeing my eyes roll. This guy enjoys drama. I now face a tough choice. Do I identify myself or not? The knowledge that my father is the superior of these guards may change their behavior considerably. However, this incident may also reflect poorly on him, and I would not want to be the cause of that.

Probably better to remove ourselves from this situation anonymously. In all likelihood, Liam will not recognize us. He has never set eyes on Lydia, and the only time he saw me was when my older sisters and I attended Prince Harold's engagement ball earlier this year, and I doubt he even remembers.

Toward the beginning of the evening, we were briefly presented to the royal family where they sat together on a dais. My father introduced each of us by name, and we curtseyed. It was not a particularly memorable occasion except that while the King, the Queen, and Prince Harold all gave us respectful attention, Prince Liam just stared off into the distance, as if bored by the whole affair. At the time, it struck me as quite rude.

Since he barely glanced my way when my looks were at their best, the chance he will recognize my disheveled state after crawling under a wall and being dropped on the ground is slim.

"Nevertheless, I think I am perfectly capable of dealing with *these* particular intruders myself. You may go," the Prince commands.

The guards all scurry away like obedient little mice. A spiteful shower of dirt sprays my face as the leader passes me. He walks around the bushes, then stops to ensure he is still within earshot of the Prince.

Lydia and I arise as well, my head bowed more out of concealment than deference. It strikes me how Jayne and Anne have made a career out of trying to maneuver into the Princes' circles at any social event. They consider just standing on the fringe of their crowd a triumph of magnificent proportion. Now, here was Prince Liam not two feet in front of me.

Lydia squeals, "Oh! Midnight! You found him!" She dashes at the Prince to retrieve her cat.

"Lydia!" Shocked by the lack of propriety, I let her name slip through my lips, unbidden. Hopefully, I did not just give our identities away. Prince Liam merely laughs, kneels down to her level, and hands off the cat.

She sits down on a nearby bench stroking and rocking the cat like a baby. The cat, too squeezed to move and in completely unfamiliar territory, lies in her arms with an expression of resigned tolerance. "Don't worry, Midnight, we will have you home soon," she coos.

Prince Liam and I face each other in awkward silence. A cardinal trills its guttural song in the distance. Errant dandelion seeds float about like confetti on each small gust of wind. If there is a protocol for interacting with royalty when you have trespassed on their property, I am unsure what it is. I feel his keen eyes on me, burning like the sun's rays concentrated through the lens of a magnifying glass, but I remain mute, staring at the ground.

Snatches of a conversation with my mother float around my mind, a tugging thought of her instructions that one speaks to royalty only when she is specifically addressed. Yes, through the foggy swirls of recollection I hear her voice drilling this fact into my head. She did so for days before we attended the royal ball, worried that I would utter something inappropriately. On the one hand, this instruction is helpful because it means I don't need to say anything; but on the other, the quiet air, charged and heavy, threatens to collapse my will with every second.

What should I do if he never says anything? How long could I be expected to stand here? I want to blurt out the whole story. It wells up in my throat like lava ready to erupt regardless of my wishes.

"I take it you are sisters?" the Prince finally says.

"Yes," I answer, then bite my lip to cut off the spate of words ready to spew out of my mouth. I level my eyes with his chin.

"And your cat inadvertently got into the garden?" he asks after a moment of consideration.

"Not exactly…" I squeak out and concentrate on the shadow of dark stubble just barely visible on his jaw, which sets off his full lips. His black wavy hair falls to his shoulders, framing a solid physique.

I glance sideways at Lydia. How has she managed to stay quiet so long? Lost in her cat euphoria, I imagine.

"Not exactly?"

"Technically, it's not our cat."

"Yes he is," contradicts Lydia.

Ah, so she is listening.

"At least, I want him to be," she adds sheepishly.

While the Prince muses over this information, I take a quick moment to assess the surroundings a little better. I need to get us out of here. Fast. The unpruned bushes and rusty benches imply this is not a popular space. Just our luck to find it occupied today. Directly ahead of me, Lydia's seat backs up to a stone wall. On my left is an orchard of apple trees numbering about five rows across, running deeply into the property. To my right are tall bushes, easily twice the height of Prince Liam; they form a screen against whatever may lie behind. I can still discern the shadow of the guard, who eavesdrops on this entire conversation. Unfortunately, this appears to be the lone way out of where we are as well.

I push some hair out of my face, and dirt flutters to the ground like snowflakes. My dress has been torn from hem to knee. It sits on my body like a crooked picture frame. Discreetly, I attempt to brush some of the grime off and straighten the garment out. Lydia, naturally, is no worse for wear; the only hint of anything amiss on her is a slightly skewed crown of flowers.

"So let me see if I understand," the Prince begins sternly to Lydia. "You saw the cat and chased him. He ran under the wall, at which point you decided to trespass on royal property to catch him, and broke the wall in the process."

"Yes," says Lydia until the words *trespass* and *broke* dawn on her. Confused and unsure, her eyes threaten to fill up with tears again.

"Technically," I interject, "the wall was already broken. I mean there was a hole big enough for a cat…and a four-year-old." I gesture toward Lydia and continue, "I did knock some more stones loose but this would have happened eventually anyway from erosion and neglect."

Shut up, Olivia!

"If you ask me, a breach in this wall, no matter how small, is a security risk. Technically, your anger should be directed at whoever's job it is to inspect the wall to see if it is in good condition."

Shut up now!

"I mean the whole fact we could get in here in the first place should be troubling to you. Technically, you should not be blaming this on two defenseless girls."

I cringe at this last remark since I am far from a "defenseless" girl, but at least my mouth has ceased blurting.

Prince Liam says nothing. Is he angry at my outburst? I finally glance into his eyes. Instantly, their color entrances me. In the daylight, they are a striking icy blue—a color you imagine can exist only in a pristine mountain lake. They are mesmerizing, and for a moment I feel like I have been frozen in the grips of a spell. My senses abandon me. Until I realize he is speaking to me, amused interest on his face.

"Well, I daresay, you do give your opinion boldly to your Prince, Miss Davenport."

Uh-oh!

"Yes, I do recognize you as Sir Jack's daughters," he admits, "although, I have not had the pleasure of making this young lady's acquaintance."

He crosses to Lydia and offers his hand. Once her tiny fingers are in his, he raises them to his lips. Lydia just stares at him awestruck. Even if Prince Liam feels, for some reason, that this encounter is not worth mentioning to my father, Lydia will *never* be able to keep her hand-kissing a secret.

A gentle stroke of his hand has her flower crown back in perfect alignment as he sits beside her. "Now tell me how you found this beautiful cat?" He leans down to her, eyes attentive, as if he has all the time in the world. Patiently, he listens to her story, then to her entire roster of animals.

"You know, Miss Lydia, I have a number of pets as well. Do you know which one is my favorite?" She shakes her head, her eyes round as saucers, as he continues, "My favorite is my horse, Hector. You must come and visit me at the stables one day and we can ride out together. That would be a fun afternoon."

Poor Lydia. She hangs on every word with no idea how so much of court life revolves around these petty little promises; ones which the promiser has no intention of keeping. The court is rife with such self-aggrandizing fops who say whatever is convenient at the time to make themselves appear significant. Granted, Prince Liam is already significant, but I suppose it is ingrained in them since birth or something.

All I want is to get out of the palace properties and start on our way home. Since I can only imagine how horrified our parents will be, I can use the walk to determine how to put the best possible spin on this escapade. Lydia will need rehearsal time for our version of the event.

"Your Highness, we are so sorry to have disturbed you. If you would kindly have us escorted out, you can get back to…um…whatever it was you were doing before we so rudely interrupted you." I get a sour face from Lydia, as if I just canceled Christmas.

"Of course. I will show you the proper gate out myself." He rises and adds coyly, "In the future, you should consider *entering* from this gate as well."

We follow him around the tall bushes where the guard leader tries to seem like he was busy with some task other than listening to everything that unfolded. My knowing glare tells him he is unsuccessful. The area is set up with a number of different archery targets of various degrees of difficulty suspended from tree branches. Each is pierced with an arrow or two, their colorful feathers bright against the shafts. A half-full quiver leans against a tree next to a large bow. Not your ordinary weapons, I note; the magnificence of their craftsmanship and stunning gilt work can only mean they belong to Prince Liam.

More picturesque gardens unfold before us. Stone paths positioned in crisp geometric patterns traverse the bright emerald grass. An elaborate fountain anchors the scene. At least fifteen feet high, it depicts Poseidon, enormous trident in hand, presiding over a court of mermaids. Water cascades over all the figures, creating tiny rainbows that dance in the spray. On our right, a large koi pond comes into view with fish darting just beneath the surface like bright orange jewels. In my life, I never imagined such tranquil beauty.

When we pass a tennis lawn and bowling green situated among meticulously manicured hedges, Prince Liam points to another large contingent of bushes across the way.

"Do you see that, Miss Lydia? It is a garden maze. One day soon, you and I will have a fine afternoon playing hide-

and-seek in it." Lydia jumps and claps her hands as best she can with Midnight still in her grip.

Really?

Now he has promised her two different, extremely special things. Her young mind will not realize he says these things to make himself feel important. She will be devastated when these events do not come to fruition. Clearly, dealing with children is not Prince Liam's strong suit. I wish he would just be quiet.

A staircase leads us to a long open hallway. I hear Lydia inhale at the sight of the high ceilings adorned with lavish murals and the large mullioned windows lining the sides. Ahead of us is an archway crossed by an intricate wrought iron gate. Beyond it, I can make out two guards standing on either side. Finally — the way out.

"And your sister Jayne, she was recently married to the Earl Davis's son, Thomas? I trust it is working out well?" Prince Liam inquires.

I nod, astonished he remembers anything about my family. The time I met him, he seemed so distinctly uninterested.

We reach the archway, and at his gesture the surprised guards jump to open the gate. Prince Liam bends and again kisses Lydia's hand in departure. Then he faces me.

"Yes, Miss Davenport, I do know a bit about your family. For instance, I know you are the daughter who trains with the squires."

Dumbfounded, I stammer out, "Um…yes…I guess you could say that…um…I do train with them…sort of…in a way…I mean…" I desperately search for the right word.

"Let me see, I believe I know the word you are looking for," he says with a mischievous smile. "'Technically'."

My mouth opens, but for once nothing comes out. Prince Liam just bows, then turns on his heels and strides down the hall, out of sight.

Lydia and I emerge from the small gate into a large courtyard situated to the left of the grand palace staircase. Instantly, we are engulfed in the busy flow of people carrying out their daily duties. The atmosphere is abuzz with the sound of merchants. Many shout out last-minute deals before having to pack up for the day.

"Jasmine? Cardamom? Saffron?" A short, swarthy woman sweeps her hand across a number of jars sitting on her cart. They fill the air with an intoxicating blend of spices and perfumes, like the pomanders Lucy makes for our dresser drawers.

When Lydia and I step into the main thoroughfare, we are greeted with the less pleasant smells of slaughtered animals and unwashed bodies. The stench of the daily refuse piles assaults our nostrils. A current of foul water slinks along the gutters, running off to some unknown destination, quite a contrast to the peaceful scenery inside the castle grounds.

"Did you just come out of the palace?" a voice from behind us queries. It is Ellen, an expression of utter bewilderment on her face.

"Yes!" Lydia exclaims.

Will I be able to quell her excitement enough before we get home? My hope is the less we make of the incident, the less trouble I will be in. Lydia gushing out every single detail is not going to help my cause.

"How on earth did you get in there? And Olivia—" Ellen eyes me from head to toe,"—what happened to you? You look frightful!"

Lydia is about to launch into a full-scale explanation. I hold up my hand to cut her off. For all I care, Lydia can blather the entire walk home, but the sooner we get going the better. Grabbing them each by the arm, I march for the city gate. The watchman has not moved an inch off his slanted chair since we left. People travel in and out the gate unchecked. If this is how he usually handles his responsibility, I better discuss it with my father later.

"Aww, whose cat?" Ellen reaches down to stroke its glossy black fur.

"Mine!" says Lydia happily. "His name is Midnight. Let me tell you all about how he found me."

As the sun begins to set, I lead them on the path toward home. While Ellen plies Lydia with questions, I am deep in thought. Our mother is probably furious at us. We are long overdue for dinner. When she finds out why we are late, dinner is going to be the least of her complaints. The chance that my father will get in trouble for our escapade is more upsetting to me. Somehow letting him down is a much bigger deal than letting my mother down. *This* is such a frequent occurrence, I have long since stopped letting it bother me. Honestly, for the most part Mother doesn't know what to make of me. My two older sisters conformed exactly to her idea of how good daughters were supposed to behave before I came along.

The oldest, Jayne, an attractive blonde, had no problem generating a number of interested suitors after her introduction into society. She was married three years ago at the age of twenty to a man whose stature had surpassed even my mother's expectations. It had taken Jayne all of about six weeks from meeting Thomas Davis, son of the distinguished Earl Davis, to marrying him. In my opinion, six weeks is not long enough to ascertain someone's character. A sentiment not shared by my mother, who seemed to wonder why the six long weeks were needed to decide on such a flattering offer.

Mother had been aghast that when I was thirteen, Father had let me start to train with the squires. At first, she had ranted that allowing me to be so unladylike would ruin all prospects I had for marriage. When that did not move him, she argued that my face was risked daily by being just one stroke away from horrible disfigurement—which would ruin my prospects for marriage. My father still unyielding, she insisted that the strenuous nature of the training would leave me barren, which would—once again—ruin my prospects for marriage. They forged a compromise. I was to cease working with him when I became seventeen. At the time, I had readily agreed to the terms—four years had seemed so far into the future—but now the time to give it all up is disturbingly close. I don't know how I am going to survive.

"You saw *who?*" Ellen's banshee shriek brings me out of my reverie. Her reaction, I am guessing, will be tame next to my mother's when she hears his name.

"Prince Liam. He was nice. He caught my cat." Lydia beams, reliving the moment.

Ellen's mouth hangs open as Lydia details the entire exploit, complete with the promises to meet his horse and play in his maze. See, I knew she took those seriously. She will be devastated when she realizes Prince Liam didn't mean any of it. I should have let him know when I had the chance that he should not toy with my sister. But there are bigger problems to worry about at the moment.

"All right, so let's just keep this whole story between the three of us," I suggest.

"Why?" they ask in unison.

"Because Father's job is to protect the royal family's safety. It looks bad for him if just anyone can go waltzing into the royal garden with no problem."

Two blank faces stare back at me. Do they need me to draw them a picture?

"And I don't want him to get in trouble because of us. All right? So keep it quiet!"

The sun dips halfway below the horizon like an overturned bowl. Its long shafts of light are thrown out across the land in one final effort before they are extinguished. We can't waste much more time on this. Finally, my words sink into their brains and they understand the need to protect our father.

"So we should lie? We aren't supposed to lie, you know. Father may lash us!" Lydia frets, fright clouding her face as she buries it in Midnight's fur.

In my whole life, our father has never once lashed any of us for anything. I point this out to Lydia, but it doesn't put her at ease.

"All right, so do not lie per se, but do not volunteer any information unless directly asked. Keep the details sketchy. Lydia found a cat and we had trouble catching it to bring it home."

The cat itself presents another problem. Mother is entirely and devoutly superstitious. A black cat will conjure up all sorts of horrible omens in her mind. My father finds all her notions ridiculous, but there is no reasoning with her on this subject. I tell Lydia that if she is interested in adopting this cat, she should keep it away from our mother at all costs.

My mother is not alone in her beliefs. The numerous and bizarre superstitions in Stewartsland were beyond count. The higher one got up the social ladder, the more likely the person was to subscribe to them. Father confided to me once that the King and Queen are both fastidious in this kind of thinking; rumor has it the King even has a witch who provides him counsel.

The sun is now a small orange sliver shimmering like a candle flame. Ellen and Lydia start an animated discussion about how to keep the cat's presence a secret. I lag behind, lost in a jumble of thoughts and feelings—the encounter with Prince Liam, the unexpected circumstances, and the humiliation of facing him. This moment or that comment ricochet like rubber balls in my mind.

Now that I think about it, he actually gave the impression of enjoying my discomfort. He must love wielding such power over us "little people." It must be like sport to those court people. And the "technically" comment! How condescending that had been. A good laugh for him at my expense, no doubt.

Yet I had to admit, his eyes did not have malice in them. His absorbing eyes, so clear and blue that they had riveted me to my spot. For a split second, I feel a softening toward him. But then I remember his promises to Lydia and my indignation wins out. Oh well, it's not like I will ever have to deal with him again. There is no sense wasting time thinking about him…or his eyes.

A strange thing though, that moment when our eyes met I felt a connection. My whole body warmed from the center out like nothing I had ever experienced before, as if some timeless energy between us was released. It was a calmness in the middle of my chest, a feeling that can be described only as recognition. The sensation you get when you meet someone for the first time and are sure you have known him before. Remembering the moment now makes me somewhat giddy, and it becomes hard to focus on anything else.

This Prince Liam train of thought has to stop; it is so out of the ordinary for me. For goodness sake, Puck would say I lost my mind if he heard any of this. And he would be right. Clearly this is just a passing delusion brought on by the stress of the whole situation. The Prince surely has not wasted a single thought on me since I left. Surprisingly, this idea makes me feel empty, like someone scooped my heart out of my body. I try to console myself with the fact that he did remember my name and he knew I trained with the squires. When that doesn't make me feel better, I convince myself to just forget the whole stupid thing.

We round the last corner before our property and enter our front gate into the compound. Our land holds not only our home, but a stable, an armory, training grounds, and a number of fields and gardens. At the back of a small dirt courtyard, our house sits like a mother hen around her chicks. It's not impressive—only one story—but is quite sprawling and roomy inside.

I expect to see my mother outside, hands on hips, pacing back and forth, muttering about her ungrateful children. But instead, the house is all lit up and a pair of royal guards' horses stands outside.

Oh no!

Ellen and Lydia eye me with trepidation. Boy, they don't waste any time at the palace do they? These guards were dispatched before we even left the palace grounds. Otherwise, they would have passed us on our walk home. If that was the case, then I bet Prince Liam purposely detained us so they could have a head start. It takes all my self-control to not march right back to the palace and let Prince Liam know exactly what I thought of him, his empty promises, and his tattling like a child.

Well, someone is going to have to go inside and face the music. My sisters don't deserve to get the brunt of the fury. Ellen was not even involved and Lydia is just an impulsive child, a child I should have been watching better. I will shield them from my parents' wrath; let them get it out of their systems first.

"Go hide the cat in the barn while I go in and explain everything," I instruct.

"Are you sure?" says Ellen. "You shouldn't get all the blame."

"Yeah," adds Lydia, "it was all Midnight's fault."

"I'll be sure to point that out," I say sarcastically.

With a deep breath, I square my shoulders and step through the front door. Directly on my left in his office, my father is seated at his desk reading something while the two guards stand waiting. *Great.*

My father glances up from the documents, glances at me an instant, then continues reading. A charge of trespassing against Lydia and me will not go over well with him. I linger just past the door trying to assess the situation.

"Did you find your sister?" My mother's voice causes me to jump visibly off the floor. "Because she never came back here."

Cautiously, I revolve around to her. She dries her hands on an apron. Her eyes show no anger, just the usual frustration that Lydia's meanderings cause.

Mother is still a fine looking woman for her age. She is about my height with the enviable blonde hair that Jayne and Lydia inherited, which still has no trace of grey. Her lovely face has finally, through time and the stress of raising five daughters, begun to show some signs of age, with lines around her eyes and lips. Yet somehow these do not detract from her beauty, but add an air of wisdom.

"Um…yes. I found her. She and Ellen just had to stop by the barn for a moment."

"The barn? Whatever for? Oh, never mind. I am sure I don't want to know."

She spins and heads back toward the kitchen muttering about how the last thing we need is another one of Lydia's pets and how no one around here but her cares if we ever eat tonight.

All right. So Father has obviously not told Mother yet.

A peek into the office shows my father leaning back in his chair, rather relaxed as he gestures and chats with the guards, who also are curiously at ease. He does not look angry, his face has not reddened, nor is the vein popping out of his neck. Something isn't adding up here. Time to figure out what's going on.

I saunter into the kitchen, my favorite room in the house. Large and airy, it still feels cozy and warm, with French doors opening up to the vegetable and herb gardens, which sprawl among the worn cobblestones out back. The scent of mint and parsley intermingles with baking bread and roasted meat. My stomach grumbles with longing.

As usual at mealtime the space is a hive of activity. We have a cook, Grace, but Mother likes to be "in the mix," as she says, at meal preparations. They work along with Lucy, our housekeeper, to get dinner on the table. All three maneuver around each other in an intricate dance; this one grabbing a bowl and that one rotating the spit, every movement performed flawlessly with complete awareness of the others' positions. If ever they ask me for help, it is like throwing a pig in with graceful ballerinas. The rule has become to seek assistance from me only under circumstances of utmost duress.

"So what's up with the guards?" I try to keep the edge off my voice.

"Your father needs to get a party together to go on some mission with the King," Mother says distractedly. She stirs a big pot on the hearth and dips the spoon in for a sample.

My mouth opens, but before a word escapes, she cuts me off.

"Please, Olivia, let your father explain this business to you later. Right now go and get your sisters or we will be eating at midnight." She grabs a cloth to pull a hot loaf out of the brick oven. Then, she surveys my physical state for the first time. "And for Heaven's sake, wash up!"

Thankful that, for now at least, we have not been discovered, I exit the back door and head toward the barn. My sisters are relieved at the news and agree to stick to the plan. We stop at the pump at the side of the house to wash up. As I splash the cool water on my face, the grime rinses away down the drain and carries my worries along. Our parents are distracted. There is no reason they have to find out anything about our little royal incident.

When we enter the kitchen, the guards are exiting, each with a hunk of cheese and a large slab of the fresh bread. "Good evening, fair ladies," one says. "May I wish you a pleasant night." Their casual manner convinces me their visit did not involve Lydia or me.

My sister Anne, the second oldest, materializes from her bedroom. "What took you so long? It's not good for my complexion to be eating so late!" She brushes past us with a sigh of displeasure.

Anne is considered quite a beauty with sapphire eyes and a shining mane of dark chestnut hair. She has been out in society for about half a year now and is reveling in her new role as eligible young lady at court. According to Anne, the only way for a girl to advance herself is by playing the coquette to attract as high a noble as possible for marriage. I hadn't thought it possible for someone to make Jayne seem sensible and selective in her handling of prospective matches, but Anne does it in spades. Her goal appears to be to flirt with every man she comes across and then pit these men against each other in their pursuit of her attention. And to give her credit where credit is due, her games work marvelously, bestowing her with an innumerable amount of suitors.

We finally sit down to dinner and I yearn to ask my father about the letter and the mission. His brow is creased, as if he ponders over some substantial information. This is the type of issue he loves to discuss with me, especially since no one else in the family shows the remotest interest in his work.

But before I can get a word out, my mother starts right in. "Lydia Marie, how many times have I told you not to wander off?"

"A whole lot," Lydia mumbles. Her fork pushes food around her plate, a solitary pea rolls off and bounces to the floor. The crown of flowers, though wilted now, still graces her head, but her posture—head down, eyes on her plate, elbows on the table—is decidedly unprincess-like.

"And yet, you continue to do it regularly. Not only is it dangerous, young lady, it wastes time and puts me into such an awful state of worry." Mother places a hand on her breast for the proper melodramatic flourish. "Well, let me be clear, the next time this happens you will go to bed without any dinner!" She slams her hand on the table as she finishes this threat.

An empty threat. This is about the thousandth time this exact conversation has taken place, and for the record, to date, Lydia has never missed a meal.

"Oh, but mama I found a cat! The most beautiful black cat," Lydia croons.

"Black? Well, be sure to keep that creature out of the house. We have no need of any unlooked-for bad luck around here. And that goes for all of you." She shakes a finger in a circle around the table. Everyone nods reflexively, no one wishing to start Mother on a topic that would surely last for the entire meal. Confident she has protected us all from an evil fate, Mother concentrates on her plate.

Finally, about to burst with curiosity, I say, "So tell me Father, what is the nature of the letter you received from the King?"

His eyes brighten with eagerness. "Yesterday, King William received a letter from King John of Lindenwood indicating that he would like to meet with him to discuss the treaty and the land. He has invited King William to

Lindenwood for this meeting. The King has asked me to arrange a small party to accompany him."

This is big news. There are so many things I want to ask that I don't know where to begin. Anne beats me to it though. "Please, Father, no business at the table. It is ever so dull. And besides, we need your opinion. Mother and I were talking about the coming winter. We want to get new coats. You know, in the more stylish Mainland cuts."

Thus Anne launches into an entire conversation that I—and I feel safe to say, my father—have absolutely no interest in whatsoever. She proceeds to go on ad nauseam about coat length and collar design. Soon Mother and Lydia pipe in their opinions about hats and matching muffs.

Seriously? After what my father has just revealed to us and all of its possible implications, they want to talk about winter apparel?

My father catches my eye, gives my hand a squeeze, and whispers, "Tonight, you and I will sit in my office and discuss the whole thing with each other."

Thank goodness for my father.

Two hours later, a tray of hot tea and honey cakes in hand, I enter my father's office. The room is not large or grand in scale. Its paneled walls contain little decoration other than two maps: one of Stewartsland and one of the larger region illustrating where our island lies in the sea just beyond the Mainland. A large oak desk anchors the setting, papers strewn across it like driftwood brought in with the tide.

While I love the homey feeling of our kitchen, this space I regard with great reverence. Father and I regularly lock ourselves away here from the bustle of the house to engage in serious talks, lively debates, and enlightening lessons. In this place, my father has educated me on all phases of his work and divulged many issues regarding Stewartsland's security. This room is an extension of my father, of the special relationship we share—a place that is almost sacred.

When I was a young girl, I surreptitiously hung around the training grounds to watch the squires at work. The whole idea entranced me, and I replicated their moves in the shadows. Puck was the only one who knew about it. He took to practicing with me in his off time in an effort to enhance his own skills. We tried to keep it a secret, aware that it would be unseemly for a girl to participate in such activities. One day my father caught us, but instead of being angry with me, he was ecstatic to learn that I had a natural talent for swordplay and, as it happened, a number of other qualities desirable in a future knight, including tracking and battle planning. Luckily for me, he has always indulged my enthusiasm for his livelihood. In many ways, I think my keen interest and aptitude make him see me as the son he never had.

Father leans back in his chair, feet up on his desk, tamping down leaf in his pipe. At the request of Mother, he smokes only in his office. Over the years, the scent of his tobacco has seeped into every crevice and object in the room, claiming its territory. The distinct smell reminds me of everything that is important in life: trust, security, and love.

A big man, Father is imposing. He is tall and broadly built, with brown hair that is thinning at the crown. Years in the outdoors have left his skin somewhat weathered, which only adds to his overall presence as commander of the knights. Although he is twice the age of some of them, no man would willingly choose to oppose him. His reputation is that of a man you do not want to challenge.

I place the tray on the edge of his desk next to a globe and some books whose pages have yellowed with time, then prepare us each a cup of tea. My usual seat awaits me by the unlit fireplace. The soft leather of the chair closes around my body like an embrace, my legs are tucked underneath me. On my right, a small table overflows with papers about our latest area of study, the uses and placements of castle escape tunnels. But any conversation about that subject is on the back burner tonight.

"Well?" I ask, on tenterhooks.

"Well—" he draws in a large breath, "—it seems a letter was sent to King William from King John quite out of the blue. It hints he is interested in dissolving the Territory Treaty and ceding the land back to Stewartsland."

"Really? Well, I suppose it makes sense; he is getting older and has no heirs," I reply. King John has always been eccentric. There was a brief marriage to a village seamstress, but both she and a baby had died in childbirth. "Why do you suppose he never married again?"

"Who knows. He has always been a loner—no advisors to help him in decision making. Not that Lindenwood is big enough that he would need any assistance." Father inhales a drag of his pipe, then slowly exhales a cloud of smoke.

Though not a large kingdom, Lindenwood's land is profitable, rife with lush forests that provide both valuable timber and game to be exported to the Mainland, plus vast quarries full of much-coveted stones. In truth, though, Lindenwood is no more than a glorified village with a miniature castle at its center.

"Do you think King William will be receptive to his offer given their past?" I ask.

King John is the bastard son of William's father, King Bernard. When William was only twenty and still trying to establish his young monarchy, a man named John Linden arrived claiming he and his seven-year-old brother, Otto, were Bernard's sons by a long-term mistress from the Mainland, and demanded a portion of the kingdom for his own. When not originally acknowledged by King William, John left Stewartsland, but returned soon thereafter with an army behind him. After many months of battle, King William finally forfeited the land, and John crowned himself King of Lindenwood.

"I believe so. Their dispute happened decades ago. And there has been no trouble ever since. I still think King William did not want to honor this bastard's claim for recognition, but the war it caused was too costly, so at the time he conceded and awarded him the land in return for stopping the constant attacks on us." He lays his pipe in an ashtray and takes a sip of tea.

"Yes, costly because a Mainland king funded the entire operation so he could get his hands on our valuable assets," I say, indignant that Stewartsland has this blemish on her history.

"Well, as I have told you, that is merely speculation," Father says; we have had this conversation many times before. "We will likely never know the true answer."

"Given King John's age and lack of an heir, it does make sense for him to discuss Lindenwood's fate with King William. Isn't this good news?" I ask, absently running my finger over the decorative nails on the chair arm.

He makes no reply.

"Father?" I ask, confused that, now sitting erect in his chair, he seems weighted down by some worry.

"On the surface, yes, and yet I feel rather uneasy about it. Why now? Why request King William go to Lindenwood rather than King John coming here? The letter implies that John would like to show William the current state of the land, but there is just something…" he trails off.

"Something like what?"

"Something I can't quite put my finger on. A gut feeling that this proposal is not what it seems. The kind that, after my many years of service, I have learned not to ignore." Judging by how well my father's instincts have served him in the past, it would be prudent to listen to them now.

"I expressed my misgivings to the King, who more or less laughed them off. In fact, in the message he sent over this evening, he suggested that I have been doing this job for so long that I see suspicion in everything." Father shrugs, chews on the stem of his pipe.

"So what did he order you to do?" I shift my feet out from under me and take a sip of tea. I know my father. He will not risk the King's safety.

"The King commanded me to get a small party together for the trip to Lindenwood. A handful of guards is all he requested. He does not want to appear belligerent toward King John, like he is marching there to reclaim his lands. I managed to deceive him into taking more protection though," my father confides with a mischievous grin.

"How?" I ask through a mouthful of honey cake.

"By telling him it would be a good training exercise for the oldest class of squires since they do not get to see a whole lot of action. I explained that if the squires go, then I need to bring a few extra knights to ensure the squires will be properly drilled. Thankfully, he agreed to this with no argument." Father exhales, sits back again, and takes a long drag on his pipe. Smoke wafts from his mouth in a long, white trail.

For a moment, I am stunned silent. A mission that includes the squires – my class of squires! Giddiness bubbles up in me at the mere thought of it. Never did I think I would be lucky enough to participate in such an operation before my mother had me yanked out of the group. I feel light as air, buoyant with excitement.

"When do we leave?" The thrilled words squeak out, unnaturally high.

"The day after tomorrow," he answers still focused on the success of his ploy. Then abruptly his eyebrows fly up. "Wait…'we'?"

"Yes, you said all the squires from the oldest class were going. So when do *we* leave?"

For one second he is baffled, then, as realization sets in, his face softens.

"Livy, dear," he says gently, "I let you train with the squires, but that does not make you an actual squire."

Surely I did not hear him correctly. But his expression tells me my hearing is just fine. Tunnel vision closes around my eyes, blood pounds in my ears, my body deflates, the exhilaration of a moment ago dispersed into nothingness.

"But I work just as hard as the boys. I'm faster and more skillful than some of them too. And I am smarter than almost all of them. You have said so yourself!"

"Yes, I know you are," he agrees with a sigh, "but this trip will be all men. There is no proper way for a young lady to accompany us."

"But I am *not* a young lady, I am a *squire!*"

All reasonable arguments are obstructed by the throbbing in my skull. My father, who has trained me, stood by me, groomed me in his likeness, can't destroy my dream like this. I leap from the chair, knocking my plate to the floor with a clatter, and kneel at the desk, my hands clasped together. "Please, Father, there will never be another chance like this for me again! Please let me come…I'll do anything!"

My father stares down at his hands. He is still for a long moment. When he raises his face to mine, I see not the eyes of a doting father, but those of a Master of Arms. "I am sorry, Olivia, but the answer is, and will remain, no. This matter is closed. Good night."

His brusque tone is all too familiar; any further discussion is pointless.

Tears cloud my eyes. I grope my way out of his office. Anger burns through my body, radiating out my fingers and toes. I am surprised objects don't smolder from their touch. A rug, its corner upturned, trips me; my hurt so consuming, it disorients me in the familiar hallway. The unfairness of life weighs down on me like the load of the sky on Atlas.

Bursting through the door of my room, I flop face down on my mattress. Ellen and Lydia jolt up from their shared bed.

"What's the matter, Livy?" Lydia whispers. My weeping is the only answer she receives. So rarely have my little sisters seen me cry, they are unsure how to handle it. After a moment of quiet consultation, they decide to let me be.

Once I have started crying it is as though a plug has been pulled from a dike. All the resentment I have tried so hard to push down comes pouring out. Why do I have to give up what I love most? How can my parents expect me to be someone I am not? My childhood had been full of sparring, riding, and the like with Puck while my sisters played house, embroidered, and learned to cook. These dull domestic tasks are what I dread having to learn. A life full of these responsibilities and not my beloved ones looms over me like a giant black cloud. The bitterness is so acute, it is a living presence.

Time passes. The tears subside eventually, all spent. Then, I just lie there listening to my sisters' sleeping breaths. I feel empty, like someone has amputated the core of my soul and only the lifeless husk of my body remains. The bleak future stretches out before me like an abyss ready to swallow me in one bite.

The open window carries in the sounds of night. Owls hoot in search of prey, crickets perform their nightly concert. At a light thump, I glance up. It is Midnight; he has hopped onto the open sill. Our eyes meet for a long minute of appraisal. He leaps onto my bed, kneads around for a moment, then lies down right next to my head. My pillow vibrates with his purring.

Blasted cat. Just what I don't need right now. But his soothing presence lulls me to sleep.

5

"Well, what did you expect?" asks Puck.

We are in the armory shed where all the equipment is kept. Puck organizes swords and supplies for the mission, a task assigned to each squire for their appointed knight. In an effort to gain more esteem from his fellow squires, however, Puck double-checks everyone's gear. His diminutive stature makes him try extra hard to impress our classmates. Yet, I fear, rather than viewing his extra assistance with respect, it causes them to disregard him even more.

Since we were little, we have been inseparable playmates. Puck's father, who had been a knight, was killed in a border skirmish when Puck was only two years old. Father has since taken the role of surrogate father to him, and now that he is of age, he trains under my father's tutelage.

People are often under the impression that Puck and I are twins. Even now the likeness is still pointed out; we share the same coloring and are virtually the same height. Our builds are also noted to be alike, a comment we both find insulting since a young man does not like to be recognized as scrawny and a young woman does not want her lack of curves pointed out. As for temperament, Puck's natural easy-going spirit nicely complements my obstinate strong will. I feel more comfortable with Puck, more myself, than I do with anyone else. He gets me and I get him. We work well together—unfortunately not romantically. My future would seem easier if this was the case.

"What did I expect? To be taken seriously. I train with you guys. I expected to go!"

I lean in the open doorway, staring outside at the sky. The air is hot and heavy as dark clouds filter swiftly across the sky ahead of an imminent storm. The scent of water and earth fill every breath. A low rumble of thunder groans far off in the distance. The weather matches the tempest that brews up inside of me.

Puck just peers at me sidelong. "On a trip with all men? How did you think that could happen?" He asks in such a matter-of-fact tone I want to slap him. "I mean, training is one thing, Livy. On a trip this long, there are all sorts of things to consider."

At my disgusted face, he elaborates, "It could be dangerous. Maybe not once we get to Lindenwood, but what about the outlaws we may encounter on the way?"

Good point. The forests of Stewartsland are notorious for outlaws. Their favorite target is the bimonthly transport of tax money to the northern ports for shipment to the Mainland. Originally the outlaws were comprised of small groups of men who were either escaped criminals, fugitives from the Mainland, or just unsavory men who found a life of crime more profitable than an honest living. A decade or so ago the problem of bandits robbing even the poorest of travelers had become so severe that King William was preparing to intervene.

Then out of nowhere the problem dissipated. Rumor spread of a man named Athos, who took it upon himself to regulate the outlaw community. He ordered an end to the needless terrorizing of innocent travelers. Men who were willing could join his band, and those who were not simply vanished from Stewartsland altogether.

Although he did establish some honor among the thieves, Athos is still a practicing criminal, and the tax transports are still fair game, along with any other party of ostentatiously rich persons. For the most part, King William leaves Athos alone since he solved the traveling problems for most ordinary citizens. Athos is now something of a folk hero among the people, a fact which peeves my father to no end. His bold exploits are quite the tales of legend around Stewartsland, but I question if he is audacious enough to attack a party led by the King.

"Besides," adds Puck, "there are other more…delicate matters as well."

"Oh yeah? Like what?" I spit out nastily, more aggravated with him by the second.

He stops packing, takes a second to decide on his wording. "Well, how about sleeping arrangements? Or better yet—bathroom arrangements?"

All right. So I have not considered either of those things. But they are just technicalities. Surely we can come up with a mutually agreeable arrangement. However, when I envision discussing any of this with my father, the impossibility starts to sink in. Stark realization washes over my face. When I glance up, Puck's eyes are filled with pity.

"Look," he says, touching my arm consolingly, "I know the training means a lot to you and everything. But you had to know, on some level, that it was just for fun. You can't actually become a Knight of the Guard one day."

Wounded beyond words, I still manage to find some. "I can't believe you would say that to me. It was just for *fun?* You know how much I love it! How much it means to me!"

"But Livy…"

"No! No *buts*! I thought you of all people would have my back on this. Instead you are just like the rest of them!"

He sighs, but says nothing more, then resumes packing. I fight back tears, simply devastated. Puck was supposed to share my outrage and brainstorm with me on a way to be included. If I don't even have Puck on my side, what hope is there?

But he is right. On some level, I know I cannot grow up to do a man's job. In my heart, I want to become one of my father's knights. My head knows there is no possibility of this, but I nurse the fantasy that one day it will be all right for a girl to think differently and act differently. Why can't a girl have a life of adventure and accomplishment of her own? Only the husband is allowed this? Mother says it will all make sense when I fall in love. Yet, how could I give up my passions all for the sake of a man? I can't imagine ever loving anyone *that* much.

This mission is a once-in-a-lifetime chance for me. There will never be another opportunity like it before I will be expected to get married. It would be my one shot at utilizing all the training I have dedicated so much time and effort to these past years. This morning I had woken with a sense of resolve, counting on the fact I would have Puck's support. Now the sense of utter hopelessness from last night slams back on me full force.

"So what was Prince Liam like?" Puck says cheerily, an effort to change both the subject and the mood. He already heard the story from Lydia this morning. She was bursting to tell someone. Ellen and I had to convince her that Puck was the safest audience.

"Well, I guess he was at least nice enough to let us go without making a big deal and informing our parents," I mumble. The ominous clouds converge over our property like a thick blanket.

"But not nice overall?" Puck questions. He separates and lays out waterskins to be filled. Empty, they are as deflated as I feel.

Thunder grumbles menacingly.

The memories of my encounter with Prince Liam, which until now had been forgotten, freshen in my mind. I recall his behavior the night at the engagement ball. Prince Harold made a point of walking around to converse individually with the guests. He asked my father several intelligent questions on the subject of horse training, then addressed me by name and asked if I was enjoying myself. His charming manner put everyone around him at ease.

On the other hand, there was Prince Liam, who spent a good part of the evening appearing to sulk in his chair on the dais. Eventually, Queen Helen sat next to him and whispered something in his ear that caused him to wade into the crowd. He made a turn of the room, only nodding in acknowledgement to a precious few. When he passed us, my father wished him good evening, to which he received a curt, "Sir Jack." Then he eyed me up and down as if weighing whether I merited any acknowledgement. Apparently I did not, because he abruptly spun and walked away.

"I don't know. I had the feeling he was mocking me or something. I mean he knew about my training with you guys and made a point to mention it."

"Hmm. I wonder how he knew that?" says Puck, who gathers saddlebags and places them in front of each knight's pile of gear.

"Yeah, me too. I mean it's not like it's a secret, but it doesn't seem like important enough information for someone of his rank to know. Anyway, he was rude about it, like he knew I was in an embarrassing situation, so he felt the need to make me feel even more uncomfortable." Suddenly my feelings of self-pity over the mission are replaced by all the irritation I feel toward Prince Liam and his attitude.

"So you are embarrassed that he knows you train with us?"

"No, of course not. It's just..." I pause while I try to decipher exactly what did bother me about it. When it hits me, the words fly out. "It's just that he made it seem like it was such a cute, frivolous whim of mine. I mean, he doesn't even know me and I have to justify myself to him? Why? Just because he is a Prince? He thinks it's all right to just make snap judgments of people and look down on them and…" I trail off when I notice the crooked smirk on Puck's face. "What?"

"Oh, nothing," he says, a hint of amusement in his voice. "It just seems like he really got to you."

"And that is funny to you *why?*" I ask through clenched teeth.

Thunder claps louder outside.

"Because I haven't seen you this fired up about someone since we were eleven and that traveling carpet maker's son was in town. Remember how you two antagonized each other for days before you admitted to having a crush on him? And then you were dreaming of marrying him and spinning wool with him for the rest of your happy lives." Puck chuckles over this memory.

"First of all, there never was any dreaming of wool spinning. And second of all, are you implying that I have a crush on Prince Liam? Because I most certainly do not!"

"Yeah, sure, if you say so."

"I *do* say so. Why are you being such a pain again?"

Puck's face softens. "Sorry, my mistake." His tone is unconvincing.

I rub my eyes with the heel of my hands. "Look, I'm tired of arguing. Why don't we go outside to practice our new footwork before the rain makes everything too muddy."

"I can't, Livy. There's too much to do. First, I have to get all the equipment laid out for everyone. Then I have to make sure all my gear is packed and ready to go in the morning. Most importantly, I have to re-lace the left side of Sir Michael's jerkin before the old lace snaps."

Just listening to him detail it all makes the anger rise up in me like a tide. I should be preparing for the mission with him. The unfairness is almost too much to bear. Jealousy eats at me so viciously I cannot even bring myself to offer him help. Maybe I should try to beg my father one more time. Come up with a new angle to persuade him.

"Don't worry. I will tell you every detail when I get back. It will be just like you were there with us," Puck assures me.

Thunder booms in earnest outside and the rain, as if waiting for this cue, pours down in immediate torrents.

"Yeah, just like it." My voice breaks with emotion.

"Livy, please don't be so upset," Puck starts, but I am already sprinting away from him into the teeming rain. I crash into the gardens at the back of the house and stand there soaking wet, not sure what to feel or where to go. My whole image of the world and my place in it has been crushed like the plants drooping miserably under the downpour. Gushing streams of water sweep soil and leaves over my feet, now sodden in my shoes. The bottom of my dress soaks up the wetness like the roots of a tree.

The realization that I have to sacrifice my passions leaves me feeling more desolate than ever. I knew all along it had only been a dream, but somehow that doesn't make the pain in my heart any less. If only I had this one chance, this one mission as a farewell to that part of my life before I am forced to move on. Perhaps I should appeal this idea to my father; maybe considering it a good-bye present would change his mind.

As if he senses I am thinking of him, my father's voice roars out of the house, "Olivia! Come in here this minute!"

Now what? In no state of mind to deal with anything else, I try to stall.

"I'm dripping wet," I call back. Mother freaks out at any messes coming into her house. Hopefully, she is standing nearby and will concur with my excuse, but no such luck.

"*Now!*" he yells. His tenor leaves no room for further delay.

I slog into the kitchen. This cannot be good. The last time I saw Father in this room I was six and in trouble for letting one of our cows escape. It does not bode well that he has come in here searching for me. Mother stands nearby quite baffled by the unusual circumstance of Father's presence. Grace and Lucy bustle about in an attempt to seem as though they are not hanging on every word.

"Olivia, is there something you would like to tell me about yesterday?" he asks knowingly.

Uh-oh.

Unsure how much he found out, I don't want to add any more incriminating information than I absolutely have to. Better to play it safe, see if I can get him to reveal exactly how much he knows. But I bet I can guess who told him about the whole incident. Someone who, I am certain, relished the opportunity.

"What exactly do you want to know?" I keep my demeanor calm and ingenuous while inside I am infuriated. Prince Liam sold us out. But what else would I have expected from that smug man?

"Don't get pert with me, young lady. You know quite well what I am referring to." While I silently stare at the floor, he prompts angrily, "About breaking a wall and disturbing the Prince!"

My mother gasps, her hand flying to her forehead. "Heaven save us," she murmurs and, ever the dramatist, proceeds to cross herself.

"Oh, that," I mutter, but do not continue.

Drips from the hem of my skirt create a pool of water around my feet. The fact that Mother is not concerned at all by the mess this makes on her floor conveys the magnitude of trouble I may be in. My nervousness combined with the muggy kitchen causes a bead of sweat to form at the nape of my neck. It runs slowly down my back like my sinking feelings. Grace and Lucy have stopped the pretense that they are not listening and stand wide-eyed.

"Well?" my father snaps.

I have to say something.

"Well, let's see. If I remember correctly, Lydia chased a cat through a hole that was *already* in the wall that leads into the royal gardens. I may have broken it some more when I went after her, but it was, in truth, only a matter of time before that happened." That is all I am owning up to at the moment.

"And that was where you disturbed Prince Harold?" Mother interjects, completely horrified. Her pale face and unsteady footing remind me of a ship's seasick passenger.

"Not Prince Harold. Prince Liam. And I wouldn't say we disturbed him. The guards had us in their custody. He voluntarily interceded on our behalf." No need to mention about being on the way to the jailer or our further conversations with the Prince.

Mother just stands there with her mouth agape. She is actually speechless, an extremely rare occurrence that I would have heartily enjoyed under other circumstances. Grace and Lucy clearly try not to laugh as they exchange a conspiratorial glance.

My father takes a deep breath in an effort to control his anger. "And why didn't you tell me this last night?"

"You have a lot on your mind. I didn't want to add any more troubles since it all worked out okay," I say, hoping my concern for his welfare will buy me some points.

"And you thought it would be less troublesome for me to hear it all secondhand from the guards, my guards, who were involved?"

All right. I should have figured out that the news would get back to my father sooner rather than later. Usually, I am much sharper at recognizing such details, but thoughts of the mission have consumed my mind since last night, leaving no room for other matters. On a bright note, at least Prince Liam was not the one who got me in trouble. Not that this should matter to me—yet somehow it does.

"I am truly sorry, Father. I sincerely hope that I did not get you in trouble," I say in a voice that notoriously works like a charm on him—one of the benefits of being his favorite.

"No, no," he says, half-amused, "I just took some good-natured ribbing about not being able to guard the royal family, even from my own daughters."

My mother gives him an acerbic glare, her displeasure at me being let off too easy very apparent, so Father adds seriously, "Consider yourself lucky, young lady, that this time there were no serious consequences. Keep that in mind in the future." He walks brusquely out of the room.

Everyone stands silent for a second. Then Grace returns to chopping up carrots and Lucy retrieves a mop to work on my puddle. Mother finally finds her voice and her litany starts. "Olivia, do you see why you need to pay attention to Lydia? If you had, she wouldn't have wandered off and none of this would have happened. Imagine! Being thus embarrassed in front of royalty! It just goes to show…"

Her voice fades as I push through the swinging door and follow my father's path into his office. He sits behind the desk, piled high with a mountain of papers. No doubt most of them concern the stipulations of the Territory Treaty. I stand in the doorway and adopt my most guileless pose.

"Father," I say, in my same manipulative tone, "I was wondering if I could speak with you a moment."

He glances up distractedly. "Yes, what is it now, dear?"

Presenting this perfectly will be my only hope, so I choose my words carefully. "I've been thinking about how I am almost seventeen and I need to start considering my future. It won't be long before I have to give up the training sessions with the squires. Soon we will need to have some serious talks about the next phase of my life."

My younger sisters cavort outside his window in the courtyard, indicating that the storm has passed. Lydia loves to play in the mud, much to Mother's dismay. Their laughter carries across the air, the perfect song of childhood innocence.

"Well, it's nice to see you being so sensible," he says absentmindedly while he thumbs through some documents and sorts them into piles.

The sun breaks through the clouds. Its rays reflect through the raindrops on the window, make dappled shadows dance across the surface of the desk. Father only partly listens; maybe this is a good time to get him to agree with me.

"So I was wondering, you know, about this mission. Maybe I could just go on this one, like a culmination to all my training—a farewell present, if you will."

There is no immediate reaction. Instead, he gathers one pile of paper and taps it down on the desk into a neat stack. He lays it down to one side then looks me straight in the eyes. I have his full attention now. His tired face is drawn with concern over the upcoming trip. It becomes clear that his silence, which I was taking as his possible consideration, is just him mustering up the energy to refuse me again.

"Livy," he sighs, "I know you are disappointed, but I already explained to you that it would not be possible to bring you on a trip like this. It is all men and it would not be proper."

"But…"

"No *buts*!" he says, exasperated. "Now if you will excuse me I have a lot to prepare before morning. Please, Olivia, just try and come to terms with the fact that you cannot go." He turns his back on me and thumbs through a book on the credenza.

Conversation over.

I drag myself to my room and sit in the open window. The sill is wet from being left open during the storm, but I don't care. Sounds of Lydia's squealing and Ellen's admonishing echo through our courtyard. Blankly I stare outside, too despondent to even cry. Midnight crawls out from under my bed, his refuge from the thunderstorm. He jumps up in my lap and begins to purr. Absently stroking him, I note this is the second time he has come to comfort me when I was upset. Odd, that he should have such an affinity toward me when Lydia is the animal charmer of the family.

The assortment of emotions I feel after these past twenty-four hours is indescribable. There is not one word that could encompass them all. What is important for me now is to not be devoured by them. One thing all my training taught me is to stay focused in the face of adversity.

Every problem has a solution if you just focus. There has to be a way for me to go on this mission. I examine the problem from all sides, determined to find an answer, but I keep coming back to the central problem—that I am a girl. Face it, if I were a boy none of this would be an issue.

And then, like a flash, an idea enters my head. A crazy idea that would best be forgotten. But the longer I sit with my crazy idea, the more achievable it seems. Soon a reasonable plan of execution has formed to go along with it.

"Well, Midnight, what do you think? Should I give it a try?"

The cat just glances up at me from his comfortable perch and, to my surprise, he winks. If I had not seen it myself, I wouldn't have believed it. I take this as a sign that he gives my plan his blessing.

6

I sit a long while, engrossed in contemplation. The sun falls low in the sky, the vibrant collage of oranges, pinks, and blues resting on the horizon. Soon it gives way to the inkier hues of twilight. The chill of the autumn night coils around my shoulders, and I close the window. Midnight remains a contented ball of heat curled in my lap.

If I am going through with this, all the details need to be carefully considered. I put my battle-planning skills to work and make a mental list of the items required: a basket, food, ale, scissors, and most importantly a vial, which will be the hardest object to obtain unnoticed. My senses are heightened in anticipation as I review all the imaginable snags I may encounter. The plan is divided into five steps, but each successive step hinges on the completion of the one before it. And one final detail remains uncertain. Hopefully, a solution will present itself sometime this evening.

By dinnertime, I am as ready as I will ever be. Most important for now is to contain my nerves and act low-key. My mother and Anne are just beginning to lay the table when I come in and cheerfully offer help. If this is met with any surprise, it is not noted by anyone, although I do ignore a questioning glance from our cook. Grace is tall, unusually tall for a woman, with a wiry frame that suggests she does not enjoy the fruits of her labors. Her austere features and tight black bun impart upon her an air of severity. It is hard to get anything past Grace.

My mother mutters to herself again, distracted enough by another of Lydia's antics. Lydia herself, with the help of Ellen and Lucy, is being made presentable after her excursions in the mud. Anne hands me the plates to distribute while she lays out the cutlery. Grace places a large roast garnished with vegetables on the center of the table. When the family finally sits to eat, Anne is back on the coat subject in full force.

"I was passing by Herman's Apparel today and they have a whole new selection of the latest fashions on display. All from the Mainland, of course. Have you thought any more about whether we can get new coats this year, Father?" she asks, hopefully.

"No, dear, I can't say that I have. I am rather engaged with business at the moment." Father addresses Anne in the same manner as he does Lydia. It is the patient way one speaks to a small child, one who is still so young she needs everything spelled out for her. Anne never notices the condescension.

"Oh, yes. I guess that makes sense," Anne says, unable to hide the disappointment in her voice. Her inability to grasp the importance of what Father deals with highlights her ignorance and self-involvement. And *this* is what Mother would prefer I was like?

But for right now, I have a charade to pull off, so I quickly set to work.

"What colors did they have, Anne?" I ask with feigned interest.

At first she gazes at me with surprise, as if I had grown another head, but of course the temptation to talk about the coats wins out. She begins a long dissertation on the variety of colors, making sure to differentiate between the two "vastly different blues" she saw. While she rattles on, I glance sideways at my father. He watches me with a quizzical expression. It is imperative he thinks all thoughts of the mission are out of my head. Knowing I have his attention, I simply sit back and pretend to give Anne mine.

The rest of the mealtime conversation is much the same, and when it is over, I am confident I have lulled my family into an unsuspicious frame of mind. My father retreats to his office for the evening while the rest of us clear the table. We enter the kitchen balancing bowls and plates to find our housekeeper, Lucy.

"Mrs. Davenport, Grace has taken ill and gone to bed. I will be shutting up the kitchen this evening," Lucy informs us.

Good. This works to my advantage. Lucy's round face with large expressive eyes gives away her every thought and emotion. If she starts to suspect I am up to something, I will be able to throw her off track easily enough.

"Mother, I had a bit of a fight with Puck before," I say with just the right amount of remorse.

She and my sisters prepare to settle in the sitting room just off the kitchen. A cozy space, we usually gather around the fireplace for after-dinner activities. Mother is full of sympathy, happy this is something I have chosen to confide in her and not my father.

Mother has high hopes for Puck and me. She knows my aversion to marriage, knows I have never truly had feelings for any boy. Oh, I have had the occasional crush but it wore off quickly when I pictured a life as somebody's wife and property. In all likelihood though, it will be someone who holds Puck's station in life, when he makes knighthood, who will be considered an appropriate match for me. My mother views a marriage to Puck as the obvious resolution to a complicated problem. And believe me, I really *want* to love him, but all I can ever seem to muster is a serious *like* for him. Admittedly, it is my best chance of retaining even a modicum of my interests on a regular basis. I am sure no ordinary husband would be so tolerant. But it will be hard to watch Puck get to live out the life I truly believe is meant for me.

"About what, dear?" she asks, eyes brimming with concern.

"Oh, it was so silly that I don't remember. Anyway he is sleeping in the armory tonight. Would it be all right if I brought him some food now as a peace offering?"

"I think that would be nice of you. After all, Puck has a big day tomorrow," she replies.

Her mention of tomorrow's mission irritates me immensely, but I need to focus. The important thing is that I have obtained permission to go to see Puck.

Step One—done.

Lucy immediately cuts a nice hunk of cheese and wraps it in a towel, grabs some of the leftover chicken, and cuts a nice slab of bread. Then she searches around for something to put it in. I have anticipated this and stationed myself next to the pantry. A crucial part of the plan hinges on the next few moments.

"Oh, I'll grab a basket out of the pantry, Lucy, while you get some ale for Puck," I offer casually.

"That would be a big help, Livy." She pours some ale into a carafe and searches for a mug to serve it in.

Our pantry is dim and cluttered. Overstuffed shelves sag in the middle with jars, cans, and cooking supplies. The corners, stuffed with brooms, mops, and umbrellas, close in on one like an intruder. Various containers, baskets, and jugs create a maze on the floor. Yet, despite all the nooks, crannies, and hidden hazards, its organization has never been attempted.

A crooked cabinet hangs on the far wall. This is where my mother keeps all her remedies. Its door eases open without a sound. I take a small vial from a box of empty ones on the bottom shelf, then grab a large amber bottle from the high left corner. Carefully, I uncork it, fill the empty vial with some of its clear liquid, and stopper the vial closed. Then I return the bottle to its former position.

Step Two—done.

"The baskets are in the right corner," Lucy's voice calls from just outside the door.

Startled, I almost drop the vial.

Focus.

"Oh yes, I see them now, thanks!"

Stumbling around a butter churn, I grab the first basket my hand touches off the pile. There is one last item I need. Grace's box full of knitting and sewing supplies sits nearby. I rummage through the pile of yarns, threads, and needles, a jumble of softness penetrated by the occasional pierce of metal. Finally, my hand lands on the desired object—a pair of scissors. I lay the vial and the scissors in the bottom of my basket and cover them with a towel.

Step Three—done.

I exit the pantry. Before I can stop her, Lucy snatches the basket out of my hands and begins loading the food and ale into it. My breath ceases while I pray she does not discover the secrets hidden at the bottom, but Lucy is none the wiser.

"You be sure to tell Peter that Lucy sent him some of Grace's famous pecan pie," she says, the basket outstretched to me. Peter is Puck's given name. His father took to calling him Puck as a baby for some unknown reason and the nickname stuck. The only people now who ever refer to him as Peter are Sir Michael, the knight for whom Puck squires, and Lucy.

"All right, I will," I say, anxious to get out of the kitchen and on with the crux of my plan.

Thankfully, everyone is busy in the sitting room. My mother works on her needlepoint. Ellen reads a book. Anne mends some shirts and Lydia strums a lute as well as her tiny fingers allow. I reach the back door and push it open. A rush of cool air fills the room.

"Olivia," my mother says sternly. I stop in my tracks, one foot already outside. Lydia happens to strike a harsh chord at that exact moment.

"Yes?" *Keep calm.* She could not possibly know anything about what I just did or what I am about to do.

"Don't keep Puck up too late, dear. They have to leave early tomorrow," she replies, never even looking up from her stitching.

Does she think I need that pointed out to me? Again? Her appalling lack of regard for my feelings is, as usual, hurtful. But I will give her one thing—she is consistent in her insensitivity where my training is concerned.

"Of course, Mother," I answer sweetly and step out the back door to head for the armory.

Now for the tricky parts—Steps Four and Five.

The armory door is ajar and light emanates out, a thick chunk of yellow against the dark night. As I approach, I see Puck hard at work polishing a sword. Framed by the doorway, he appears every bit the soldier preparing for battle. He exerts so much effort shining Sir Michael's weapon that he does not notice me. Shadowy fingers of guilt creep into my mind, but I brush them aside.

"Hey," I say.

Puck stops in mid-stroke and glances at me. An expression of surprise registers on his face, but he does not reply. He concentrates on the sword in his hands.

"Sorry about my outburst earlier. I guess I was just angry," I continue, a bit too much contrition in my voice. If there is one thing I am not known for, it is apologizing graciously. Puck pauses again and regards me warily.

"Um…that's…fine," he says, skepticism dripping from his voice.

Not a good start for me. He can't be suspicious or my plan will never work. "But I still think I should be allowed to go." I huff, then stamp my foot, cross my arms, and put on my best pout for good measure.

Puck inspects the sword, but I see the small hint of a smile tug at the corner of his mouth. I have taken him off his guard. Now I need to keep it that way.

"Look what I have here." I hold up the basket. "I brought you dinner, which even includes Grace's pecan pie, as a peace offering for our disagreement earlier."

Before I can think, he pulls a stool over to a closed barrel and sits down to eat. This is when I need to be careful.

"You know what I was thinking?" I say cheerily. "I was thinking we could eat in the barn." His face curls up in distaste at the idea, so I quickly add, "You know, like when we were younger and we would have those picnics in the loft."

"Well…I don't know…I still have some things to get in order and most importantly I need to re-lace Sir Michael's jerkin."

Anxiety builds up in me like steam in a kettle. The lynchpin of my plot involves persuading Puck into that loft. However, I suspected he might hesitate, so I have a trump card to play.

"Well," I say wistfully, "I guess you could eat here. It's just I was hoping to hear one of your stories about the constellations. They always cheer me up when I am down."

Bingo.

Puck gets a dreamy, faraway look in his eyes. He is obsessed with the stars, their movements, and the myths regarding each constellation. After some internal debate, he decides to go, if only for a little while. I promise him I will keep him on schedule, so he stands up and heads for the door.

"Wait!" I blurt out, hoping he does not notice the tinge of hysteria in my tone.

"What now?" he asks, startled. "Why are you acting so strange?"

Focus.

Puck knows me better than anyone. I need to be extra sharp to fool him. *Take a deep breath. Be the picture of calm.*

"Why don't you finish with the sword while I go set up in the loft. That way everything will be ready when you get there. It will waste less time."

Whether I give a credible performance or Puck just has too much on his mind, I do not know, but thankfully, he is convinced. He agrees to meet me there in fifteen minutes.

Step Four—done.

The barn is about fifty yards away from the armory on the property by our fields. A simple structure with the requisite color scheme of red and white, it houses a handful of animals. I pass the hen houses that flank the entrance. These coops, a bevy of activity in the day, sit silent, their outlines sharp shadows in the darkness.

The wooden door groans in protest as I slip inside. A crude ladder set against the wall leads to the hayloft. I light an oil lantern and carry it to the top. Scents of hay and animals permeate the space. I push open the loft doors to reveal the open sky. Cool, fresh air rushes in while I stand and admire the view. Twilight has diminished into night. The first stars begin to twinkle, scattered sparkles in the thick expanse of sky.

An old blanket lies rolled up in the corner, a forgotten relic of times past. I shake out the dust and hay, then spread the blanket on the floor. Next, the contents of the basket are laid out. I remove the bottle of ale and empty the contents of the vial into it. After swishing it around for a minute, I examine it closely. It looks and smells like plain ale. My pinkie finger dips in and collects the tiniest drop to sample. Tastes like plain ale too.

I smooth out my skirt when I sit down, brushing off the ubiquitous pieces of hay. Everything seems normal, like any one of a thousand picnics we have shared up here. No reason for him to suspect anything. While I wait, I rehearse how I want things to play out. In no time, the barn door creaks on its hinges and Puck's head emerges from the top of the ladder.

"I could smell that chicken from the door. Yum!"

Without pause, he hops down on the blanket and shovels in hunks of chicken, cheese, and bread. His mouth is barely able to keep up with the pace. There was so much preparation today that Puck likely had no time to eat.

"Good?" I ask, cutting more chunks of cheese and slices of bread to match his ravenous appetite. Crumbs fall all around him in his haste. They stick on his lips and litter the front of his shirt.

After the moment it takes for him to swallow, he responds, "Delicious! Thanks so much for bringing me this. I was starving." Then he adds sincerely, "And thanks for coming back and spending time with me. I didn't want to leave with you angry at me." He ruffles my hair in a sweet gesture.

Remorse slithers into my conscience, spirals around my insides. Hurting Puck is an unfortunate consequence of my plan. Maybe I should rethink things. After all, it isn't too late to back out. I am torn about how to proceed.

"Maybe we should make this a tradition," Puck says.

"Um…what?" I ask, addled at being driven from my thoughts.

"You know, you serving me dinner before I go out on a mission," he says in a tone so unassuming I know in my heart he is not trying to be unkind.

However, at the words "serving me dinner," my outrage over the whole situation is rekindled. Any thoughts of halting the plan are snuffed out. Careful to conceal my emotions, I grab the wooden mug from the basket and fill it to the brim with ale. Its frothy top sloshes over the rim.

"Here, you must be thirsty." I hand it over.

He takes a big swig, wipes his mouth on his sleeve, and sighs with contentment. As he continues his feast, I watch him intently for any sign of the ale's effect—a twitch or unusual movement. I am so engrossed in my scrutinizing it takes me a moment to register Puck's confused expression.

"What?" he asks.

"What what?" It is imperative Puck does not get suspicious. *Focus!*

"Um…why are you staring at me all weird like that? What's going on?"

"Oh, was I staring? I guess I was just thinking…uh—" *please let me think of something to say,* "—of how we probably won't get to spend as much time together any more. Times like this. Now that we are getting older, everything will change."

This sentiment probably comes to me so easily because it is true. Our time has been so predictable these last few years, but the future approaches unclearly. My resolve slightly cracks and regret seeps into the fragile openings. Puck is important to me. Can I risk his anger at my betrayal? I twirl a piece of hay around my fingers and wonder if my plan is worth it.

"Yeah," Puck replies, "it is too bad that you won't be able to continue training with us any longer. But just as well I guess, since the older we're getting, the harder it is for you to keep up with us guys."

Really, Puck? How easy do you want to make this for me?

All lingering guilt is washed away. It is now the point of no return.

"More ale?" I ask. He holds out his cup for a refill.

"Puck, like I asked for before, would you please tell me one of your stories? I always loved the one about Cassiopeia."

"Sure." He moves to the loft opening and sits, his legs dangling out. I settle down next to him and place my head on his shoulder as he points to a place in the north sky.

"She should be appearing over there shortly. Of course, we will see her better in a few months." He pauses and yawns before going on with the familiar story of the vain Cassiopeia, the beautiful Queen of Aethiopia. When he explains how her vanity led to her downfall, I think of Prince Liam and wonder if this type of conceit is a trait that all royal persons share.

Cassiopeia's arrogance insults the god Neptune and almost leads to the death of her daughter, Andromeda. In the end, the hero Perseus steps in to save the day. But, in my favorite part of the story, Neptune has the last laugh when he immortalizes Cassiopeia in the stars. He positions her seated on a throne with her head pointed at the North Star. Her revolution around it causes her to spend half of every night in a humiliating upside-down pose. A bit of humbling, that is just what Prince Liam needs.

When Puck is finally finished, he can barely keep his eyes open. "I don't know why I am so tired all of a sudden," he mumbles.

"Well, you did do an awful lot today." I lead him back inside and close the door behind us. Puck stumbles down, lolls back on the hay piled up against the wall.

"But I can't fall asleep now. I am not done getting things ready," he says, panicked, and makes a half-hearted attempt to stand, but he is so unsteady he drops right back down to his knees.

"Maybe you should close your eyes for a minute or two. I'll wake you up after you take a short nap. I am sure that will refresh you enough to finish getting ready."

"I'm not sure that is a good idea," he protests, but even as he says it he curls up in a heap of straw. Soon he curls into the fetal position, with his head resting on the crook of his arm.

I force myself to wait while I watch Puck's breathing regulate into heavy sleeping. Gingerly, I walk over to his prostrate form.

"Puck?" I whisper.

No response.

"Puck?" I say louder and tap him slightly on the legs with my toes.

No response.

"PUCK?" I yell and give his leg a good swift kick.

No response.

Ah, Mother's sleeping draught—works every time!

Step Five—done.

I collect the remaining food, empty carafe, and mug, and deposit them into the basket. Puck lies sprawled out on the hay, arms and legs curled into his body. His chest rises and falls with each peaceful breath. A shake disperses the crumbs and straw off the blanket that I use to gently cover him. Maybe it makes me a bad person, but excitement replaces my sense of guilt.

With the basket and lantern in hand, I descend the ladder. The quiet barn is laden with the scent of animal. A glance around shows me nothing is awry. Several cows huddle close in their stall, tails swaying ever so slightly in their sleep. Our fat pig reclines on her side with no idea that the coming winter signals her doom. Someone will likely be in early to milk the cows, but there should be nothing to indicate that Puck is passed out in the loft above. He should remain undisturbed until he wakes up sometime tomorrow afternoon or evening.

Back at the armory I double-check everything for tomorrow's journey. Puck's armor is all laid out alongside the gear for the eight knights and their respective squires. I had never been assigned a knight like the rest of the final-year squires—a fact that still bothers me. My father says I am assigned to him, which is, after all, the most prestigious position. We both know he only says this to make me feel better.

Sir Michael's pile of gear sits next to Puck's, with the gleaming sword now back in its scabbard. Thoughts of Puck's knight give me pause. He will prove tricky to fool, I am sure. What precaution can I take to minimize his ascertaining my identity? The armory is windowless, its light obtained only from a door at one end and a fireplace in the rear, so I drag Sir Michael's and Puck's equipment into a back corner. With the hearth unlit, it is quite dim. Hopefully, this will help my cause in the morning. I remove the scissors and the vial from the basket and hide them under Puck's helmet. There is not much more I can do now.

While I stroll back to the house, my mind summons up a picture of Puck passed out in the loft. Did I give him too much of the sleeping draught? How much does Mother usually give one of us when we are feverish or ill? Surely, it is the whole vial. Then again, maybe she only uses half a vial; in which case, I probably just gave Puck enough to dose a small horse! For a brief moment, fear for Puck's safety makes my blood run cold. But then, I distinctly recall Mother giving Anne a whole vial once, and the icy dread retreats.

Now I need to focus on my last problem: how to explain why I will be missing in the morning. Since the plan's inception, no worthy idea has presented itself. When I enter the kitchen, Lucy busily puts things in place for breakfast in the morning. She takes one look at me and sighs. Anxiety must be written all over my face.

"You all right, Miss Olivia?" Lucy asks in the kind, calm manner she has used all my life. Her little round body bobs around the kitchen like a just-hooked fishing lure.

"Yes, of course," I utter too quickly.

Blurting may be the one thing that will tip Lucy off. This is the woman who spent my childhood mediating fights between my sisters and me, patching up all my cuts and scrapes (and there were many) while listening to the stories of how I had gotten them, and just generally getting to the bottom of any, as she called it, "monkey business." Lucy knows blurting equals trouble.

"I know why you are so upset and I don't blame you. You are just so disappointed that you can't go tomorrow." She takes the picnic basket out of my hands and lays it on the counter, then clasps her chubby hands together as she nods sympathetically.

"Oh, yes. Real disappointed." I play along, even staring down at the floor despondently.

"But you know, it's for the best."

Ah, one of Lucy's catchphrases. She is a veritable font of idioms. Other favorites are, "It will all work out in the end" and "Everything happens for a reason." Each of her expressions is vague enough in meaning that no matter what the eventual outcome is, she can point back to how she had predicted it. I cannot criticize her though. Her attitude is rosier than anyone else's I ever met, and these sentiments bring her comfort.

"I know." An idea that may solve my problem leaps to mind. I slump down on a stool by the counter and put my head on my arms. The surface smells vaguely of garlic and mint.

"There, there." She comes around behind me to stroke my back and hair. Lucy never feels more useful than when she is soothing away some inner hurt.

I have her right where I want her.

"Lucy," I whisper despondently, "I just don't think I can bear to watch everyone leaving tomorrow knowing that I can't go with them. It will be too hard."

"Of course it will be, you poor dear." She spins me around, clasps my face in her hands. They feel so warm after the chilly night air.

I manage to produce some tears to go with my distraught voice. Seeing this, Lucy wraps her arms around me in a fierce hug. Her large bosom crushes into my stomach, deprives me of breath. Flyaway strands of her disobedient curls tickle my chin.

"I just think that…" I trail off sadly.

"Think what, baby?"

"Maybe it would be better if I am not here, then I don't have to watch at all." Lucy seems like she is trying to reason this out, so I add, "Maybe I could go over to the big blackberry patch on the side of Fern Hill. I could spend the morning picking blackberries."

Fern Hill is quite a good walk away, at the extreme edge of the city limits. Beyond it lies only wilderness for many miles. If I wanted to be alone, there would be no better spot than this virtually uninhabited one. Lucy contemplates this idea, her brow furrowed while she searches for an argument against it.

"You always say there is nothing like fresh blackberries," I remind her, "and when I get back, we could spend the afternoon making blackberry tarts." Lucy is a sucker for blackberry tarts and for any chance to do something domestic like baking with me.

She moves to the other side of the counter and empties the picnic basket. The carafe, mug, and towels are each set out in a deliberate manner while Lucy ponders. My mother has gone to bed, so Lucy will be responsible for this decision. Under normal circumstances, she would not hesitate to let me go, but I think she is trying to decide if my mother will be upset that I miss Father's send-off. All I can do is wait. I keep my head down on my arms and try to radiate a pathetic vibe.

After what seems like an eternity, she finally sighs. "Yes, Miss Olivia, I think that sounds like a good idea. It will keep your mind off things and get us some good dessert as well. I will tell your mother in the morning where you went and why. No one could blame you for being so hurt, especially after all the time and effort you put into your training."

Now I truly could cry. Nobody in the house has ever acknowledged my hard work. Mother pretends my training does not exist and never so much as mentions it. She has heavily discouraged my sisters from talking about it as well. To know that Lucy understands my disappointment and feels it is justified, well, it is beyond gratifying. Unfortunately, it is a safe bet Lucy will have different feelings tomorrow when my real intentions become clear.

"By the way, did Peter enjoy his dinner?" Lucy asks. She ducks into the pantry to restore the basket to its proper place. Rustling and rattling can be heard as her ample form picks its way through the mess.

"Very much so," I assure her.

She comes out with the large metal pail for the berry picking and places it on the counter. My long yawn triggers one for Lucy. It is time for bed. We extinguish the oil lamps and set the stools back in order. Lucy takes her candle and we head for the hall. The kitchen fades to an outline of orderly shadows.

"Well, Peter is going to have a long day tomorrow. I hope he gets himself a good night's sleep," she muses, straightening a picture on the wall.

"I am pretty sure he will," I manage to choke out.

At my bedroom door, Lucy kisses my cheek, as she has since I was little. "Sleep well, my little Livy."

Despite my fatigue, I lie awake in bed. A hundred thoughts drift around my head like dust specks in a sunbeam. No one should be alarmed by my absence in the morning. It will take a good while of the day before that lie is unraveled. I fear how everything will play out, but this is tempered by my determination to see things through.

Clearly I will not get away with my plan undiscovered but, as I see it, the key is *when* I get caught. If I can make it out of the city and well into the first, or even the second day, then even though my father will be furious, he will be forced to let me finish the mission. I am more worried about him getting in trouble with the King. However, my father's stunned reaction at my unmasking should prove he was unwitting of the whole thing. Surely, the King will recognize my father played no part in my act of stupidity.

Anyway, all these men have no problem whatsoever dictating to me how I must live the rest of my life. They decide what is appropriate and what is allowable. So what is the worst they can do? Yell at me? Ban me from going on any other missions ever again?

Believe me, I realize that is my future either way.

Ellen's deep breathing and Lydia's soft nasal snore tell me they are fast asleep. When I had first entered the room, they were whispering and giggling with each other in their bed. Now, my sisters lie intertwined in a contented tangle of warm bodies. It reminds me of the years when I slept in that bed with Anne, while Jayne was in my current bed. Anne and I shared all kinds of secrets and stories about our dreams for the future. We had actually been close in those days.

The older girls had moved to another room when Ellen and Lydia came along. Now, with Jayne married, Anne has that room to herself. Mother had asked if I wanted to move into the room with Anne and get away from the younger girls, but I chose to stay in this room. It just felt more fitting. Sometimes I wonder at what exact point the bond between Anne and I had broken. Her dreams and mine have long since taken different paths. Will we ever again be able to resuscitate a bit of the closeness we once shared, or is it lost forever, along with the rest of our childhood?

The moon reels across the sky, a bright half circle. Its position lets me know when enough time has passed I sit up onto the side of my bed. Lydia lies close to the edge of the mattress, curled in a ball, her face angelic in slumber. Next to her Ellen lies flat on her back like a corpse, her frame so thin and delicate it brings to mind a little bird. Brunette hair, not quite as thick and lovely as Anne's, falls around her pillow. In fact where I seem the less bright version of Lydia, Ellen seems the dimmer version of Anne. A circumstance we always hold as an unspoken link between us.

Quietly, I reach under the bed to grab my sparring outfit. Father allows me to wear a tunic and breeches when training, but only on Mother's condition that I never wear them off of our property. The loose garments slip on quickly. I grab my boots and hug them against my chest, then creep out of the room. The door clicks softly behind me.

On tiptoe I slink through the darkened house to the kitchen. A drawer in the hutch eases open, and I pull out the stub of a mostly used candle and some flint and tinder. Then, I grab the metal bucket waiting where Lucy left it. The clanging noise it makes when lifted off the counter freezes me in my tracks. I count to ten and listen for the slightest sound in case I have woken someone. When I am sure I have not been heard, I sneak out the back door.

Crisp night air calms my racing heart. When I sink onto a bench to don my boots, the musky smell of firewood floats faintly into my nostrils. The methodical act of lacing them puts me into "squire mode," centered and ready for what I need to do. I slip to the armory silent as a wraith and squeeze through the door, shutting it firmly behind me.

Once the candle is lit, I check around. Everything is the same as when I left a few hours ago. The knights' and squires' gear is arranged in piles. Saddlebags stand ready to be packed with supplies, waterskins ready to fill. I walk over to Puck's things. His armor consists of a leather jerkin, breastplate, and helmet. Time to see what I look like in it.

His jerkin is made of stiff brown leather that is fairly worn in some areas. Lifting it over my head, I am surprised at how heavy it is once settled on my shoulders. An old one that my father lets me wear is much lighter. Tightening the laces down the side, I reach for the breastplate. This is actually lighter than the hand-me-down I have and fits me quite well. The helmet is bronze, with ear flaps and a nose strip down the center. I have worn one of these before, during training, so I know how well it obscures one's face. Almost a squire but for one last, important detail.

Across the room there is a barrel on which stands an old white, chipped pitcher and a crude wooden bowl. The barrel leans against a post that has a mirror attached to it at eye level. Knights and squires wash their faces and hands here when returning to the armory after a day of sparring or actual battle.

I retrieve the scissors from the floor where Puck's helmet had been and walk over to the mirror. The image I see is me in Puck's armor, which will not do. Removing the helmet I stare at my reflection for a good long moment. What I am about to do suddenly upsets me much more than I ever imagined. But these feelings must be forced aside, so I steel my resolve and grab a fistful of my waist-long hair. In one rapid snip, it is cut off to my shoulder. A few moments later, all the hair left on my head sits on my collar and the rest is strewn out around me on the floor like a pile of limp spaghetti. I allow myself one moment to glance at it wistfully, but it is not as much a shame as it would have been with Jayne's or Anne's beautiful hair. Approaching the mirror, I shove Puck's helmet back on my head. With the short hair I do appear quite "Puck-ish," surprisingly so if you don't look me directly in the eyes.

For my plan to work, I am relying on a phrase my father taught me in my lessons: "In general, people see what they expect to see." He gave an example of a raid on one of our northern settlements. The pillagers disguised themselves as traveling peasants, quarry workers, and one was even dressed as a pregnant woman. They were able to infiltrate the city and spread out to strategic positions before commencing their attack. No one had paid them any mind because they had blended in. My hope is that in the morning people will expect to see Puck, so if I play the part well enough, no one will question it.

The fallen hair is stashed in the empty berry bucket, along with the scissors and the empty vial. Now I need a place to hide it, a place where no one will find it accidentally tomorrow. My eyes come to rest on the barrel right in front of me. A tap with my foot produces a hollow ring. Removing the pitcher and the bowl, I tip it up a few inches. Sure enough, it was emptied and then flipped over to use as a makeshift stand. I deposit the bucket on the bare spot underneath and lower the barrel back down over it. No one will be searching for anything there.

With nothing left to do, I settle down in the corner next to Puck's gear. There are still a couple of hours until dawn, that distinct time of hushed, foreboding stillness. A surprising sense of calm flows over me. It is possible I may even relax a bit until morning. I remove the helmet, but decide to leave the jerkin and breastplate on. Then, I blow out the candle and darkness engulfs the armory.

There is nothing to do now but wait.

I must doze off because the next thing I hear is heavy footsteps outside. Weak light filters in from the crack under the armory door. Springing to my feet, I manage to grab Puck's helmet and shove it on my head just as Sir Michael lumbers through the door.

A large man with a commanding presence, his prematurely grey hair falls in curls to his shoulders, framing a face shrouded with a full mustache and beard. His piercing eyes, as grey and steely as his hair, and his booming voice send fear through the stoutest of squires when he is angry. One superficial nod is all I merit before he strides over to his gear.

Hopefully, Puck had everything Sir Michael needs in order, so I can keep our contact to a bare minimum. After surveying the equipment, he seems satisfied and starts to put on his jerkin without a word. And I better stop staring at him and get busy. I stock the supply bags with the food, water, and incidentals we will need. These are loaded into the saddlebags for our horses. Other knights and squires trickle in, everyone intent on readying for the journey.

"Hey, Puck," a voice says to me. At first I stiffen, but it is only Albert, one of my fellow squires. Albert towers a head taller than our biggest knight. His nickname is Blade—not for a sword, but because his painfully thin build reminds the knights of a blade of grass. The fact that he is also not intellectually sharp makes the nickname even more amusing to everyone. He is harmless.

"Hey," I answer in a gruff tone to discourage any further conversation.

He studies me a moment, and sweat forms on my brow. If Albert can tell I am not Puck, it does not bode well for my disguise. Finally, he leans down to my ear and whispers, "Um…are we supposed to wear our helmets?"

"Yes. Sir Jack's orders," I answer in the same curt manner—but inside a wave of relief rushes over me.

Albert says no more and simply sticks his helmet on his head, then continues to ready his gear. This short dialogue actually works out well because when the rest of the squires notice Albert and me with our helmets on, they all follow suit. Now I won't stand out as the only one wearing it.

"Puck, get over here and help me with this confounded buckle!" Sir Michael orders.

In a flash, I am at his side to assist. One of the brass buckles that holds Sir Michael's breastplate closed has gotten tangled in an awkward spot by his back. He cannot reach it, despite his contortions. Deftly, my fingers untangle the fastener, then see it properly closed. All the while my head is down and my eyes are firmly planted on the floor. My heartbeat pounds in my ears, as I am certain that at this proximity, Sir Michael will detect my identity. But, he is busy in conversation with the other knights regarding the journey.

"Thank you, boy." He waves at me dismissively when I start to step away. So, Sir Michael is the first to prove the point of people seeing what they expect to see.

After that, it is quite easy to remain unnoticed. There are seven other knights and seven other squires who mill around, all intent on their own affairs. I grab my saddlebags and head for the stable, where the horses are ready to go. Puck's and Sir Michael's steeds walk with me to the point of departure in our property's main courtyard. The knights each have their own mount, whereas the squires share a group of horses that we use during the training. One of the highlights of being selected a knight is a trip to the southern province to select your own stallion—a highlight I will never get to experience.

The horse assigned to Puck today is an older, white-and-black dappled horse named Pepper, who saw his share of action some years back. His tolerant temperament makes him good for training, and I have ridden him many times. While we stand waiting, he nudges my head with his nose as if to say he likes our pairing as well. Funny, Pepper is the only one who knows my true identity at the moment.

The courtyard is a bustle of activity. Servants, pages, and stable boys scurry back and forth like ants around a disrupted nest. Squires lead out their horses, joining me at the gate's threshold. Knights emerge from the armory together and climb into their saddles, and the squires follow suit. Townspeople line the main road to watch the departure of the King's party. My mother and sisters, along with Lucy and Grace, come out of our house and join the spectators. When my father steps out the front door, I involuntarily suck in my breath. Cloaked in his armor, his entire bearing commands attention, an aura of authority and intimidation emanates from him. Mounting his waiting steed, he swings around to address the company.

"Good morning, gentlemen. As you know, today's journey will find us leading King William on a diplomatic mission to meet with King John in the North." Father sits tall and confident in the saddle, his eyes scanning the crowd. The knights assemble in a semicircle around him, with their squires just behind. As much as possible, I shield myself from my father's gaze behind Sir Michael.

"I have asked the oldest class of squires to join us in order for them to gain some experience and to glean valuable knowledge from this distinguished corps of knights. I remind you all that we are traveling with His Majesty the King, and even though this trip may seem devoid of danger, we must always be on our utmost guard for the safety of His Majesty. Your behavior and comportment during this mission will be a direct reflection on your ability to operate as a knight in Stewartsland."

This last statement has the intended effect. All the squires sit up straighter in their saddles, assuming a more knightly demeanor. I even catch myself doing it. My father recognizes that without any imminent threat, young men may lose focus and become rowdy with excitement. His statements should nip this in the bud and make friendly socializing between us seem inappropriate. Good. The less anyone has reason to talk to me the better. Fleetingly, I wonder how much my father has confided in the knights his qualms about this mission. Are they aware of his misgivings?

At a wave of my father's hand, the company moves out. Our first stop is the palace to meet the King's party. The route is filled with people waving colorful pennants and cheering. Children sit on shoulders or cram through legs for a better view. As we pass through the city wall, I notice the fat, little gatekeeper, this time much more conscientious about his job. A horde of citizens packs the inner square. Shouts ring out from enterprising food and drink vendors, who capitalize on the uncommon crowd.

The King's entourage emerges from the royal stables. King William rides at the center of the troop astride a black stallion, his imperial silver armor glinting in the sun. Even in middle age, his hair still curls thickly in raven black waves to his shoulders. A hint of grey at his temples emphasizes the simple, golden circlet that adorns his head. The years as King have imparted his face with a permanently stoic expression, which may be perceived as coldness, but his kind, just leadership has bestowed on him the adoration of his subjects.

With his escort in tow, King William rides to the front to greet my father. First comes his councilor, who will advise in all legal matters. Next his feeble old priest, since the King devoutly receives Holy Communion every day. The cleric's timeworn body hunches unsteadily in his saddle. I am amazed he has the stamina to even attempt this journey. They are followed by two royal bodyguards, a staff bearer, and a trumpeter all dressed in the King's livery—a mighty oak tree pillared by two boars topped with the insignia "Vires et Honorem" (Strength and Honor). And then, one last person passes, the sight of whom constricts the air in my lungs.

Prince Liam.

For a moment, my heart stops—along with time itself. The courtyard enters a dream-like fog where everything moves in slow motion as my mind tries to catch up with what unfolds before me. Why is Prince Liam on this mission? Surely, it makes more sense to bring Prince Harold As heir to the throne, he will handle negotiations of this sort in the future. But it is Prince Liam in front of me, cloaked in his armor, his face impassive.

He glances around at the company, no trace of expression betraying what goes through his mind. His gaze stops on me and lingers for a moment. I should look away, but my body refuses to respond to my command and remains unmoving. My heart freezes as his eyes narrow ever so slightly. There is no way he could recognize me from yards away with my head buried inside a helmet, right? One second passes, then another, with our eyes locked. Then a bodyguard addresses him and points off beyond the city gates. Prince Liam turns his head, and the connection is broken. I have to remind myself to breathe again.

"Didn't know *he* was coming," I hear one of the squires mumble to Albert.

"Don't worry, Francis, he won't associate with the likes of us mere mortals," he replies.

"True," Francis agrees with a snicker.

So Prince Liam is not well thought of by the squires. This is an interesting piece of information. The guys must not discuss it around me for fear I would tell my father their derogatory remarks. What is it exactly that they do not like? He sits immobile on his horse, his face as stern and unfeeling as ever. Suddenly, I remember his smug, condescending manner from the other day; my sympathy quickly wanes. If his dealings with the other squires are anything like the one he had with me, I can understand why they think poorly of him.

"I heard Olivia had a run-in with him the other day," Albert states. *Boy, news travels fast—I wonder how he heard about it.* "That must have been interesting. You know she wouldn't hesitate to put him in his place."

"No, she wouldn't," Francis agrees with a chuckle. "It's a shame she couldn't come with us today. She has certainly earned her place among us, but I guess being a girl and all..."

"It's funny, I never really think about her as a girl—she's just one of us, you know—but I suppose Sir Jack has more to consider," Albert says.

My eyes almost tear up knowing my classmates hold me in such regard. After all these years and all my hard work, I have been unsure if they truly saw me as an equal. It's gratifying to hear their words.

A trumpeter sounds the departure signal and the horses fall in line to commence the journey. Cheers rise up through the crowd as they wave pennants and throw flowers in our path. The King's staff bearer and trumpeter lead the way, followed by the King, the Prince, and their party; the ancient priest teetering precariously; then my father; and finally the knights in two lines, each followed directly behind by their personal squire. Sir Michael rides in the middle of the pack so we are, thankfully, not right behind my father. Sir Gavin, Albert's knight, trots next to Sir Michael, which puts my non-observant friend next to me—an ideal arrangement in my book.

We proceed at a nice pace down the road and soon pass my family's compound again. Mother, Anne, Ellen, and Lydia stand on the roadside to watch the spectacle, with Grace and Lucy right behind them. Lydia, who is absolutely overjoyed at the sight of the royal procession, bounces around like a jumping bean. Her pure enjoyment makes my face break into the tiniest of smiles, until I notice Lucy staring right at me with a keen expression. For a moment, I am sure she recognizes me, but she abruptly shakes her head as if to convince herself she is imagining things. Better plant my gaze firmly forward, until we are out of the city limits.

My first day passes with surprising ease. We make excellent time, so good in fact, that it may be possible to make it all the way to Lindenwood by nightfall of the next day. In the early stages of the journey, we ride through small villages and hamlets where clusters of people file out to watch our procession. The farther we travel from Adelina, the less populous the land becomes. Open fields spread out as far as the eye can see. Every once in a while, a stray farmer at work in the sun stops his toil and watches us in bewilderment. At one point, we pass a convent, its bell tower soaring over the flat countryside, the nuns inside singing hymns that echo ethereally into the open air around us. Eventually, the landscape changes from clumps of bushes, to patches of trees, to forest on both sides of the road, and the ride becomes more monotonous. Beyond the trees, the rushing of the Crystal River sounds in the distance.

Father spends most of the day up front with the King. The knights use the ride for instruction, pointing out different terrain and how to use the natural landscape to your advantage when you are in battle. They also describe what types of areas make the most attractive hideouts for outlaws. And to think, I would have missed out on all of this. It makes my blood boil.

We stop only once, at midday, to eat and water the horses. I need to escape off on my own so that I can relieve myself. Puck was correct when he said this would be an issue. As I lead my two animals down to the river, I am dismayed to see Albert with his horses coming to join me. How am I going to get rid of him?

"What do you think so far?" he asks eagerly. "Those tactics Sir Richard mentioned about how to avoid being trapped in low ground were quite interesting, don't you think?"

Great. Albert is in a chatty mood and my bladder is about to burst. I shrug. Perhaps my indifference will make him pipe down.

"You're awful quiet today, Puck. Everything all right?" he asks, such genuine concern in his voice there is no way I can blow him off.

"I ate something that didn't agree with me last night," I mumble. An idea hits me so I add, "In fact, I need to use the bathroom." I clutch my stomach dramatically.

"Oh, that is too bad," says Albert sympathetically. He scans the area. "Why don't you go over there?" He points a bit downstream to a clump of bushes. "I'll keep an eye on the horses and warn everyone of your…um…situation."

"Thanks," I yell over my shoulder and sprint off in the direction of the bushes. They provide the perfect amount of privacy, and Albert keeps everyone else away. Now that wasn't so hard. Of course, it would have been easier if he had just known I was a girl. But Puck was wrong about it being a major problem. I feel pretty good about things when I return to the horses. Their reins in hand, I prepare to lead them back to the group.

"Oh, wait a sec…" says Albert. He steps over to a tree, lifts the flap on his jerkin and begins unbuttoning his trousers.

I almost yell out, *What on earth are you doing?* but I bite my lip just in time. Of course the guys urinate in front of each other all the time, so I can't make a big deal about it. My face flushes hot with embarrassment while I cower between my two horses. It was naive to not see something like this coming. If they just let me come as a girl, situations like this could have been avoided.

Albert finishes his business then walks over cheerily. "All set. You feeling any better, Puck?"

"Not anymore," I mutter, more to myself than him.

We rejoin our party, and the rest of the day is, thankfully, uneventful. It is late when we stop to make camp. The squires carry themselves with drooped heads and sagging shoulders, unused to the exertion of a day's march. Wispy black clouds obscure the moon's light, offering little hint about where we are, but I gather it is a place familiar to my father. No doubt a location often used as a campsite by the knights. After a quick meal of salted meat and dried fruit, I unfurl my bedroll by a tree at a distance from the main fire. Quickly, I pull off my breastplate and helmet, then duck my head under the covers.

Day One is behind me.

I fall into a sound sleep, content that whatever happens now, I will be able to finish out the mission.

I wake just before dawn, the sky a steely grey with wisps of pink hovering on the horizon. I ease the corner of the blanket off my face and peer around. In the dim light, a well-defined clearing opens before me, nestled beside the road amidst dense, green foliage. Slumbering bodies are strewn about it like dropped breadcrumbs. So far, no one else stirs.

A stream babbles through the trees at the rear of the camp. Stuffing my helmet on, I creep down to its edge and furtively remove my helmet to wash my face. One splash of the frigid water jolts any remnants of sleep away. I stuff the helmet back in place. All along the bank, the horses are tethered to trees. They whinny and stomp in the cool morning's air. I find Pepper and stroke his mane. My luck could actually hold out for the whole trip. After all, no one has given me so much as a second glance yet. I'll just continue to keep my head down. Confident with this notion, I make my way back to camp to load my pack up for the day's journey.

Others now rouse, roll up their bedding, eat a quick meal, and don their gear. There is little chatting amongst anyone. While this makes things easier for me, I am a bit surprised by the lack of discussion. The knights all have matter-of-fact expressions on their faces; this is, after all, business as usual for them. My fellow squires follow the knights' example, each one keeping to himself. Or perhaps, everyone is just afraid to disturb the King.

The royal tent is erected on a small rise toward the back of the clearing. An impressive structure, its sturdy canvas walls are canopied with luxurious navy-and-red silk. One of the bodyguards stands as sentry outside. Next to the tent stands a lesser version minus the silk, undoubtedly for the councilor and priest. So far, there is no movement from either structure.

Stale bread and sharp, hard cheese serve as my breakfast. I lean against a tree trunk and watch the King's pavilion. The flap to the royal tent opens, and Prince Liam strides out dressed in his armor, the Stewart coat of arms gleaming on his breastplate. He stands with his hands on his hips and surveys the camp, his eyes sweeping in a semicircle around the men. They come to rest on me. Once again, I feel like a rabbit in a trap. His eyes pierce me in an inquisitive way.

Calm down. You are under a tree with a helmet on, for goodness sake. From a distance, he should not even be able to tell if I am looking at him or just staring off into the distance. Of course, he is so arrogant he probably thinks everyone wants to stare at his greatness all the time. I need to breathe and slow down my heart, which pounds erratically. Prince Liam's attention has an unnatural effect on me.

His attention is suddenly diverted by Father walking up the rise toward him. They engage in a short conversation, and I take the opportunity to disappear before Prince Liam notices me again. I dust off and grab my bags, intending to fetch the horses. Only one short step later I hear an angry voice yell, "Peter! Where are you?"

It is Sir Michael. He is not happy. Freezing in my tracks, I spin around to him, as does nearly everyone else.

"Get over here, lad," he yells in my direction, "this stupid lace has broken."

In an instant, I am at his side. Indeed, the end of the leather lace that secures the left side of his jerkin has snapped off. His supply sack sits nearby. I rummage through it, hunting for a replacement cord. Surely, Puck packed an extra lace or something that can be used as a reasonable substitute.

Uh-oh!

Dread drifts in, envelops me in its icy claws. My stomach becomes lead. Puck had spoken about replacing the laces of Sir Michael's jerkin in the armory the other night. Obviously, he had planned to do it before the journey, but he did not get the chance—because I had interrupted him with dinner and…

My heart races, sweat beads on my brow. I am paralyzed with fear until a boot toe jabs my side. "Look alive, boy!" Sir Michael orders. Mechanically, I resume groping through the bag hoping to find something—anything—that I can improvise with. There is nothing.

"What I don't understand is why these laces were not replaced *prior* to this trip. They clearly needed to be," he snaps.

Unsure what else to do, I mumble an apology.

Bad move.

Sir Michael takes this as insolence and yanks me up by the armpit. Spinning me around to face him, he roars, "I am speaking to you, Peter, and therefore require your undivided attention. Do you understand?"

I stand there mutely, aware that his yelling has drawn the attention of everyone. Certainly, they all try to act as if they are not listening, but I am sure every ear is perked up in this direction. Before I can think of a way out of this situation…

"And take off that blasted helmet so you can look me straight in the eyes when I am talking to you!" In one fell swoop, he reaches out and knocks my helmet to the ground. "Surely I have taught you more respect than…"

His words abruptly cease.

Under different circumstances, his expression would be quite comical. He has stopped yelling in midsentence, his mouth agape, eyes wide and disbelieving. His face resembles those painted masks some gypsy vendors sell at our city's festivals. Lydia has one; she always tries to scare Grace with it. Since no response from me seems to be required, I stare at the ground and wait for all the pieces to fall into place for him. To my surprise, he draws his sword and points the tip right at my throat. For some reason, at this stressful moment, my brain manages to register that this is the second time in three days I have had a sword to my throat. Not such a good track record. His next words surprise me even more.

"Who are *you?*" He scowls. "Speak quickly!"

"Olivia," I say in a strangulated whisper. It dawns on me that Sir Michael does not have the first clue who I am. For all he knows, I mean them harm, particularly the King, whom he is sworn to protect with his life.

"Who?" The point pushes painfully into my neck.

"Olivia?"

This time the voice isn't mine. It is my father's. He rushed over at the sound of the commotion and now stands with much the same expression Sir Michael had a moment ago.

"How…? What are you…? Explain yourself, young lady!"

All right, I have not thought this part out particularly well. Here I am surrounded by knights, most of whom have their swords drawn ready to assist Sir Michael, followed closely behind by the squires. It is a fairly safe bet no one is going to take my side in the "I just found it unfair that I was not allowed to go on this trip in the first place" argument.

Shifting my feet uneasily on the ground, I blurt out the first thing that comes to mind, "Well, I told you I wanted to come."

In life there is plain old anger and then there is outright betrayal. I see the latter in my father's eyes. A look Puck will no doubt duplicate when I get home. Two of the people I care most about in the world have been hurt by my selfishness. Somehow this consequence did not seem as horrible when I planned this all out. It does now.

My father marches forward, shoving the sword tips out of his way. As he grabs my arm and pulls me away, he gives a hard glare at all the men. "Don't just stand around. Make ready to depart!"

The circle around me disperses like seeds blown from a dandelion, but there are more than a few smirks on their faces when they saunter away. Father yanks me over to a large fallen tree that lies rotting on the ground. He pushes me down on the trunk, then spins to face the camp. I know better than to speak while he tries to get his anger under control. My fingers nervously play with moss and fungus covering the bark.

"That you pulled this stunt doesn't surprise me as much as the fact that you got Puck to go along with it," he spits out through clenched teeth.

"Well, um…Puck didn't exactly agree to this willingly," I mumble, pulling off a clump of moss and breaking it up. Clumps of green fuzz crumble to the ground, the pigment discoloring my hand.

"How do you mean?"

"I sort of…drugged him." I drop the rest of the moss and wipe my hands on the legs of my breeches, where it leaves a vivid stain.

Father spins around. "You *what?* What on earth did you give the poor lad?"

"Mother's sleeping draught," I say, still unable to meet his eyes. "Then I cut my hair and took his place. He knew nothing of my plan. I expect he will be even less happy about it than you are."

"I am not sure that is possible," Father says sternly. "I cannot express my disappointment in you right now, Olivia. Did you ever even stop to think that the repercussions will not just be for you, but for me as well? How do you think this makes me look in front of the King? Will he now think that anyone who wanted to could have snuck into this party right under my nose? That is almost as bad as him thinking that I cannot control my own daughter. Which is obviously the case. And when he already has your garden trespassing incident fresh in his mind!"

He gives a long sigh and gazes back at the camp. Now I just have to wait for him to realize the only solution to this dilemma: that I continue on the mission. I cannot go back home alone, and it would be unseemly for him to send me with any of the men except himself, but from a royal security standpoint that is not an option. So what else can be done but to bring me along?

I feel horrible, though, that I embarrassed him in front of all the men. If there had been more time to come up with a suitable plan, I would have tried to avoid that. When my father dismissed the men, Sir Michael made a beeline for the King's tent. He must be worried I made him look bad as well. And King William must be annoyed by my antics and the holdup it now causes. At least we won't have to wait long to find out, because the King and his entire escort are making their way over to us right now.

Under his breath my father mutters, "Don't you say one single word when they get over here. Do you understand, Olivia? Not. One. Word."

"Yes, sir," I whisper back at his wasted warning; I have no intention of saying anything. The party comes to a halt in front of us. King William scans me from head to toe, sizing me up. Is he trying to decide what to do with me, or how to punish me? Maybe I will be meeting his jailer after all.

"Your Majesty," my father says, bowing. "First let me offer my utmost apologies for my daughter's behavior. I assure you I had no prior knowledge she was planning this little escapade."

"Yes, I think that was made rather clear by the horror on your face when she was discovered," the King replies, a hint of amusement in his voice.

"Secondly, I am most sorry for the inconvenience and delay this has caused."

As my father makes his apologies, I peek up at Prince Liam where he stands just in front of me, his arms crossed haughtily over his chest. The arrogant expression on his face annoys me. Why did he have to come over here anyway? This in no way involves him. Maybe he wants to mock me again. Although he does not so much as glance at me, I sense his attention radiating toward me.

"Not at all," King William says, waving his hand unaffectedly. "I came to offer the young lady one of my guards as an escort home."

What?

That is not part of my plan! And besides, my father could not seriously consider sending me off into the woods with a strange man, royal guard or not. It takes every ounce of my restraint to not jump up and protest.

"That is gracious of you, Your Majesty," my father answers. "However, I am concerned about the propriety of that arrangement. Not," he adds hastily, "that I would expect anything less than the highest scruples from one of your men."

Good. So Father has a grasp on the situation. Sending me back with any strange man and no female chaperone is entirely inappropriate. And there are no other women on the trip. Too bad Puck isn't here; my father would trust him with me. Now, they will all have to work out the only viable option—that I continue on the trip. I merely sit quietly and wait for them to come to this inevitable conclusion.

"Well, I certainly understand your feelings. Especially since the young lady in question is your daughter," King William agrees. "I am sure if I had a daughter of my own, I would feel much the same way."

They discuss me as if I am not sitting right here, as if I have no capacity for thought—or hearing. I am actually quite capable of taking care of myself and could get home without help from any man, thank you anyway. Not that I will suggest this as an option, of course.

Time drags into a prolonged silence. Birds chatter in the trees, the river bubbles happily by, the men are all packed and ready to go. They stand in a huddled mass waiting for instructions from their superiors. Come on guys, surely one of you can figure out the answer. My father must be aware of the only solution, so why isn't he saying anything? Perhaps he is waiting for the King to suggest it, so it appears he thought of the idea and can take credit for it.

"If I may make a suggestion, Sir Jack…" Prince Liam begins.

I am so happy someone is finally going to state the obvious, I don't even care that it is coming from his egotistical mouth. But then, he decides to become the next person to throw a wrench in my plans.

"Why don't I accompany the young lady home along with one of the guards. I give my word that everything will be handled with the utmost discretion."

Really?

So just because you are Prince Liam, "your word" should be enough?

To my surprise, though, both my father and the King sigh with relief. Will my father just send me off with these two men on Prince Liam's word alone? Then I remember, to my dismay, in the eyes of the law and the church, a royal promise is sacred. My father is in no position to argue with the offer even if he is unhappy about it, which is not the case anyway. Why would he be? This proposal easily resolves the problem for him.

"Thank you, Prince Liam. That would be a most fitting solution, provided it is agreeable to His Majesty." My father's voice sounds hazy through the anger ringing in my ears.

"Oh, quite all right by me," the King replies, then addresses Prince Liam. "You won't feel that you are missing out on anything, son?"

"No, Sire. Not at all," Prince Liam answers in that half-amused voice I am growing to hate. I'm glad I can provide such entertainment for him. Again.

My gaze is planted firmly on my feet. I fear if I look up at him, I will lunge and scratch his eyes out for ruining my carefully crafted plan. Wrath consumes me, like a flame on a green leaf, it burns, curling and warping my insides, blinding me with its heat. Deep breaths. I need to concentrate on a way to control this fury on the humiliating trip back home. Father will be in enough trouble because of me, I don't want to make it any worse.

"Well, it's all settled then. I will have her packed and ready to depart in a half an hour," Father assures them.

He speaks about me as if I were an object to be transported rather than a human being. But I guess that is what I am now — a nuisance parcel that needs to be returned. The royal entourage all nod in accord and walk back to the now-dismantled royal pavilion. Father finally faces me. I do not meet his gaze for fear of seeing the disappointment in his eyes.

"All right then, Olivia, not only can I not undo the trouble and embarrassment you have caused here, but I also do not have the time to deal with you accordingly. *That*," he says ominously, "I will do when I get home."

"I am sorry, Father," I mumble, trying to sound contrite instead of irate at being sent home under such unpleasant conditions, while I push a small pinecone around on the ground with my toe.

"Hmm, for which part I wonder? For disobeying and undermining your father? For putting your mother into what I am sure by now is a theatrical state of anxiety? For drugging your best friend and eliminating his chance to participate in this mission? Or just for the simple fact that you got caught—which was inevitable, I hope you realize? And all this when you knew my misgivings about the safety of this trip!"

This is all said in a calm voice that belies my father's clenched jaw and the pulse throbbing in his neck.

We remain in silence for a few moments, each contemplating our own feelings on the situation. Sparrows merrily chirp, hunting our camp's perimeter for any errant crumbs. The men await orders to march, and I see more than one sly glance in our direction. My eyes meet Albert s, and I can't help but notice his mortified face, no doubt remembering our break time yesterday. Sir Michael glares at me outright, peeved at being deceived by my ruse in the first place.

"Gather up any traveling supplies you will need to get home. Leave anything that will be of use to Sir Michael, who—" Father notes pointedly, "—will now have to share the service of a squire for the remainder of the trip."

When I rise to retrieve my belongings, my father takes my arm in one hand, lifts my chin with the other, and instructs, "Remember, Olivia, Prince Liam is a member of the royal family. You may not speak to him unless you are spoken to first. And please, Livy, for my sake, speak as little as possible to him. You have a tendency to volunteer too much information without thinking."

"So no blurting," I say to show I understand his train of thought perfectly.

"Exactly."

I don't particularly need the advice. There is nothing to say to the arrogant fool who ruined the plan I had for the only mission in which I will ever be likely to participate. Nothing good at least. Besides, I think, remembering what Albert said, I am sure he will not want to associate with a mere mortal like myself.

Packing takes me less than five minutes. Dismally, I saddle up Pepper while I wait for the Prince to join me. My part in this mission is over.

The King's party heads north for Lindenwood. Prince Liam, a guard, and I set off in the opposite direction back to Adelina. When we mount the horses, the guard, whose name is Adam, and Prince Liam share some brief, quiet words. Then we ride in single file, Adam in front followed by Prince Liam. I bring up the rear, my head down in disgust and defeat. This is not how I imagined my journey home. Prince Liam and Adam must be irritated with me for abruptly ending their mission. Escorting a disobedient, stowaway girl home is probably not on their list of ways to spend the morning.

Every once in a while I peek up from my misery at the Prince's back. He rides proudly in his saddle, shoulders back, head held high. Even with no one there to see him, the royal bearing remains, the entitlement and haughtiness too innate to falter. My sisters will absolutely die when they find out my proximity to him. And Mother will absolutely die when she finds out the reason. I have to admit—he is quite handsome. From behind, I have a nice view of his broad back and his muscular thighs—a strong, athletic build. Thick ebony locks fall in perfect waves to gently graze his shoulders. The dark hair is such an amazing contrast to those sky blue eyes that I remember so well.

Why is it some people receive more than their share of desirable attributes while the rest of us must survive on the leftovers? Life would seem a lot more just if he had some detectable flaw—other than his arrogance, of course. But who wouldn't be arrogant in his place? An existence of royalty, riches, and the looks of an Adonis, where the world is at your fingertips and the path always cleared before you. Most of us "mere mortals" cannot begin to imagine it.

My gaze falls down to my hands, dirt crusted in the creases, nails torn and ragged from the past day's excursion. I run my fingers through my chopped-off hair then try to brush off my dirty squire clothes. It is fair to say that if Prince Liam has snuck any peeks at me—which he probably hasn't—I have not made the same favorable impression on him. Not that this should matter to me. But it would be nice just once to be in his presence and not have the appearance of a beggar.

The morning is uneventful. We backtrack along our previous route as it cuts through the forest and soon runs parallel with the Crystal River about ten yards to our right. A breeze filters across it, cooling the air. Sunlight glimmers through the leafy canopy above, creates patches of gold that flicker all around us. The only sounds are the songs of birds and the rustle of brush from whatever small animal disturbs it. Clearly, Adam cannot speak until spoken to either, and so far Prince Liam is not saying a word. We ride in silence for a long couple of hours.

Around midday, after a coma-inducing period of quiet, the Prince finally says, "Adam, let's stop here and take our lunch."

"Yes, Your Highness," Adam replies.

The river snakes its way only a few yards from the road's edge. Not wide here, its current tumbles along gently. Clusters of trees dot the shore, their leaves changing to yellow. Adam gathers up the horses and walks them down to the riverbank. While the animals drink their fill, Adam reaches into one of their packs and pulls out some strips of dried meat for his meal. I stand awkwardly nearby, not sure what to do. I notice the Prince staring at me, his eyes casting their hypnotic effect. It is a good thing I am not allowed to speak until spoken to because, at this moment, I don't believe my mouth could produce an intelligible sentence if it had to. Prince Liam's brow furrows, his eyes run from my head to my toes, appraising me silently.

"Miss Davenport, let us go downriver and see if we can find a bit of shade to relax in while we dine." He grabs a supply pack and says to the guard, "Adam, do stay here and see to the horses."

"Yes, Your Highness."

Are these the only three words Adam will get to say on this trip?

The Prince takes a few steps and then peeks over his shoulder to make sure I am following. Of course I am. It is not as though I have a choice. My feet mechanically follow his commands. Why do I let him drive reason from my brain?

We walk along the embankment for a few yards and step around a clump of bushes right where the river flows over a small rock waterfall to form a small pool. The circular pond is densely surrounded by willows whose leaves bend to kiss the surface. Lush wildflowers of every color and size dot the landscape, their vibrant hues reflected back on the water. Butterflies flit about them, the splendor of their wings momentarily frozen each time they alight. At the other end, the current pours through a narrow opening down another waterfall. There it becomes a flowing river again and at intervals breaks off into some smaller streams. The lazy drone of insects mixes with the flute-like sound of wind through the reeds. It would be hard to envision a more beautiful setting, as if the earth itself heard Prince Liam was coming and designed this Edenic place for his personal use.

The Prince sits in the shade on a wide, flat rock whose edge overhangs the water and motions for me to sit. I sink down next to him. He gestures to the surroundings. "There. Now isn't this a tranquil place to relax for a bit?"

"Yes, Your Highness," I squeak out. *Great.* Now I sound like Adam. I wonder if Prince Liam ever tires of hearing these same three words over and over.

As if reading my thoughts, he says, "Miss Davenport, I realize that protocol dictates I must address you before you may speak to me. However, I would be delighted if you would just speak freely to me until we get back to the city. It will make the trip more pleasant for the both of us. Don't you agree?"

"Yes, Your Highness." It is out of my mouth before I can stop it, and he heaves a heavy sigh of defeat. Little does he know what dangerous ground this is for me. Goodness knows what I will come out with when allowed to "speak freely." Actually, on the long, silent ride, I had been preparing some not-so-nice things to say about him messing up my trip, but now that I sit here with him, it hardly matters. Inwardly, I debate what would constitute a safe topic, but for me there probably isn't one. Then, I remember the one thing that I am truly curious about. In true form, it is out of my mouth instantly.

"Did you know it was me? I mean, before my identity was exposed?"

Prince Liam's eyes dance. He seems happy to have been asked a question.

"Well, no. I did not know it was you, per se. When I first noticed you, I thought perhaps your father had decided to bring you, but then, when nobody mentioned anything, I figured I was mistaken. I assumed you were that other boy, the one you are with most of the time. When you were unmasked, though, I realized that you were not meant to be along."

Yeah, you and everyone else.

He removes food from his pack—a slab of dried pork, a hunk of cheese, and some fruit. Taking a knife to a red apple, he cuts off a wedge and hands it to me. The tips of our fingers touch, the merest brush of contact, but a jolt of energy surges through me, tingles right out my toes. I bite my lip to suppress a gasp.

"Thank you, Your Highness," I murmur and take a miniscule bite.

I feel nauseous—well, maybe that is not quite the word, more like extremely aware of myself, as if all my senses have been heightened. It is as if my very soul is sitting bared on this rock, as if Prince Liam can see into the inner recesses of my being. This is both terrifying and exhilarating all at once. Never has one person had so much of an effect on me.

Prince Liam glances out over the water, quite at ease. His face shows no trace of smugness or arrogance. It also shows no sign that he experiences any of the tumult of emotions he is currently inflicting on me. How could these intense sensations be one-sided? They seem to reverberate in the air all around us, so thick I could reach out and grab them.

My mind is muddled; better to just sit here quietly and compose myself. But, as if some spirit has taken control of my voice, I hear myself whisper, "I'm sorry."

The Prince cocks his head to one side and questions, "Sorry for what, Miss Davenport?"

"For messing up the mission for you. For getting you stuck with the job of escorting me home."

Prince Liam seems surprised. Then with a gorgeous smile, he confides, "I did not want to be on the mission in the first place. I am actually rather happy to be going home and washing my hands of the whole thing."

"Oh, I thought you would be disappointed to miss out on it like I am." I sigh.

"I think what you did was brave," he states softly.

Now it is my turn to be surprised.

"Um…brave?" That is the last word I expected to describe my antic.

"Yes, Miss Davenport, to try and do what you truly wanted to do even though you were ordered not to."

"I am pretty sure no one else is going to view it that way. Especially my mother."

In fact, I can imagine quite a few other words with much different connotations that will be coming out of her mouth by this time tomorrow. And I think we can safely say that my training days are over. Which is probably just as well, since Puck will likely try to spear me over all this.

"Well, at least you will have the comfort of knowing that one person thought it was brave," he says warmly. And I must admit, that will be a comfort.

"I might have thought it out better, though. I did get caught after all. But I did figure that was going to happen."

"Exactly!" he says triumphantly. "*That* is what made it so brave. Sometimes I wish I had the guts to…" he trails off.

"To what?" I ask against my better judgment. A prince should not be expected to elaborate.

He answers though. "To break the rules, to stand up for what I want."

"But you are a prince!" I stammer. "Isn't getting to *make* the rules part of being a prince in the first place?"

"No, in fact, nearly every aspect of my life and choices were dictated before I was born, even if I am only 'the spare.'" At my startled face, he admits, "Yes, I know that is what people call me. Honestly, I am twenty years old and I have barely ever made a meaningful decision for myself. There are traditions and obligations even for second sons that date back for centuries dictating where I can go, what I can do, and who I can marry."

His face hardens, the stony expression I have seen before like a door slamming against a warmly lit room on a cold night. A million questions parade into my head, but I am unsure what to say. His candor has unnerved me. It never occurred to me before to think of his life in such terms. I just assumed he more or less did what he wanted to do all day with the entire palace staff at his beck and call. My whole perception of him is reframed.

We wordlessly eat some meat and cheese with the sun cresting in the noonday sky. The pool laps rhythmically at the edge of the rocks, a constant gentle hum. Insects flit about, swarming in tiny cloud-like formations around our heads. Butterflies hover among clusters of blooms. Birds coast from tree to tree, a chorus of song.

"So what would you do if you could choose for yourself?" I ask.

He stares at me, shocked. Maybe I have crossed a line in even asking such a thing. But in wonderment he replies, "You are the only person who has ever asked me that." After a moment's consideration, he continues, "What I would like is to be able to serve on military duty. To go on a real mission to the coast."

The coast is the only outlying area where troops are stationed. Occasionally, there are raiding parties from other islands or from the Mainland, usually a ragtag band of invaders who don't pose a threat to Stewartsland as a whole, but need to be dealt with nonetheless.

"But I thought you had already been to the coast?" I distinctly remember my father arranging for Prince Liam to make a couple of trips.

"Yes, but not much happened during the two times I was sent. And the one time when a more significant battle occurred, everyone's main intention was to keep me as far from the danger as possible. It seems unfair that I spend all these hours in training, but will never actually be allowed to put my skills to use." He twists a strip of pork around in his hands.

Well isn't this ironic? Someone who can totally relate to my problem.

A small snort of disgust at the unfairness of it escapes my lips. The Prince's head shoots up, his eyes filled with hurt. He must think I am belittling his problem.

"No," I blurt out to clarify. "I am thinking that I feel the same way about all the training as you. I have spent countless hours at it and hear over and over again what a natural talent I have for it. But clearly, in the end, no one is ever going to give me the chance to use any of it for fear of my safety."

The comparison seems obvious to me, but maybe he will see no similarities in our situation. After all, he is a prince and I am only a girl.

"Well then," he muses, "it would seem as if you and I are in the same boat, wouldn't it?" Then he holds my gaze and I swear my body begins to melt right into the rock.

Conversation now flows effortlessly between us, the topics merging seamlessly one to another. I have never felt so at ease with someone. We are amused at the same stories, indignant at the same injustices, and passionate about the same pastimes. Total synchronicity. The shadows grow longer around us, even as time seems to stand still.

The subject of Prince Harold's upcoming marriage to the Lady Emily arises. I have seen her only one time before, at the Introduction Ball when the betrothal was announced. She is slender and blonde and beautiful, with every grace you would imagine a future princess should possess—beauty, charm, and a demure sense of self. When I note this, the Prince says, "My brother would seem lucky in the girl my father has selected to be his wife. She seems a well-bred girl on the whole except..."

He stops himself abruptly, as if he is suddenly aware that he should not be sharing information of such a personal nature with someone outside the royal circle. Although I am curious to hear what he was going to say, I decide it is wiser not to pry. And for once, my mouth obeys and stays shut. Prince Liam seems deep in thought. I am not sure if he is trying to decide what to say, or if I should consider the matter dropped. While I enjoy the picturesque scenery, I take some more bites of the tangy cheese. I feel a tickle on my hand and find a ladybug crawling across it. As I raise my arm up, she marches up to the tip of my finger, then spreads her wings and sails across the water.

At length the Prince says, "I probably shouldn't be telling this to anyone. My father would certainly frown on me for mentioning anything. It's just that Lady Emily seems a bit too eager to be a princess. I mean, not that it isn't an honor any girl would desire."

Oh yes, because this is every girl's ultimate wish. I don't get the princess fantasy—the adult-perpetuated myth that every little girl should dream of becoming a princess. Because you live happily ever after, right? This presumption is unconvincing to me. True princes are a rare find. So let's face it, the odds of becoming an actual princess are slim at best. Girls should be taught to create their own happiness.

So maybe this is what Lady Emily dreams of and can actually attain, but not every girl desires this. I would love to enlighten him on that sentiment.

"She just seems a little materialistic and power hungry. I can't exactly put my finger on it, I have no specific example. It is just a weird feeling I get from her."

"Why would your father be upset if you mentioned this to him?" I ask, thinking about the close relationship I share with my father. He definitely likes to hear my input on people and trusts my judgments as well.

"It was a long, arduous process to choose the 'perfect girl.' She needed to have the right family credentials, the proper education and music training, a sense of propriety and decorum, a knowledge and respect of royal protocol. And she had to be likeable enough that the people would be excited to see her as princess," he explains.

"Wow, given all these criteria, it amazes me you were able to find one such girl, let alone being able to choose from among several."

"My father spent many sleepless nights weighing the pros and cons of all the eligible ladies before settling on Lady Emily. Once his mind is made up, he does not want to hear anything contrary to his decision."

"Goodness, didn't Prince Harold get any say at all in who would be his wife?" I ask, noticing the boldness of my tone a bit too late.

Prince Liam is taken aback. "No. Normally the nobility does not get a say in such matters. And I wonder," he adds knowingly, "will you get such a say when it comes time for your father to arrange your marriage?"

Good point.

"Well, I hope he will at least ask my opinion before accepting any offers," I answer quietly, my tone belying the tiny bit of uncertainty I do feel about this matter.

"Your Highness?" Adam's voice calls from above. "The horses are watered, fed, and rested. I suggest we press onward and cover the most possible ground this afternoon." Adam wants to either make it back to Adelina tonight or at least be close enough to the city walls to eliminate the threat of running into any outlaws.

"Yes, Adam. We will be right with you. No sign of any 'dangerous sorts' out there, is there?" Prince Liam jokes.

"No, Your Highness. But one must always be on guard," Adam answers, all business, and strides back to the road.

I collect the remnants of the food and stand up to sprinkle some broken bread crumbs on the rock for the birds to enjoy. What was a companionable silence between us a moment ago, now feels awkward. A hollow feeling creeps up from my toes to engulf me in disappointment more intense than I have ever experienced. Our time alone is about to end.

"Miss Davenport, I would like to thank you for the conversation. It was a pleasure to talk, and I mean genuinely *talk* to someone. I don't get many opportunities to do that."

"The pleasure was mine, Your Highness," I say. "And you have my word that I will keep what we have discussed in the strictest confidence."

The Prince graces me with his entrancing smile. "Then I thank you for that as well."

We remount and continue on as before with Adam in front, then Prince Liam, and then me. My emotions are a jumble of contradictions. Besides the disappointment, part of me is a bit euphoric after this private interlude with Liam. I am surprised by how much my sense of who he is has changed. He is a person I can actually respect and relate to. There is a synergy between us. A feeling of closeness, as if so much unspoken by us had just been understood. Puck and I always "got" each other, but it had never occurred to me that there could be something deeper. With Prince Liam though, it had felt as if a part of my soul had rejoined me back where it belonged; as if all the pieces had finally slipped back into place.

Momentarily, I become lost in the sense of completeness, and then like a hammer striking the nail, a jarring concept rams me back into reality. After this journey, I will probably rarely, if ever, see the Prince, and I will never have the chance at such an intimate conversation with him again. The thought of this fills me with such despair that it takes all my self-control to keep tears from filling my eyes. It isn't like me to have such an emotional reaction to anyone, especially someone that I barely know.

At first, I cannot wrap my mind around the sensation hurtling me from one extreme to the other. Then it dawns on me. This matter involves not my mind, but my heart. With full force I am hit with an utter realization—I am in love with Liam. Me! Of all people! The girl who scoffs at love in general, let alone the inane "love at first sight" theory. Yet from the moment our eyes met in the garden two days ago, something in me has changed.

Suddenly, the meaning of every trite love song and saying about broken hearts, every melodramatic complaint from my sisters, every sentiment that I found so laughable becomes crystal clear. This is a relationship that can never happen. Even if Liam feels the same way, which I doubt, we can never be together. Had we not just had a conversation about the exact subject of how the King chooses his sons' wives? Not only do I not meet the requirements of birth, but I am guessing that my little escapade has not exactly given me the best standing in the King's opinions. How low must my ranking be on the propriety and decorum scale at the moment?

After a few moments of uncharacteristic self-pity, I try to reason with myself. It is time to face the hopelessness of being in love with a prince. This is not how the world works, and I know it. "Happily ever after" is a myth. There are some obstacles even love cannot overcome. Nothing good could be accomplished from me admitting my feelings either to Liam or to myself. When we are home, I must dispel this notion and must never acknowledge it again—not to anyone, especially myself.

For the present, all I can do is try to absorb every second of this trip, to memorize and retain every small detail of this first and last time that I will ever be so close to Liam. My life will move on. I will marry Puck and things will be as they always were. Slowly, this passion will be suffocated by the ordinary. Yet, when I am old and grey, today's memories of what love briefly felt like may ease the pain of long years lived without it.

Adam and Liam debate how hard to push the horses, while I stare at Liam's back, trying to take in his figure, his energy. Every minute detail of sight, smell, and sound must be noted.

I am so absorbed in him that when I hear the *whoosh* pass my ear, its meaning does not immediately register. A loud twang sounds from the tree bough right above my head.

And that is when I see it: a silver blade stuck fast in the branch—a dagger that has just been thrown at us.

With lightning speed, Adam swings his mount around, sword drawn. Liam jumps from his horse and runs for me. His arm hooks my waist. He tosses me to the ground with a thud. For a moment, we remain frozen, scanning the woods for the source of the attack. Footsteps crunch the underbrush to my left. Whoever the enemies are, they are not relying on stealth. Two men armed with swords clamber out of the trees.

Liam springs to his feet. Adam leaps to his side. They stand shoulder to shoulder, weapons raised. I stay low and scoot my way behind a large oak on the side of the road. Its thick trunk provides ample cover. The horses stand nervously on the path, stomping their feet in bewilderment at the turn of events.

"What business have you in the woods of King William?" Adam's voice booms.

I rise to my knees and peek out from the side of the tree. The men are dressed in nondescript armor, but one carries a wooden shield with the Lindenwood crest, a broad linden tree. Their tall, broad-shouldered frames and long blond hair, however, suggest a Mainland lineage. The attackers do not reply, but in a glance at each other, a mutual agreement is tacitly formed. They pounce. Adam and Liam meet their assault with vigor and the loud clang of sword upon sword rings out through the forest. Our horses, spooked by the sudden commotion, run off in different directions.

Recovering from my shock, I assess the situation. If these men had seen there were three of us, they certainly would have mistaken me, in my current dress, for a servant. I would not be their first objective. However, if they had heard only Adam and Liam speaking and did not notice there was a third person, then I have the element of surprise on my side. Whichever is the case, neither of them gives me any thought at the moment, and this can be used to my advantage.

Adam and his foe exchange mighty blows. The force of each one drives them closer and closer to my position. My left hand brushes metal on the ground. Lying at my feet is the dagger just thrown at us. It came loose and fell from the tree bough above. A small weapon, it is no match for a sword, but if skillfully placed, could prove useful for Adam.

They are nearly on top of me now. Their sweat flies through the air like raindrops with every exertion. The enemy has his back to me. Adam propels him closer and closer. It is now or never. I fly from my place of concealment and sink the knife into the unsuspecting fighter's calf. His knee buckles, one arm flails back in my direction, and his shield bangs into the side of my skull. He crumples down, grabbing for his injured leg. Adam takes full advantage of this second of lost concentration and delivers a fatal blow to the man's neck. Bright blood spurts out in a high, wide arc, splattering everything in the surrounding area, including me. Though I am seeing stars, I register warm liquid soaking my skin.

Adam, a well-seasoned fighter, runs to Liam's aid without missing a beat. My eyes follow him, and I force myself to focus again. His adversary may be the largest man I have ever seen. It takes all of Liam's strength just to block the onslaught of strikes being aimed at him. Every blow forces him toward the side of a large rock. Once he is backed up against it, Liam will be at a severe disadvantage.

While I watch in horror, the enemy drives him into this ill-fated position. With a great swing, he knocks Liam's sword from his grasp. It clatters to the ground a few feet away. The fighter audibly grunts with satisfaction. He mutters menacing words that I cannot understand and raises his sword high above his head to deal the final blow. His arms never deliver it though. Adam runs him through from behind with his sword. The fighter stares down for one brief moment at the point of a sword sticking out of his chest before he falls lifeless to the ground.

Liam and Adam collapse to their knees, panting.

"Your Highness, are…you…all right?" Adam gasps, still trying to catch his breath.

"Yes, Adam. And you?" Liam places his hand on Adam's shoulder in concern.

"Fine, Your Highness." He stands and wrestles his sword out of the dead man. After inspecting it, he wipes the blood off on a patch of grass.

"Thank you, Adam," Liam chokes out.

"He was huge, Your Highness. I don't know how you fought him off for so long. Why did you not tell him that you are the Prince? That may have given him pause."

"I do not think it would have mattered to him who I am. My royal robe indicated my rank if he had been interested. Did you hear him speak? He is clearly a paid mercenary. He may not have even understood our language. In any case," Liam says, finally catching his breath, "one more moment and he would be the one standing here now. Thank you, Adam."

"You are most welcome, Your Highness. However, had it not been for Miss Davenport I would never have been able to dispose of my man so quickly."

Their heads swing around in unison as if they have forgotten I was with them. I stand on unsteady feet not two yards behind them. They race to cover the space between us.

"Are you all right?" Liam asks, alarmed by my blood-spattered tunic.

He checks me over for wounds from head to toe. His hands linger on my face as he gently wipes some warm liquid off my cheek. Concern is evident in his eyes.

"Yes." I quake. My voice matches the shakiness I feel throughout my body. But whether the cause is the blood, or the bodies, or the fact Liam touches me, I do not know.

"Are you sure?" Liam asks, his eyes following my hand that now rubs the walnut-sized lump on my head.

"It is his blood, not mine," I assure, pointing to the corpse. Adam recounts how I stabbed the enemy in the leg, which caused enough of a distraction for him to slit the man's throat.

"That was quick thinking, Miss Davenport. Smart combat skills," Liam praises.

"She took a bit of a blow to the left side of her head," Adam notes. Impressive that he noticed that in the midst of his battle.

"Let me see," Liam says. He softly feels the affected area and, even though it is tender, the touch of his fingers sends tingles through my body. "Does it hurt?"

"Not really. Just sort of a dull ache," I answer truthfully. "I'll be fine."

Slowly, his hand falls from my temple and cups my chin. We stare at each other a moment before it drops to his side. I am sorry when it does, but try to shake the cobwebs out of my head. There are important matters to address.

"I don't understand. Why would King John have soldiers roaming the woods? Why did they attack us? Adam is in King William's livery, surely they know about the meeting between the two Kings." My mind reels trying to make sense of it all.

Adam and Liam glance gravely at each other and a notion that has been flitting about in the recesses of my mind surfaces. There is something sinister going on at Lindenwood. My father's misgivings were correct after all.

"They were scouts. Scouts who were to make sure no one made it back to Adelina to send out a warning. There is obviously evil afoot with this meeting. My father is walking into a trap." Liam sighs heavily.

"What would you like me to do, Your Highness?" Adam asks.

"Did either of you see where the horses went?'

"Yes, two ran down the road toward home, while the other bolted off to the left," I say.

"The first two are probably well out of our range by now. Adam, will you search for the one that went into the woods?"

"Yes, Your Highness."

"Well now," Liam says to me, "let's see if these gentlemen can provide us with any clues as to whose orders they were following."

We roll over the man at our feet, and Liam begins to search him. I cannot help but notice the man's face. He seems fairly young, but with the edge of a man who spent most of his short adult life soldiering. His thick brown hair, matted and clumpy, unshaven face, and stale smell lead one to believe he has been without the comforts of bathing for quite some time. But his eyes captivate me the most. They are wide open in terror. When I reach down to gently shut them, I wonder if he has a wife and children somewhere who love him, who are counting the days until his return. A count that will now be in vain. Even with his eyes closed he still looks ghastly, not at all a face peaceful in death.

I can feel Liam's eyes on me, and when I raise mine to meet his he says, "I assume it is safe to say that this is your first real combat experience?"

"Yes."

"It is a lot different than sparring. When you stab someone, they actually bleed." He rubs my arm sympathetically.

"There was so much blood. I never thought there would be so much."

My mind drifts back to the lectures my father would give to the squires about not losing one's focus amid all the horror of battle, but I never understood the full impact of what he was trying to say—until now. Instinctively, my hand massages the injury on my own head, and I know it could have been so much worse.

"Better his than yours," Liam says, squeezing my arm for effect. "Remember that. He would not be standing here feeling sorry for you."

This must not be Liam's first experience with combat. His brief trips to the coast were enough to provide him this lesson already, even if his men had tried to shield him from it.

Our investigation of the mercenary produces little more than a few concealed knives. The second body provides no additional clues. We search the surrounding area and find my saddlebag caught on a branch. It had been torn from Pepper in his hurry to escape. A short while later Adam appears with Liam's steed after tracking him a good way into the woods. He still seems a bit skittish, but no worse for wear overall.

"If the other horses ran off down the road, they will most likely continue on it toward home," Liam says to Adam. "You will no doubt catch up with them on the way."

"On the way?" Adam asks, confused.

"Ride as hard as possible to Adelina and warn Prince Harold of the treachery. Tell him to muster the army and march in all haste to Lindenwood."

Adam protests abandoning his duty to Prince Liam. But Liam assures Adam that he and I will follow after him on foot. We will eventually cross paths with Prince Harold and the army when they make their advance. Additionally, he asks Adam to make sure there is a fresh horse for him to use when he joins the army and an appropriate escort to see me the rest of the way home. My head shoots up at this statement, about to object, but then the futility of the situation sinks in. Men are back to discussing me as if I am not here, so why even bother? I absently touch my head to check the lump. It still aches dully, but doesn't seem any worse.

"Your Highness," Adam hesitates, "given what we just went through, I do not feel it is altogether safe to leave you alone and unguarded."

Alone? What am I? Don't I even count? Did they not both just commend my actions?

"Nonsense. These were likely the only scouts in the area. We will be following you swiftly on foot. All will be fine."

I have my doubts about how Liam can be sure that these men were the only scouts around, but keep my opinions to myself.

"If I may suggest," I interject, "perhaps Prince Liam should remove his royal robe and continue on in the guise of a simple traveler. If we appear to be ordinary folk of no importance, other scouts may simply ignore us."

Liam and Adam stare at me stupefied. Maybe to suggest that the Prince appear "ordinary" is not to be borne. But Liam's face breaks into a wide grin.

"Brilliant idea, Miss Davenport."

He slips off his robe and the richly brocaded tunic underneath and stands before me in a plain white shirt. "Will this do?" he asks, modeling flamboyantly.

"Honestly, your pants are stained and ripped and your boots are dusty from the fight. But the shirt is as white as new fallen snow. You should dirty it up a bit so it seems more congruous with the rest of your attire." Again dead silence and stares from the two men. Perhaps I spoke too familiarly to Liam so I hastily add, "Um…Your Highness."

Liam slaps Adam on the back and laughs. "You see, you needn't worry for me. I will be in good hands with this clever girl. I mean 'squire,'" he says, winking.

He gathers some dirt in his hands and rubs them with relish over the pristine white material, taking great pains to make sure none of the shirt escapes attention. Then he gently addresses Adam. "Truly I will be fine. Time is of the essence, so please ride hard and warn my brother."

Adam finally relents. He mounts the royal steed and hands down Liam's supply bag, then offers the Prince his own sword.

"No, I have mine. There will be no need for anoth…" Liam pauses. "On second thought, yes, we will take it. I hear Miss Davenport can handle one quite well." I feel myself blush at his compliment, but also notice Adam suppresses a smirk. He hands the sword with its belt down to me. "We also have several daggers recovered from the enemy to choose from. All in all we are well armed—now go," he orders Adam, giving the horse's hindquarters a slap. "And be careful."

"You as well, Your Highness."

We watch him gallop down the road and out of sight. Hopefully, he will make good time. The sooner Prince Harold and his army get to Lindenwood, the better. I am worried about my own father's safety, but try to remind myself that he, of all people, can handle it.

Now for the long walk home. Admittedly, the idea of a little more alone time with Liam is appealing. Maybe I should admit my strong feelings for him. Maybe it could change things. But who am I kidding; once we meet up with the oncoming army, he will be gone, off on an adventure, while I am relegated to my house and my punishment. The thought of me will likely never even cross his mind again once we make our separate ways. I heave a long, deep sigh. It echoes back at me from the forest.

Liam watches me with an expression that can be described only as mischievous. My eyes narrow in question.

"So what do you think, Miss Davenport, should we really start for home? Or…"

Or what? I puzzle for a second, and then it dawns on me. My ensuing grin certainly mimics his as I voice his unspoken idea, "Or go after the King and his men?"

"Yes," he agrees, smiling wider, "or go after them."

Excited to the point of giddiness, we take stock of our provisions then gather up the knives, bows, and arrows from the dead men. We deduce that these mercenaries, who had been on foot and carried no food or water, came from somewhere nearby—a home base for the scouts. This means that more could be out here searching the woods.

"It is probably not a good idea to leave the bodies out in the open," I note.

So, Liam and I, with much effort on my part, drag them off the road and cover them as best we can with brush and leaves. Any decent tracker would spot them immediately; however, if no one is searching for them yet, it will buy us some time.

"How long before the other scouts notice they are missing?" I wonder out loud, my head throbbing from the exertion.

"Hopefully not until nightfall, when they are all likely to rendezvous. But we can't count on that." Liam points at the nearby water. "This stream continues on and feeds into the Crystal River beyond the pool where we ate lunch. It runs pretty much alongside the road. Let's backtrack to that point and then decide how to proceed."

It is as good a plan as any.

"First, we should try to throw off any would-be trackers. Once the bodies of their comrades are found, they will want to avenge them," I say.

At my direction, we spend a few minutes walking all around the area, sprinting off several times in different directions before crossing back. I even run back and forth across the stream a few times hoping to confuse any dogs the trackers may have with them.

"We should walk in the water if possible. It will be much harder to track us that way," I instruct.

"It's like you don't even need me, Miss Davenport," Liam jokes. He steps into the knee-deep water along the banks.

"May I please ask a favor, Your Highness?" I ask softly, following his lead into the cold stream. "Would you please just call me Olivia?"

"Of course, Olivia, and please, while we are out here alone where there is no need for formalities, please just call me Liam."

At home, it would be tantamount to heresy for someone the likes of me to call him by his Christian name. Knowing my tendency to speak without thinking, I wonder if it is a smart idea for me to get used to not putting the Prince title on his name. That could definitely get me into trouble at another time. Then again, what are the odds I will have reason to directly address him again? The truth of it is, calling him Liam will make him seem attainable, make him much harder to forget.

"Why do you think King John would be luring your father into a trap? Why now after all this time?" I ask, pushing some low-lying branches out of our path.

"I am not sure. I have been wracking my brain trying to make sense of all of this."

The water deepens, soaking me to my midthigh. Midges dart around us in tiny transparent clouds, biting any exposed skin. I swat them away to no avail. My ears are on high alert for any sound of pursuit, but hear only the trickle of the stream over the infernal buzzing of our companions.

"Even if King John had enough men to overcome the small party my father brings, he would undoubtedly know an attack would be mounted against him from Stewartsland. He has lived peacefully for so long in his little corner of the world. It would seem an unusual move to risk open war. But how does one explain the mercenaries? That is a most troublesome detail. Who is to say how many men he has paid, and for what?"

"Could he be hoping for ransom money?" I ask.

"Yes, perhaps, but to what end?" Liam questions. "Once the ransom is paid and my father released, surely John knows an attack would follow in retribution for the audacity of the act." He pauses, runs his hand through his hair. "No, there is something more at play here."

"My father had misgivings about King John's invitation. That is why he brought the squires along on an 'exercise.'" I slog hard in the muddy streambed, the water now at my waist. We must be nearing the junction to the river for the current to be so strong. My breath quickens with exertion and my head starts to throb a bit harder.

"Yes, I know. Your father warned me as well that this whole meeting didn't seem quite right. He even asked me when we were alone if I could try and reason with my father. But, my father has a blind spot where Lindenwood is concerned. I think he covets it too much. If only he had listened to your father, they would both be safe right now."

In what I judge to be a half an hour, we make it up to the place where we ate lunch. Just below the waterfall that cascades down from the pool, we climb out of the water by the rock we sat upon. Was that merely an hour ago? It seems a lifetime.

Mounting the narrow path up a small hill, we decide to abandon the rough river waters and keep within the cover of the trees in hopes this will minimize our chances of encountering any more scouts. Our silence fills the air as we skirt the edge of the pool and disappear into the forest. Liam's soft, careful footsteps, learned from his years of hunting, are as undetectable as the ones I have developed through my years of tracking.

Liam pauses and inhales deeply. "It is so wonderful to be out here with just you."

Not certain what the statement means exactly, I don't reply.

"I cannot even remember the last time I was anywhere at all without at least a guard hovering nearby. My every move is shadowed and I can never quite drop the royal pretense, you know?"

"It must be pretty awful to never be alone." I had never considered this before.

"The air, the forest, the excitement—it's all so liberating. Look, I can even do this!" He proceeds to make a bunch of silly faces and we both laugh. "Goodness help me if I ever tried that in the palace. I must follow protocol at all costs."

This is not the Liam from home at all. All his haughty mannerisms and dry comments are gone. Could his apparent smugness there just be the self-control he forces himself to display to keep from going crazy? I would find life under constant surveillance simply torturous.

"It's hard to conform to what everyone else wants all the time. Sometimes I feel like no one knows the real me, like it doesn't matter *he* even exists," Liam confides.

"I know. My mother wants me to be something I am not. And even after I have worked so hard to be a squire, everyone thinks I can just give it up—like it's a hobby and not part of who I inherently am."

"See, I knew you would understand," Liam says, rubbing my arm, "not having any choice in the most important areas of your life."

"Yes, this is exactly the kind of situation I have trained so long for. I was dying to put my skills to the test I was heartbroken when my father forbade me to come on this mission. But he had misgivings from the start, and he could not have been more right."

Our conversation halts at the mention of my father. The thought of what grave danger my father is in weighs heavily on me. He will never leave the King's side willingly, and he will fight to his death to defend him. For all I know, he could be dead already. Desperately, I try to remember the last thing I said to him before our parting, but I cannot recall. Since we were both so upset at the time, I did not tell him that I loved him or how much he means to me or anything. What kind of daughter am I? How can I live with myself if something has happened to him? Knowing that the last thing I ever did was disappoint him?

As if he can read my thoughts, Liam says, "Your father is an extremely intelligent man and a gifted fighter. The kingdom is fortunate for his service all these years. And I can think of no one else who I would wish at my father's side when he is in danger."

"Thank you."

My father loves his work. He can talk battle plans, strategy, and defense systems all day long to anyone who will listen. Some accuse him of being meticulous to a fault. This gives me some hope that Father, who was already suspicious, may not have let the King walk into the trap after all.

"Obviously he has a masterful pupil in you, Olivia; you have certainly held your own out here."

"I think it would be more to my father's dismay than anything. If I had been a son…well, that would be a different story."

"Believe me," Liam murmurs bitterly, "sons dismay their fathers just as easily."

Progress is slower now on the uneven ground of the forest. Although the trees provide concealment, the undergrowth is difficult to navigate. Dead leaves and scrub choke the ground, our steps as careful as if quicksand threatened to swallow us up. Water squeezes from my sodden boots with every stride, like a sponge being wrung out interminably. My supply bag is rather damp, too. We will need to light a fire later to dry things out.

My mind, jolted by the attack, finally settles down. I assess our situation and have to ask myself: what in the blazes do we think we are doing? Here we are, two people not particularly well-seasoned in battle, and one a girl no less, planning to march into the aftermath of an ambush. I, for one, have no concrete ideas about what we should do if and when we reach Lindenwood, other than scouting out the area and waiting for Prince Harold and his men to arrive.

Liam and I should probably be discussing this, but he proceeds with such an air of confidence that I do not want to seem foolish by bringing it up, especially since he had just said I was "holding my own." At that compliment, my fingers and toes had tingled with exhilaration. I don't want him to think that I doubt his abilities.

In a small glen, edged on one side by a sprawling patch of brambles, and on the other by the path we are shadowing, we stop for a break. Liam sits at the base of a large oak tree and motions me to take a seat beside him. He offers me drink. It takes me a moment to react and take the waterskin. Being so near to him, I find it hard to concentrate on anything, and the dull ache on the side of my head does not help matters.

"So, Olivia, what do you think our strategy should be?" Liam asks in a quiet voice just above a whisper.

My simple name sounds so melodic coming from his mouth. Again. If I was going to be childish and count, I would note it was the third time already. I wonder if he notices I have been avoiding using his.

"Well, I suppose if we can arrive at the outskirts of Lindenwood undetected, we should scout out the area to garner whatever intelligence we can so it is ready to report to Prince Harold when he arrives," I reply, glad we are finally devising a strategy.

I go on to theorize that if King John's intention is to abduct King William for ransom, and I pray it is ransom and not some more nefarious aim, he will be sure to lure him inside the castle walls first. This will not likely leave many details for us to scout.

What I don't tell Liam is that the thought of an out-and-out assassination of King William has also crossed my mind, though it is not the most plausible course of action. For that, King John might have merely paid someone to poison King William or arrange an "accident" that could leave King John entirely without implication. Summoning King William to Lindenwood indicates there is more to this than just a murder attempt.

Liam agrees with my spoken summations. We believe we can reach the outer border of Lindenwood by morning. And hopefully, if Adam made it back to Adelina without delay, then Prince Harold will not be far behind us.

For the first time, it occurs to me that Liam and I will have to spend the night together in the woods. Not that I would have any problems with the camping aspect. Puck and I pitched tents many times in my family's outlying fields, where we spent the night pretending we were soldiers on a patrol mission. At the thought of Puck, I feel a terrible pang of guilt; our eventual reunion may not be pleasant. It also strikes me that Puck and I have not had a "patrol night" in the past few years because my parents, and by that I mean my mother, had deemed them inappropriate. I can only imagine what she would have to say about my current situation.

Suddenly, I am conscious of just how alone Liam and I are as we sit shoulder to shoulder against the tree. Just thinking of the logistics of the night gets me so nervous that I blurt out, "You know, we won't be sleeping together tonight."

Liam's eyes whip to mine a bit startled at first, but then his face breaks into his crooked half-smile of amusement.

"Beg your pardon?" he drawls.

I take a deep breath to try to calm myself. Why does he transform me into such a fool?

"I meant to say, that we will need to take turns tonight being on guard while the other sleeps. So we won't be sleeping at the same time." He just continues smiling at me, so I add, "That is pretty basic patrol rules."

"Indeed it is." He chuckles with an expression that is quite frankly starting to annoy me.

"And you find that funny? Why exactly? Or do you just find me funny?"

"Not funny. Just amazingly unpretentious. The ladies of the court I come in contact with have manners of such pronounced decorum."

Somewhere in the back of my mind, I can hear my father warning me not to embarrass myself or him in front of the Prince. So much for that.

"Sorry for my indecorous nature," I mutter.

"No, no, I mean that the court ladies are so rehearsed and disingenuous while you are so…well…refreshing." He puts his arm around my shoulder.

I tilt my head up toward his. His face is earnest and also incredibly close to mine.

"Well," I say, hardly able to hear myself over the pounding of my heart, which for some reason is quite loud in my ears, "I don't spend much time with the ladies of the court."

"To your great benefit, it would seem."

Staring into his eyes, I feel a sensation that can be described only as familiarity. The feeling of immense calm and contentment one feels after returning from a long, arduous journey and finally resting one's gaze on home. We draw closer to one another even though I have no sense of either my or his body moving. It is as though we are being drawn to each other by a force that emanates from us magnetically, pulling the other inward.

In my life, I have experienced a few crushes, but they were felt only in my heart. The powerful feeling I have right now radiates through my entire being. As our lips are about to meet, I have the sense that I am floating on air, weightless and never more alive.

Abruptly, the moment is broken when Liam and I both start at the same sound—voices.

Our faces change in an instant to ones of alertness. The voices come from a good way up the road, but they are getting closer. I scan the area and decide the low-lying brambles are the closest possible hiding spot. Silently, I touch Liam's arm and point. He nods in understanding.

We cross the space in a flash, lie down on our bellies, and shimmy our way underneath. It is a tight squeeze and I can feel the thorns scratching the back of my thighs between my jerkin and my boots. My arms and neck don't make out much better. Our bodies wedged together, there is hardly room to breathe.

Hopefully, the men will be so engaged in their conversation, they will pass right by this scraggly patch of brambles without a second glance. Liam and I lie immobile side by side, our chins touching the dirt. The approaching voices become distinguishable.

"So, we make for Lindenwood tonight if we have received no word of any escapees. There we will wait for battle."

"I don't care where we go or what we do so long as we get our promised pay," the other responds gruffly.

They have emerged into view, walking slowly toward us. From our vantage point, I can see them only from the waist down, one fat, one thin. I pray they just move on by. A gentle gust of wind blows their sour smell our way.

"Lord Otto has not disappointed so far," the first points out. At the name Otto, Liam stiffens and I suppress a gasp. Is King John's younger brother involved somehow in this matter?

The men stop and are silent for a moment while they both take a drink from their skins. I try to will them on their way. But no such luck. My heart sinks when I hear the first one exclaim, "Hey, look, footprints—*fresh* footprints."

With swords drawn, they scan the area. The thinner one's eyes must fall on the brambles. Surely, we made rather obvious marks in the dirt when we slid under them. He nudges the fat one and motions toward where we are hidden. They advance on our hiding spot. We are trapped. My eyes fly to Liam's and in that brief moment, he grabs my hand, squeezes it reassuringly.

This time I do hear the *whoosh*, see the thin man stagger, gasping for air as blood pours from his mouth, the result of the arrow now lodged in his chest. The fat man first yells out in fear and horror at his comrade's fate before falling heavily to the ground himself, felled by a shot to the back. I am too stunned to react. Liam's eyes are wide in bewilderment. Before either of us can say a word, a voice rings out from the woods, "You two will now come out from under those brambles, place any weapons on the ground, and raise your arms in the air."

After a second's consideration, Liam gives me a nod of assent. We wriggle our way out on hands and knees. Then we follow the commands we have been given, lay down our weapons, slowly stand, and raise our arms. My injury pulsates against the side of my skull as I look around. A circle of about ten non-uniformed men surround us, all with their bows drawn.

A slightly built, yet devilishly handsome, man in a dark green tunic steps forward from the trees. His wiry frame and pleasantly chiseled face are complemented by a mustache with pointed goatee, which he strokes slowly up and down as he regards us.

"Well, well, look who we have here," he says and laughs.

I am unsure how he knows us, but I know at once it can only be one man standing in front of us now.

The infamous outlaw Athos.

Athos circles us, his eyes sweeping up and down our bodies. Smaller than I would have imagined, he stands only about my height, whereas the legends assure he is a near giant. Dark hair contrasts with olive skin, indicating a lineage from somewhere in the southern parts of the Mainland. His entire personage reminds me of a fox—sharp, quick, sly. Without doubt, a formidable opponent.

He flourishes his arm at his men. "Do my eyes deceive me, gentlemen, or is this our own venerable Prince Liam alone in the forest, but for a squire?"

I am too surprised that Athos has so easily recognized Liam to say anything. Liam, on the other hand, seems perfectly composed considering we are currently heavily outnumbered by a band of outlaws.

"Well, you are half-right. I am indeed Prince Liam, but if you inspect a bit closer, you may find I am with no ordinary squire."

Athos gives Liam an intrigued expression and walks over to me. We stand eye to eye. I imagine how I appear: dirty and bloodstained, with brambles stuck to what is left of my hair. Keen brown eyes penetrate mine in examination. Suddenly, his expression of intense question changes to one of understanding. He holds out his hand, and I hesitantly place mine into his. It is raised to his lips for a gentle kiss.

"My lady," he says, bowing, "I am Athos and these are my comrades in arms. We are delighted to make your acquaintance." His tone is courteous, but the tight grip on my hand reminds me who is in charge.

Feeling all eyes on me, I exclaim, "Prince Liam is attending important business. We would appreciate it if you would let us continue on our way. You have no authority to hold him here at arrow's point."

Athos' gaze bores into me. He drops my hand and faces Liam. "Does his Highness of our realm now allow mere servant girls to speak his will?"

Once again, I realize I have spoken out of turn. Liam must think there is something wrong with me. Protocol, obvious even to lifelong criminals, is beyond my grasp. I sneak a glance to see if my impertinence has angered him, but his eyes are locked on Athos.

"For your information, she is no mere servant girl," he answers icily. "And she speaks the truth, our time is of the essence."

Athos is silent for a moment. Finally, he orders his men to lower their bows. The command is obeyed instantly. His total authority over the men, though some are nearly twice his size, is evident.

"Prince Liam, I am astute enough to recognize that the whys and wherefores of your current traveling circumstances are extraordinarily…unusual. And yours are not the only unusual circumstances I have observed today. I have a distinct feeling that we may both possess some information that would be of interest to the other. May I suggest that, before there is another unfortunate encounter—" here he gestures toward the dead bodies, "— we move this conversation to a more private location?"

Liam is silent. I bite my lip hard to prevent any more commentary from flying unbidden out of my mouth.

Instead, I assess our situation. There are currently a good number of King John's, or maybe Lord Otto's, men patrolling the woods. The fact that now four of these men would not be reporting to their post could only raise an alarm. As a result, more men will be dispatched, which will greatly lessen the chances of Liam and me getting to Lindenwood undetected. Athos may know something that will shed light on exactly what is going on. Contradictory as it sounds, I will actually feel more secure in the company of outlaws than I would with just Liam alone. And to be honest, my head has really started pounding since we were discovered under the brambles.

Liam's voice interrupts my thoughts. "By all means. Please lead the way, Sir Athos."

With only a nod, Athos leads the way back into the forest. Liam and I are sandwiched in between several of his men on all sides. Even though we are not their prisoners, I definitely get the sense we are regarded as such.

I make a mental note to ask Liam why he referred to Athos as "Sir." My father had once briefly mentioned something about Athos being a famous war hero on the Mainland. Then there was some sort of incident. It seems like something I should remember, but right now the thoughts in my head are fuzzy and hard to organize.

We walk at a brisk pace. Several sharp bends cause me to lose all sense of direction. Normally, I pride myself on keeping my bearings, but the sharp thudding in my head distracts me, it takes all my effort just to keep going. I try to reckon what time of day it is, note that by the sun's position it may be late afternoon, but again my thoughts are slippery, hard to pin down. My legs are as heavy as cement, every step a Herculean effort.

Liam is silent by my side. Have I annoyed him by speaking out of turn? It would certainly be understandable if he feels I undermined his authority. Some part of him must recognize if I had not snuck on the mission, he would not be in this mess right now. In fact, it must make him happy that he has some men around now to confer with instead of a bratty, disobedient girl. My face flushes, burns so hot it is hard to concentrate on anything else.

"Are you all right? Do you need to rest for a minute?"

Roused, I find Liam's face painted with worry.

"Why, because I am a girl? Because you don't think I can take care of myself?" I snap out of my trance, even though I would like to rest more than anything. My feet feel as though they weigh a hundred pounds each.

"No," Liam sputters, "because you took a good hit to the head before. I thought it may be bothering you."

The men behind us try to suppress a snicker at the mighty Prince being berated like a child. I close my eyes. How many times am I going to embarrass myself and Liam with my uncontrollable tongue? My head is pounding and I have stopped moving…and so has everyone else. When I open my eyes, every countenance is fixed on me.

I want to shout, *What are you staring at? Just keep going!* but I can't get my mouth to form any words. My brain feels too slow. Liam moves closer to me. He says something, but what exactly, I cannot seem to process. It sounds as if he is talking underwater. His concern makes him all the more handsome though. So handsome, I could stare at him all day. *Wait—what?* The practical part of me registers that I need to snap out of it and pull myself together. But that voice gets farther and farther away. Then, I am floating on the air. Am

I being carried? I am not a weakling. I should protest, but I am just too tired. And then, there is peaceful blackness.

The smell of bacon rouses me from sleep. My head hurts slightly, but even with my eyes closed, I can almost taste the scrumptious breakfast Grace prepares.

Yet something about my surroundings doesn't seem quite right. My eyes open and focus not on my bedroom, but on the landscape of a sheltered glen. Memories and recollections scatter through my brain like snowflakes that finally fall into place to form a complete picture.

Oh yes, we must be with Athos and his men. I feel the side of my head. The bump is still there, but the tenderness has lessened quite a bit.

Where is Liam? When I prop myself up to glance around, my elbow bumps into something behind me. He is right next to me; we had both been sleeping on his cloak spread out on the ground. An unfamiliar wrap is draped over me like a blanket. A broad pine tree fans out above us a good several feet, providing natural protection from the elements.

Liam is sprawled out on his back, sleeping peacefully, his hands behind his head. Anne will die of envy if she finds out he slept right next to me all night. My mother, on the other hand, will die of embarrassment. Although taking into account all I had done to this point, maybe this will seem like a lesser infraction to her. It is a shame I was too incoherent to even remember a second of it. Until now, that is. I recline next to him just to watch him breathe for a few moments. This situation will *never* happen again, so I take a few moments to drink it all in. Even in my enjoyment, my heart feels little stabs of pain that deflate my mood. If only every morning could start this way.

The smell of the bacon sends pangs to my stomach. I am too hungry and thirsty to lie here anymore. Oh well. I did get to steal my one little minute to remember in the future.

Careful not to wake Liam, I peek out from under the tree branches. We are in a small clearing surrounded by tall evergreens. Men are scattered about haphazardly, some on the ground, some in makeshift hammocks. A pinkish glow tinges what little sky I can see. It is just past dawn. The only other person who appears to be awake is a man tending the fire from where the bacon aroma emanates.

I walk over in his direction. A shock of grey, shoulder-length hair sits atop his skinny frame. He is bent over his skillet, intense in his work, yet when I am a few steps away he speaks out softly, "Sleep well mi'lady?" Startled, I am silent. "It was a fair night I would say. By now you must be famished, having missed dinner."

His raspy voice is heavy with a Mainland accent. He lifts his head, and his face breaks into a kindly smile, absent of more than a few teeth. Odd that this frail, old man is so far from his homeland in the company of outlaws. What a story he must have to tell.

I find my voice. "I did sleep well, sir, thank you for asking. And yes, I am hungry and thirsty too."

The man is back to tending the food. He flips the bacon, fat sizzling over the grill, then pours some grain into a pot of boiling water. A stack of plates and cups sits at his feet. Cutlery sticks out of a half-opened sack. Where any of these items came from, I can only guess.

"Excuse my poor manners. We don't get many ladies in our camp. In fact, I should say this is the first time…well, I mean…a proper lady, if you get my drift. In any case, I was able to scrounge up a change of clothes for you. I left them over there with some soap." He gestures toward a nearby tree trunk, then points further across the camp. "There is a fine-running stream on the other side of those hemlock shrubs if you wish to wash up."

I could well imagine the types of women who would frequent a camp of outlaws. Suffice to say, they probably earn a fine night's pay in exchange for their "services." What I did not want to imagine was the types of clothing any of these "ladies" would leave behind. Certainly, it couldn't be anything in which a decent woman should be seen. And to have to wear the clothes of some harlot in front of Liam would be humiliating. A polite refusal is about to cross my lips, when the man, who notices my stricken expression, adds, "Not to worry mi'lady. The garments are the likes of what you are wearing now, only…um…clean."

At the word "clean," I am instantly aware of the fact I have not bathed in over three days. A wash in a fresh stream with fresh clothing would feel wonderful. In fact, I don't think I can even consider eating until I have taken care of this matter.

"Thank you, sir."

I retrieve the items while he mutters to himself about being called sir. His eyes dance as he tries out the title. "Truly mi'lady, the name is just plain Claude."

"Well, thank you, Claude. Your hospitality is most appreciated."

I bow and head off toward the hemlocks. He nods awkwardly at my courtesy. Clearly, it is not something to which he is accustomed.

"And no worries mi'lady," he whispers after me. "I will make sure your privacy is respected."

Claude should have no problem keeping this promise. I wend my way around one man after another deep in slumber.

A thousand different thoughts burst into my mind. What went on while I was passed out? Where are we now in relation to Lindenwood? Did Athos know anything about the fate of my father or King William? When he found us, were Athos and his men following the mercenaries, or were they following Liam and me?

There are so many questions that need answering, but when I hike down to the shore, the stream beckons me. All other concerns quickly disperse when I slip into the blissful, cool water.

To call the stream refreshing is an understatement; it is heavenly, its chill long forgotten the second the grime of three days dissolves off my body. Dirt mixed with the frothy soap bubbles drifts downstream until it is only a bad memory. The meager weight of my cropped hair in my hands startles me. As I comb through it with my fingers, there is regret, not only about how chopped it is now, but at how scraggly it will look while growing back. Beauty was never a concern for me before, but that was before I met one specific person.

The fresh clothes provide another blissful moment, caressing my now dry skin. They are merely the simple clothes of a peasant boy—tan breeches, and a dark green tunic over a white undershirt—yet to me they are as luxurious as fine silk. An attempt to wash out my old clothes is fruitless. Their stains won't budge and they are ripped in any number of places, though I do manage to scrub out most of the stench. Hanging limply on some branches to dry, they don't even seem fit for a scarecrow.

Confident I am as presentable as possible, I slip on my boots and mount the hill. The crisp air fills my lungs, revitalizes me, and I breathe in and out with purpose. Time to face everyone after my embarrassing show of weakness yesterday. Time to start behaving as though I deserve to be taken seriously. Time to rescue my father.

When I return, the camp is a hive of activity. Some men eat in small clusters, quiet snatches of conversation humming as I pass. Others shave and wash by small pitchers, while more tend to weapons or repair gear. A large, dark-skinned man sharpens his knife on a rock, the metallic scrape resonating off the trees with every stroke. He barely glances up at me before focusing back on the task at hand. In fact, no one speaks, nods, or in any other way acknowledges me.

Liam sits on a long, fallen tree trunk near Claude where he eats bacon and some type of gruel. When our eyes meet, his face lights up into a spellbinding smile. He waves me over, then pats the spot next to him on the log. No sooner have I sat down then Claude offers me a bowl of gruel and some bacon of my own. My stomach rumbles at its aroma.

"Enjoy, mi'lady."

Then he goes back to guarding his gruel pot, scrutinizing who takes what for breakfast. He even calls out a few he feels take more than their fair share. The men all tease him good-naturedly. Claude is obviously well liked and well thought of among these bandits. But I imagine it must behoove them to be nice to the person who feeds them.

"Sleep well?" Liam asks.

Does his expression hold a bit of amusement? Goodness knows, I have supplied no shortage of that. Passing out certainly did not add to my credibility of being knight material. And although I am a bit thrilled to have spent the night next to him, I am uncomfortable about discussing it. My acute hunger is replaced by acute nausea.

"I made sure to keep you close to me last night so that no harm would come to you. I did promise your father I would look after you," Liam states.

"Um…thanks," I barely whisper, a little bothered that following the promise to my father was the only reason he had slept by me; because I was a helpless girl, not because he had just wanted to be that close to me.

"Are you feeling better today?"

"Yes, fine now. Thank you." I can't meet his eyes, but feel the need to add defensively, "You know, I have never passed out before."

"Yes, well, I think that a bloody attack, a knock on the head, and a run-in with outlaws all in one day qualify you for an exception."

The tone is so kind I finally get the nerve to meet his gaze. His clear blue eyes swim with genuine concern for my welfare. They also alter me into a mute idiot who cannot form a sentence. We should be talking about saving our fathers, but all I can concentrate on is the dark stubble that outlines his jaw, frames his lips—the lips I almost kissed yesterday.

Enough! I force myself to pry my eyes away. It takes formidable effort.

"So what do you think we could possibly do today that could top yesterday?" he muses, not seeming to notice how my cheeks have flushed.

"I am sure he will think of something." I motion toward an approaching Athos.

He bids us a good morning, then leans on a large rock across from us and crosses both feet and arms.

"After giving careful thought to all the information you shared, I decided that the story required some more investigation. Therefore, last night I sent two of my men to the castle at Lindenwood to see what they could ascertain about the goings on. If your story is confirmed, then I may have something of interest to share with you."

I wonder what details Liam did and did not share with Athos.

"But right now, as a show of good faith, I would like to know the *real* story of who this girl is and what business she has traveling alone with you."

Liam speaks first. "I don't see what that has to do with anything…"

"Wait," I interrupt, "I will tell you the whole story."

Liam's expression warns me against saying anything, but then he just sighs in resignation.

"I am Olivia Davenport, daughter of Sir Jack Davenport, King William's Master of Arms. I snuck on the mission in the disguise of a squire. I have been performing weapons and horse training with the other squires for years and I did not think it was fair that I was not allowed to go just because I was a girl." When I pause, Liam stares at his feet with a smirk and Athos regards me, hands steepled to his lips, in utter fascination.

"I was discovered on the second day of the mission and my father sent me home. Prince Liam was kind enough to volunteer to be my escort. He, his guard, and I were attacked by men in the livery of King John. We sent the guard to Adelina to warn Prince Harold, then decided to go after the King's party ourselves. When we were almost attacked again, you rescued us."

"You expect me to believe that you deceived not only your father, but a whole group of trained military men for over a day?"

"Well, I knew I would never get away with it for the entire trip undetected, but I was counting on the fact that, for the most part, people see what they want to see to at least buy me some time," I explain with a shrug at his disbelief.

He is silent for a long while, stroking his small beard into a point. Liam and I wait for his response. Meanwhile, the camp is quickly being packed up. Claude leads a small mule into the clearing and proceeds to load up all his cooking utensils on the beast. Bedrolls and hammocks are gone, the fire pit has been doused over and camouflaged, and all traces of encampment are erased. Once the men themselves leave the clearing, only an expert tracker would be able to tell they had been there at all. An ordinary person would pass right by unaware.

Finally, Athos rises and speaks. "Well then, it would appear I am all caught up with how we came to meet. It would seem, Prince Liam, that this girl being sent home was a stroke of luck. It kept you from walking into a trap. As for you, young lady, if you have half as much talent with that sword as you have courage and gall, then I would guess you can well take care of yourself."

"Oh, she most certainly can, Sir Athos," Liam says, and a warm spot forms in my chest.

Two men hurry into camp. Athos excuses himself and strides over. They confer softly amongst each other. At one point, all three glance toward us, then continue with their intense exchange.

While they debate, Liam and I again discuss how out of character this behavior seems for King John. He had been happy to secure his little kingdom, and tales of his lack of ambition and lazy disposition are legendary. There are no offspring to goad him into fighting for more land; in fact, he has only a small number of men to protect him as a matter of course.

Liam remarks that when raiders were hitting the North Coast hard, King John had sent only a handful of men to fight along with King William's forces, not out of apathy, but because there simply were not many trained men. Free protection from Stewartsland's army had been a large bonus King John has enjoyed all these many years. Why would he deliberately pick a fight with us?

Of course, the piece of the puzzle we cannot reckon is the mention of the brother, Lord Otto. Perhaps it is he who instigated King John to cause all this trouble. When we finish comparing notes, our confusion and uncertainty hangs in the air around us like fog.

Athos, finished with his debriefing, approaches.

"Well?" we ask expectantly, rising in unison.

"Well, according to my scouts, there is more going on at Lindenwood than meets the eye." I feel an icy sensation creeping into my body, but what Athos says next makes my stomach drop. "I fear that your father may already be dead."

"What?" I whisper in horror.

Then it occurs to me that Athos speaks of Liam's father, our King. Even when I realize my error, I know if King John had killed King William there would be little reason to keep anyone else alive. Besides, my father would have fought to the death to try and save his King. Up until this point, there have been so many distractions; it's been easy to push the fears for my father's safety to the back of my mind. Now that we have this conversation, I am not sure I can face it.

Liam says nothing at first; he simply stares off into the distance not focusing on anything in particular. Finally, he says quietly, "Yes, I have feared that as well."

"There is one interesting twist some of my men found out on their reconnaissance a few weeks ago. My men liaised with an associate, Hawk, who is the main intelligence supplier for Lindenwood. Hawk relayed that a few months ago an unknown gentleman, who appeared to be of some importance, arrived and had been personally welcomed by King John. An event that had never before taken place to Hawk's knowledge. Since then, more and more men, mercenaries by their looks, had been arriving from the Mainland, an unprecedented occurrence for the quiet realm of Lindenwood.

"But the strangest part of all is that Hawk has not seen King John at all since the initial meeting with the stranger. He even questioned a number of local people he trusted. They reported the same. All of them, though, have seen the other gentleman carrying on business in and out of the castle.

"My scouts found the castle gates shut tight last night with an array of guards manning the walls. More patrolled the nearby woods covering the road that leads to the main entrance. The village itself seems more or less deserted, but for a few stalwart citizens who cater to the eating and, more importantly, drinking needs of the mercenaries."

"And this *gentleman*, does anyone know who he is?" Liam asks, although we both already have a pretty good idea. It seems Liam did not share his knowledge of Lord Otto with Athos last night when they spoke.

"From what we hear, the gossip is that he claims to be King William's brother."

"*Half* brother," Liam says emphatically.

Half, indeed. But when the half is the father's blood, and that father is a King, it is the only half that matters. I try to remember every detail my father ever spoke regarding these brothers. But the only fact I recall for sure is they are both King Bernard's bastard sons born to a longtime mistress on the Mainland about twenty years apart. By my calculations, King John was probably conceived long before Bernard was crowned, and Lord Otto, not long before he died.

Athos and Liam sit back down and continue talking, each supplying the other with information on this subject. I sink down beside Liam and quietly try to absorb it all. They agree that the half brother has somehow usurped power over the kingdom. That seems fairly obvious to me as well. Then for some yet unknown reason, he lured King William there under the guise of King John wishing to cede back the land.

From there, he can either use King William as a bargaining chip to gain more land, or kill him outright and fight Prince Harold's army in an attempt to win even more of Stewartsland territory for himself. Liam and Athos become silent for a moment while they weigh all this information out.

"In my honest opinion, he will try the bargaining first," I say. Both men's heads bob up, startled for a moment, as if they had forgotten I was even there.

Typical.

"For one, it would cost him less in money, time, and resources. And for two, everyone knows that the loyalty of mercenaries changes with the breeze. If they are faced with a massive army approaching, it may alter their idea of what is and is not worth fighting for."

To my surprise, they both listen intently, even nod in agreement when I pause. "I was thinking that we may have a bit of an advantage. They are clearly expecting Prince Harold to come northward to the main entrance. But what if we were to come at them from behind?"

Liam appears intrigued by the idea, but Athos scowls. "Just who do you mean by *we*, little lady? Surely, you don't think my men and I would want to insert ourselves into this skirmish of kings?"

It is imperative we have Athos and his men to help us achieve the element of surprise. I quickly think of a way to win him over.

"Athos, any long, unresolved conflict will most certainly result in almost all locals and merchants migrating south, taking their money and goods with them, effectively shutting down all fairs and seasonal festivals."

I take particular care to mention this. Exploiting regular trade routes and festivals provides a good part of his band's living. But, Athos waves his hand dismissively, as if this were no matter to him.

"Of course, the area would then be filled with a glut of soldiers and mercenaries who will pick over anything these migrants leave behind long before you can get to it. And who will also prove a much more challenging group to extort. Ongoing fighting would put a dent in this nice little niche you have carved out for yourself," I add.

I say all of this with an air of surety, even though I have no idea if it is true or if Athos will even care. His band could just migrate south along with the merchants. Yet, that would mean leaving a landscape they know by heart. It would also mean dealing with the King's brother, Prince Arthur, who is less likely to turn as blind an eye as his brother has for all these years. However, the fact remains that without his support and his men, there is no one who can carry out my proposed sneak attack. Still, I stare Athos down, my face a mask of indifference, as if his coming or not will be inconsequential.

Athos stares back at me, his face a mixture of amusement and exasperation. He nods at Liam and says, "I see what you mean about her impossible nature!"

They both chuckle knowingly.

What is that supposed to mean exactly? And why is it now so amusing to them both? The thought of them discussing me while I was out cold is humiliating. I feel heat creep into my cheeks. But then Liam's hand gently rubs my back, a signal that I did well convincing Athos. Whatever was said last night, it was meant as a compliment to my spirit more than an insult.

Without giving any answer, Athos lounges back against the rock again with his feet stretched out and crossed in front of him. A small bag at his waist produces a pipe and a roll of leaf. He unfurls the leaf packet and leisurely tamps some down into the pipe. Striking a match on a tiny flint box, he takes several long drags while he lights the pipe.

All the while Liam and I are immobile in suspense. Birds sing, soaring above from tree to tree. A light morning haze has all but burnt off in the face of the climbing sun. The air has a heaviness to it, indicating a warmer than average day for this time of year.

After a few languid puffs that float up and gradually dissipate, Athos finally cocks his head at us and says resolutely, "We've got plans to make."

My strategy to attack the castle from behind is adopted. Athos immediately dispatches scouts with orders to make sure our intended path is unguarded and to gather any other useful information. He orders the remaining men, who loll about waiting for orders, to make for Oakhill Glade. They melt silently into the forest in groups of twos and threes. Athos, Liam, and I are the last ones to leave.

We follow the river on foot as it winds north. It continues on this course until it is parallel with Lindenwood, then it curves sharply to the east and eventually flows out into the channel that separates Stewartsland from the Mainland. Along this eastern bend, it passes directly behind the castle at Lindenwood, providing a natural protection for its rear walls. The bank on the castle side is narrow, too narrow. Eventually the men will need to muster on the opposite shore and cross the water to the dock at the time of attack. This means we are currently on the wrong side.

"How will we get across the river?" I ask Athos.

"We have our ways," he replies without elaboration.

We hike in the cover of the trees on the river's right bank. The forest is overgrown and difficult to traverse. Light filters through the canopy, golden beams dancing on a carpet of rotten leaves. Dead branches and toppled trunks litter a floor choked with brambles. Every few yards, some startled creature scurries away across the haphazard maze, the underbrush undulating in its wake.

Athos, however, knows the location of every tree, rock, and downed limb. He nimbly picks a path through the undergrowth. Liam and I try valiantly to keep up. Clearly, these are ways well known to these outlaws, having probably been created by them. Our footfalls are soft and careful, which is second nature for Athos—sneaking up on unsuspecting people is a job requirement for him. But Liam and I hold our own.

If Athos raises his hand, we are to drop low and immediately take cover. Twice he makes this signal in response to something that he alone hears or sees. The first time, it is a few of his men, and they simply nod in acknowledgement before continuing. The second time, it is a magnificent stag crossing not three feet in front of us. About eight feet tall from hoof to antler tip, he bears a regal air. For a moment, he stops and deigns to gaze down at us, his muscles rippling beneath his tawny coat, before he strides away. I hear Liam's admiring intake of breath and guess he probably wishes for his bow.

The bandits communicate through a series of whistles that resemble bird calls. So far, I have counted three different patterns, each one just a bit shriller than an actual bird. What they mean exactly, I can only guess, but a three-note singsong tune like a cardinal's is used the most.

At midday, we stop next to a clump of bushes down by the river. This area is rife with apple trees, and we all enjoy one, crisp and fresh from the branch, along with some salted meat. I remove my boots to stick my tired, sore feet into the water. Tiny fish surface to nibble my toes in hopes of a snack. The tickle of their mouths combined with the cool current soothes the aching.

"How long will it take us to reach Lindenwood?" I ask through crunches on my apple. The juice runs down the sides of my chin.

"If we continue at this pace, we should probably make it by dusk tomorrow," Athos speculates.

Liam calculates that Adam should have made it back to Adelina last night. If Prince Harold left on horseback this morning, he should arrive about the same time. In this case, he will wait for the next morning to engage King John or Lord Otto in any way. Hopefully, we can come up with a way to contact him during the night to let him know where we are situated and what our plans are.

"That is assuming the heavy rain to our south does not hold them up," Athos says.

"Rain?" Liam and I say as one. Our eyes rise to the cloudless, beautiful sky, puzzled. The chance of a storm seems improbable. Athos stands and brushes off his pants, a knowing grin on his face. At my questioning glance, Liam just shrugs.

We trudge along our course northward for the rest of the afternoon. The air is oppressive amidst the densely packed trees. Sweat pours down my face while I glance longingly through the forest at the riverbank. There, a soft breeze carries gently over the water, the grass bending ever so slightly at its touch. I sigh, my perspiration-soaked clothes clinging to my skin in the muggy air. And sure enough, fast moving, streaky grey clouds approach from the south, carrying Athos' promised precipitation.

When the river curves to the right, so do we. A short way after this bend the river narrows considerably. Without warning, Athos motions us to leave the cover of the forest and make toward this part of the river.

"You ready to cross the bridge?" he asks over his shoulder.

I scan around, baffled. Nothing that even remotely resembles a bridge is visible, nor do I remember ever hearing about a bridge this far out in the wild. We are still a few dozen yards from the shore, and I wonder if Athos is just having some fun at our expense. But as we near a couple of large trees on the riverbank, a man steps out from behind them. While he and Athos whisper to each other, I notice two ropes spanning the river attached to trunks on either side. Although they are parallel, one is about two feet above the water and the other is about four. How they have come to be positioned in such a way is anybody's guess. Athos motions for us to come forward.

"Follow me please, but one at a time."

He deftly hoists himself up onto the lower rope, faces sideways to grasp the higher one, and shimmies his way across the water. The river is narrow here, but it also flows downhill in a swift current. Large, jagged rocks point up through the flowing white rapids. None of this seems any bother to Athos, who springs lightly onto the opposite shore.

"You go next Olivia," Liam mumbles. His face wears a pained expression and has an almost green cast. Before I can see if he is okay, Athos' man, who stood stock still to this point, orders me to hurry along.

I step up onto the lower rope and grasp the upper rope in my hand. After a deep breath, I slowly edge sideways. It is not very wide across, but when I check from up here, it seems like a long way to the other side. The water below churns menacingly; rough rapids rise up to wet my feet. Pointed stones jut out like sharp teeth from the white foam, granite jaws waiting to swallow me up at one wrong move. Looking down is probably not the smartest idea if I want to get through this. My full focus is on sliding my feet and hands along the ropes, only remotely aware of the burns my tight grip inflicts. While the ropes stayed nice and steady for Athos, they bob up and down like a cork in water for me.

Finally, I reach what I deem to be the halfway point. This gives me the motivation I need to finish. Athos waits, arm outstretched, for me to touch down. He again raises my hand to his lips. "Well done, my lady."

Now that my feet are firmly planted on dry land, a sense of exhilaration surges through me. The thrill of it reminds me of the pleasure I get from training.

Athos and I both direct our attention back across the river at Liam. He is about to mount the ropes when he says something to Athos' cohort. The man roars with laughter and slaps Liam on the back while he replies.

"Ah, such a charmer that Prince is. But I guess you know that already since you were making to kiss him just before we met," Athos notes.

My cheeks redden. Athos and his men were under cover in the woods when we were discovered by the enemy scouts. It is beyond embarrassing to think that Liam and I were being watched in that intimate moment. I want to tell Athos to mind his own business, but my attention is focused on Liam. He is even more uncomfortable crossing than I had been. The ropes quiver far more vigorously, too.

"You know, the more tense you are, the more the ropes shake. Remember that next time," Athos instructs. I am guessing there will not be many more "next times" for me in this department, although part of me is excited about the idea of getting to try it again.

Suddenly, a thought that doesn't add up occurs to me. "Wait a second, Athos. When you saw me about to kiss Liam, didn't you still think that I was a squire—a *boy* squire?"

"Miss Davenport, I make no judgments," is his only reply.

Liam reaches the halfway point and freezes, suspended over the water with his hands clenched tightly on the rope, his eyes squeezed shut. A moment passes, then another, but he remains stock-still. The rapids kick and froth, spattering him with showers of spray. Should I shout encouragement? Or should I make my way out to him? What could possibly be wrong? A thousand different thoughts are flying through my head when Athos shouts, "Come on, Your Highness, we don't have all day here."

Woken from his stupor, Liam wobbles the rest of the way across. When he alights on our side, Athos just shakes his head disgustedly. "Finding a little leisure time to sun ourselves are we, Your Highness?"

Liam makes no reply. I move next to him and rub his back in an attempt to comfort. His shoulders shake from the pounding of his heart. Still, he takes my other hand in his, giving it a squeeze. When he glances at me, my heart skips a beat.

Athos whistles a short, shrill whistle three times. The man on the opposite shore unties the ropes from the tree and Athos then pulls them across, unties our side, coils them up, and stuffs them into a hole in one of the trunks. Then without a word he strides away. Liam and I scramble to follow, but I cast one glance back across the river. His accomplice has vanished without a trace.

"How will your man get across now?" I blurt out, flustered and trying to work out their system in my head.

"You leave the worrying for my men to me, little lady."

On this side of the river, the trees are spaced apart nicely. While this proves much easier to navigate, and, thankfully, less stifling, it provides little cover for either our safety or from the elements. The rain clouds have caught up to us. Thunder rumbles loudly and almost instantly, just as Athos predicted, a tremendous downpour drops from the sky. We race to take refuge under a natural rock shelf nearby.

All in a row, we crouch underneath, our knees pulled up to our chins. Cramped but dry, we wait for the deluge to pass. Each of us keeps to the silence of our thoughts until Athos asks, "Just out of curiosity, Your Highness, what did you tell my man that he thought was so funny before you crossed the river?"

"I told him I couldn't swim," Liam admits.

After a split second of silence, the three of us burst into laughter.

That night, after rejoining his men at Oakhill Glade, Athos regales them, much to their delight and amusement, with the story of the Prince who couldn't swim. Liam himself laughs the hardest of all, especially when he shares that the man, named Hob, had replied, "Oh, do they have someone at the palace who does that for you too?"

A circle of men recline around a large bonfire, its logs crackling sharply in the night air. Some smoke pipes while others enjoy warm ale. Even Claude and his donkey made it here somehow. The bandits crane forward, intrigued to host such an esteemed guest.

I am next to Liam on his spread-out cloak. The firelight frames his face in a soft glow, softening the stubble on his jaw. His ebony hair gleams like black silk, and sparks of orange reflect in his clear blue eyes. He is even more handsome, if that is possible. My whole body radiates warmth, but whether from the fire or my proximity to Liam, I do not know.

It strikes me how at ease he seems with these men. His chances to interact with ruffians and outlaws are certainly few and far between; in fact these would seem the type of people expressly kept away from Liam and his family. Yet, anyone watching tonight would think he spent most nights sitting around a fire in the deep woods with these more unseemly versions of men rather than at a court of pretentious nobility.

"So then, I asked if he had any helpful advice—" Liam laughs so hard tears form in his eyes, "—and he says, 'Yes, Sire, best be certain not to fall in.'"

The men roar in amusement.

"Never let it be said that my men are not full of the sagest advice!" Athos shouts, raising his mug to a rousing cheer from his men.

The ale flows freely, and a large deer roasts over a smaller secondary fire. It smells heavenly as it rotates on the spit, whetting my suddenly keen appetite. The meat proves worth the wait when it simply melts in my mouth, more delicious than I ever remember venison tasting. Of course, the men get in a few good-natured quips to Liam when asking if he is enjoying it. Deer poaching in the King's woods is an illegal, punishable offense. But Liam notes only that it is the finest he has ever had the fortune of tasting, which makes the men, especially Claude, beam.

The more I get to know Liam, the more of a mystery he becomes. Acting this at ease with people and laughing at himself are traits that go against the impression I developed of him at home. There it seemed he was the one doing the mocking and no one should dare make fun of him unless they were prepared for dire consequences. Whereas here, he relishes the tongue-in-cheek ribbing he is taking.

As we sit, he banters back and forth with the men, taking it as good as he gives it. Is this some secret part of himself that he can never allow out when in the confines of the palace? Will this personality shut off when we eventually return home? I certainly hope not, because this is surely a truer version of Liam than the arrogant, condescending cad from Adelina.

A few times Liam catches me watching him, which is not hard since it is pretty much all I am doing. Each time he gives me a little wink and each time it seems as if the rest of the world melts away for a second and there is only him and me alone in the universe, inextricably connected to one another. When he looks away, his attention diverted by the men, it is as if a dark cloud has eclipsed the sun from my view. Then the hopelessness of loving not an ordinary man, but a prince creeps in—a prince who told me himself that all his decisions, including marriage, are dictated to him.

Perhaps his keen awareness of the novelty of this situation explains his enjoyment this evening. The odds of him having many nights like this ever again are virtually nonexistent. As is the thought of a prince marrying a girl with no royal pedigree, and who has embarrassed herself in front of the King to boot. But what can I do now? I am in love with him. It is not as if I can command myself to just stop. If only it were that easy, imagine all the heartache people would have been spared over time. And I suspect that he may have feelings for me, too. How deep they are I can only guess. Does it make it better or worse to know that the doomed feeling might be mutual?

My eyes must reflect the resignation of my thoughts, because Liam leans in and quietly asks me, "Are you tired?"

Before I can answer Athos claps his hands together. "All right troops, long day tomorrow. Time to get some rest." He stretches out stiff legs and disappears out of the firelight. The men scatter about the clearing, preparing for the night. Bedrolls and hammocks materialize out of nowhere.

I stand up to scan the area, not quite sure where to go. When I face Liam, he has risen as well and stands right next to me. "Where do you think we should go? Close to the fire where it will be warmer?" he asks.

"Um…" is my eloquent reply.

I am thrown by his use of the word *we*. Athos reemerges with two blankets, one of fine sheepskin, the other of a richly brocaded fabric. Both are clearly items made for a wealthy household and are decidedly odd to have in the middle of the woods. He offers them to us, insisting that as honored guests, we can make use of his bedding. When we protest at his generosity, he simply notes that he has made other arrangements and slinks away.

"Thank you," Liam calls after him and then adds in an appreciative, deferential tone, "for all your help." Athos simply nods in acknowledgement before melting back into the darkness.

"So let's stay by the fire for the warmth and the light." He lowers his voice and adds, "I trust Athos, but I will not say the same for all his men."

"Yes...um...sure..." I stammer out, the picture of eloquence once more. Not only am I nervous about the prospect of sleeping by Liam again, I now wonder what bad intentions Liam feels the men have toward us...or more specifically me. Last night I was passed out and did not have an opportunity to consider all of this.

"Which blanket would you prefer?" Liam asks. His tone and manner are so nonchalant you would suppose he routinely slept next to girls he barely knew. When this thought sinks in, I feel as though I have been punched in the stomach. What if he did sleep next to girls regularly? There would be no shortage of women who would consider such a proposition an honor, or at least a foot in the door to something greater. Life as a royal mistress is purported to carry a fair number of perks.

Thoughts of any girl laying one finger on Liam make my heart feel as though it will explode into bitter shards of envy. An acute understanding about crimes of passion becomes crystal clear in my mind. Inflicting actual physical harm on any girl who dared to go near Liam would seem like a completely justifiable response. The anger I feel at the mere thought of it is taking all my concentration to control.

In response to my stupefying silence, Liam finally says, "I will take the sheepskin because it can be a bit itchy. I remember that from some sleep-outs I had with my brother as a lad. In fact, being here with you like this reminds me of that."

In the split second following this comment, I hurtle from overwhelming territorial jealousy to overwhelming indignant anger. Is he actually implying that sleeping next to me reminds him of sleeping next to his *brother?* Is this where his casual attitude comes from, because in his mind I am like a *boy?*

A bevy of emotions careens through me. Liam starts to seem uncomfortable at my prolonged quiet. "I assure you, Olivia, my intentions are strictly honorable."

"So I gather," I snap at him.

Thickheaded man that he is—and aren't they all—he must think I fear for my virtue. Because my virtue will directly affect my marriage prospects. And that is what all girls want, right? Love and marriage? It is in this moment I realize that this is, in fact, exactly what I wish for with Liam. Well, was wishing for, at least the love part, right up until his last comment comparing me to Prince Harold.

He stumbles over his words. "It's just that…well, with all these strange men about…I would feel better being near you so I can make sure that you stay safe."

"Why would you worry? As you say, I am like your *brother* so who would want to bother with me?" I snatch the brocaded blanket roughly from his hands, and I get a modicum of satisfaction from the panicked expression on his face. In one swift movement I wrap it around me and lie on the ground with my back to him. Liam says nothing. After standing quietly for a moment, he finally lies down a few feet away from me.

I am humiliated. All this time I have been falling in love with him, tormented by knowing I could never have him. And he has been thinking of me like a brother? You read poems and hear songs about crushed feelings and broken hearts, but nothing can adequately prepare you for just how all-encompassing the hurt is. And aside from the devastating pain is anger that forms a fiery ball in my chest.

Anger mostly directed at myself for being so pathetic, for letting my emotions and imagination run away with me.

The camp is silent except for some snoring, but many of the men must have witnessed our little exchange. First, they all see me almost kissing him, and now they get to watch my jealous blowup. How petulant, ridiculous, and immature I must seem. Even more annoying to me is that I now hear Liam's heavy breath; seems he fell asleep utterly unfazed, while I am still so upset and sleep is a long way off. I try to concentrate on tomorrow and the attack plans, but despite my best efforts, silent, hot tears flow down my cheeks.

I wake just before dawn after only a few restless hours of sleep. A dim sky morphs from pale grey to pink, dotted with wispy white clouds. Unlike the last two days, the air has a noticeable chill. For a few moments, I lie there feeling thoroughly disgusted with myself. Much of my self-pride rests in the fact that I do not succumb to the erratic emotions most women display in the throes of love. In fact, Puck and I wholeheartedly agree on this sentiment. Over the years, we have shared any number of laughs at the expense of Jayne and Anne on this precise subject. Now I am acting no better—and over a prince no less. What could be more cliché? The thought of Puck does little to improve my mood. Will our friendship survive my betrayal, and if it doesn't, was it all worth it?

Vaguely, I notice the sheepskin atop the brocaded quilt on my shoulder. I lift my head ever so slightly to peek and find Liam right next to me, unfortunately, still as handsome as ever. Sometime during the cool night, after the fire had gone out, he had moved closer to cover me with his blanket. My heart simply melts at the sweetness of the gesture. But my practical side rebukes me for how quickly I let the warm, content feeling build up in my heart; how quickly I cling to the idea that he cares about me. It is due time the sensible part of my mind takes over and forces the irrational, emotional part to stop dwelling on dreams. Even if Liam is in love with me—and I am pretty sure that men in love with you do not usually compare you to their brother—it is a relationship that would never be condoned by the royal family. So any more time and thought wasted on it is worthless.

Besides, any sense of interest I perceive from Liam is probably only his intrigue at the uniqueness of our situation. He is finally away from the constraints of the palace and all the prying eyes of the courtiers. Liberated for the time being, he is in love with the whole world at the moment. Not me specifically.

Perhaps this is the case for me as well. Maybe I am just enjoying the freedom and excitement of everything going on. Any *feelings* I think I have for Liam are just a transfer of this strong sensation onto a person. It is a great argument to rationalize my emotions. And I don't believe a word of it.

Pans begin to rattle. Claude is awake. I sit up. We are in a glen surrounded by oaks. On my right, trees march up a small hill leading out of the depression, and water babbles melodically from this direction. When I rise, I follow the sound and emerge onto wide flat grasslands. A small stream coils lazily through lush fields, a blue ribbon in a sea of green.

I splash cool water on my tear-stained eyes and hope it will counteract the puffiness. No one needs to know I cried myself to sleep. Several horses graze in the grassy expanse under the watchful eye of one of Athos' men. He gives me a brusque nod when I stroll over to the animals. How he knows I am not an enemy and how the horses appeared here sometime in the night are mysteries to me. Athos is certainly some sort of a magician. The horses mostly ignore me, except for one who nudges his wet nose into my side. I stroke his velvety mane for a few moments, then return to camp.

Claude hands me a plate with bacon strips, a wedge of cheese, and a hunk of stale bread. "Mi'lady," he says and bows.

"Thank you, sir," I reply. He beams and sticks out his chest with obvious pride, then resumes his breakfast preparations.

Liam already sits nearby, a plate of food on his lap. I approach and force myself not to meet his eyes. The plan is to act as if everything is completely normal and hope that Liam follows suit. My stomach, however, is uncooperative and somersaults at the sight of him. His newly emergent beard and completely disheveled hair enhance his appearance, make him seem more accessible, like a regular man, not an untouchable prince.

"Good morning." His cheery tone belies the nervous gleam in his eyes.

"Morning," I murmur, trying to sound bored. An indifferent tone I copy from Anne when she is cross with a beau. It must work because he eats in silence, concentrating only at his plate.

At length, he clears his throat. "May I clarify something, Olivia?"

He does not get a chance. Athos and another man stride over and immediately talk business. The other man, Luke, will organize the surprise attack. He apparently has extensive knowledge of storming castles—an interesting line of work. Scouts brought back the news that Prince Harold is on his way. They made camp about ten miles away from Lindenwood castle last night. Once they arrive on the outskirts of Lindenwood, one of Athos' men will enter the camp and relay all of our objectives to Prince Harold.

Liam breaks in. "And how is it that one of your men will simply be able to waltz right into a royal camp and garner a meeting with my brother?"

Athos seems irritated at both the interruption and at the implication that one of his men could not accomplish this feat. "My dear Prince, there is a special symbol presented that is known to your father which lets him know a man is in my keeping. It is a symbol with which your brother is familiar as well, even if *you* are not."

Having mollified Liam into silence, Athos further relates that King John, or whoever is in charge, expects the royal army to march right up to the front gate. His men are positioned to defend this scenario. So far, King John has deployed only a few scouts into the woods closest to the castle. They are only there to spot Prince Harold's progression and give fair warning ahead of time. An ambush is not in place. Athos concludes by saying that his men will continue to monitor the situation for any changes.

"How can you be sure that one of your men was not spotted and tipped King John off to our existence?' Liam presses. I thought of the same thing, but would never have had the guts to question Athos.

Athos rewards Liam with a glare that would shrivel the most vibrant bush on the spot. "Do you actually think that a bunch of mercenaries could compete with my men in their knowledge of this land? I can assure you my men do not get *spotted* unless I mean them too. Honestly, do neither of you have any faith in me?" We make no reply, so Athos adds coldly, "Our plans from last night stand. Be ready to leave within the next half hour."

By the embers of the fire, we retrieve our gear. The quilt and the sheepskin are gone, no doubt packed up and hidden back in whatever treasure trove they had come out of. A man leads the horses into the camp. Two sturdy geldings, one black and one white, are brought over to us. Each is saddled for riding. Wherever Athos kept his treasures, it clearly contains costly riding gear.

Funny, I always had a picture in my head when I heard the word "outlaw"—one of some dolt-headed, drunken brigand. Yes, we all heard tales of Athos that made him sound suave and clever, but I just figured these were embellishments to make the story more appealing for the masses. In reality, though, Athos was not only all this, but very intelligent and a just, admirable leader to all these men. Indeed, I rather envy the lives of his men and would like to ask to join them; that is, if I was not a girl.

Liam stands next to me and clears his throat. "If I may just clarify something…" he starts again, but then pauses, as if unsure exactly what to say, before blurting out, "You don't remind me of my brother."

Not sure whether to reply or not, I say nothing.

"I mean, what I said last night, it didn't come out the way I intended. Obviously you don't remind me of Harold…I mean…you being a girl and all…"

It is almost painful to watch him nervously try to make his point.

"Don't worry about it. A person should be flattered to be compared to the crown prince—boy or girl."

Liam gives a small relieved laugh. "You certainly could teach him a thing or two about camping. He is not overly comfortable in the out-of-doors, always complaining he misses his luxuries. I am glad to be here with you instead."

He raises his face shyly and his blue eyes connect with mine. "For a number of reasons."

We set off at the appointed time, fifty or so men in all. Our plan is to make for the forest, known as the North Woods, which lies across the river from the castle. Then our objective will be to cross it at the opportune moment. Once again Athos' men vanish into the landscape, leaving Liam and me with Athos. The day is cooler and the sky overcast; it seems a downpour is imminent, but all the clouds can manage is an on-and-off drizzle.

Athos and Liam take the lead, their horses side by side while mine trots along behind. They discuss various strategies for when we arrive at our rendezvous point. One question is exactly how many men Prince Harold will have with him when he arrives. Liam speculates it will be no more than one hundred fifty men. That would seem the maximum number he could muster to leave immediately. Harold would have sent messengers through the countryside and to his uncle at Prescott before leaving. This would add a considerable number of men, maybe six hundred, but would take more time to gather and deploy.

"How much more time?" Athos questions.

To my surprise, Liam addresses me. "What do you think, Olivia? At least one or two more days?"

I have been listening to their whole conversation, but for a moment I am startled, since I assumed to this point they were about as interested in what I thought as in what the horses thought.

"At least one, maybe two more for Prince Arthur with the time it would take for the messenger to arrive, for them to muster the men, and for them to gather all the necessary provisions for the long march. Also, if men are coming from east and west they may assemble at a central meeting point before progressing forward as a group."

The two men nod in agreement at my assessment.

What an amazing feeling! Not only to be included in the discussion, but to have my opinion respected. They continue to plan for every possible contingency. I pay close attention and include my thoughts at different points, elated to be considered part of their brainstorming.

"I am going ahead for a bit to see if one of my scouts is waiting at a usual meeting place with news," Athos announces. "Just continue to follow the path we are currently on."

Frankly, to call the route a *path* is generous. It is overgrown with thick vegetation and littered with downed limbs. The horses need to be careful with their steps as they pick their way forward. At our daunted faces, Athos assures us that if we yaw too far off course, one of the nearby men will set us right. Liam and I scan the woods, which in our eyes appear empty of anyone, but say nothing more as Athos' horse bounds off.

Alone again, we ride side by side in silence. His presence makes me nervous and unsure of myself. Usually I am quite adept at reading people, but I cannot figure out exactly what Liam's feelings are toward me. The games and innuendoes of love are foreign territory for me. No wonder my older sisters are always in such distress over men. It is a confusing and unsettling experience.

Things would be a lot easier if I could just come right out and ask him what his feelings for me are. In fact, in the past, I wondered why my sisters did not do this exact thing;

it seemed at the time as though it would have spared them so much suffering. Now that I find myself in the situation, I see how asking such a question is easier said than done. If I don't ask, I can still cling to the possibility that his feelings for me match my feelings for him; but if I do ask, well, who knows—the answer could be devastating.

"We should make it to the North Woods by nightfall easily if the heavy rain holds off," Liam comments. "At least if it is at the distance Athos claims. I have never been up to this northwestern part of the country. All my experience has been on the northeast shore. What about you?"

"Um…no…I have never been here either," I stammer. "I have only been south a few times and never farther south than Prescott where we went three years ago when your cousin married Prince Kent from Glynland. That was a terrible trip…it was so hot and Ellen kept getting sick everywhere. And such crowds, I mean the wedding alone having over 500 people…" I trail off.

In my head, I know I am babbling. Obviously, Liam does not need me to tell him who his cousin married or how many guests had attended. In fact, he had not asked about any travels other than to the northwest part of the country. But, as usual, my uneasiness makes my mouth move against the sounder judgment of my brain.

Liam just watches me, head cocked, an amused smirk on his face. But when it becomes clear my blathering has stopped, he says graciously, "Yes, my cousin's wedding was well attended."

Silence again.

Uncomfortably. Loud. Silence.

How many times can I mortify myself in front of him? Just a few moments before, my opinion had been sought, as if I were a fully capable person. This last dissertation probably dispelled any such impression. Without meaning to, I sigh in disgust.

"What's wrong?"

"Nothing," I mutter, eyes downward.

"No, really. Tell me."

He steers his horse into my path, effectively blocking me from proceeding. This leaves me no choice but to respond.

"Well, if you must know, I am a bit embarrassed that I just blabbed out a bunch of nonsense to you about your cousin, not fifteen minutes after you asked my thoughts on how long it would take the men to arrive." I have nothing to lose with being honest. In response to his puzzled expression I go on. "Because you valued my opinion as competent and then I go and blurt out a stream of idiocy."

Liam chuckles so heartily that I actually have to laugh at myself a little bit. "For the record, I do value your opinion and advice. You have clearly spent a great deal of time not only training, but discussing battle plans and strategies. You obviously have a keen mind for it. And since you must have learned the majority of it from your father, I am sure you will be a source of useful information when we arrive in the North Woods."

Now it is my turn to be puzzled. "How so?"

"Because you will know how he thinks and what course of action he would be likely to take in any given situation. You may be our best hope for getting both our fathers out of this mess alive."

The safety of our fathers has been the one topic we have meticulously avoided. I pushed it to the back of my mind while I concentrated on all my newfound adventure.

But the cold hard truth is that my father is in grave danger. He walked into a trap, a trap he had been worried about. What had I done but cause him shame and confusion just at the time his faculties should have been at the height of focus? Tears come unbidden to my eyes as the reality that I may never see my father again sinks in.

Liam gently says, "I am sure they are both still alive." He reaches out and places a hand reassuringly on my leg.

"Yes, for now while they can still be of some advantage. But what happens if and when the advantage no longer exists?" I wipe tears off my cheeks.

"I guess we will just have to get to them before that, won't we?" Liam says as he swings his horse around to the path again.

"Our little secret party will be the decisive weapon in this battle," I state, trying to marshal my confidence while Liam and I pick up our pace on more traversable ground.

"I am sure it will be. The element of surprise will avail us well," Liam says and for my amusement continues with overexaggerated bravado. "There is no obstacle we cannot overcome, no barrier we cannot cross, and no man who will thwart us from our goal. We will be unstoppable."

"Unless there is swimming involved," I joke.

My hand flies to my mouth. For a moment, I had forgotten to whom I was speaking. The conversation reminded me so much of my bantering with Puck that I let the barb fly out before I could think better. Prince Liam may not appreciate my wry humor, particularly at his expense.

Before I can apologize, Liam roars with laughter. "And *that* is why I love being with you. You keep me on my toes, make me laugh, and never hesitate to put me in my place."

Our path narrows so we have to proceed in single file. He takes the lead while my horse falls in behind. We are silent again, but it is a wonderful, easy silence that now fills the air. Speaking now would break a magical spell that has enveloped us. The rain has picked up to a steadier drizzle, which soaks everything in a dank chill. I am perfectly content, however, as I wrap myself in the warmth of the words, *"I love being with you."*

We reach the forest behind Lindenwood Castle at dusk and take cover in the thick trees that run nearly to the shoreline. Across from us, the back of the castle walls arc out in a semicircle toward the river. At its midpoint, there is a gate topped by a parapet. A sentry who mans this position slouches against the wall, arms folded. He is alone. There is no worry of an attack on this side of the fortress.

And with good reason. The narrow gate is fronted by a small pier about ten feet in length. Deliveries are made here directly to the castle from the river. The position of the gate, with its guard above, combined with its limited area makes it a problematic entry for someone to take by force. An army of hundreds squeezing through the tiny opening simply would not be a practical tactic. Thankfully, we number only about fifty.

Scouts of Athos have been stationed in these woods for the past thirty-six hours and report no unusual activity, only the normal changing of the gate sentry. King John is busy tracking the movements of Prince Harold to know the moment he left Adelina and the moment he arrives here. The second set of men Liam and I encountered two days ago were probably positioning themselves for that exact duty.

I wonder how King John reacted when he learned those men had gone missing and were possibly found dead. He would likely surmise that someone managed to escape his ambush and fled to warn Prince Harold. The Prince would not have left Adelina so soon unless he had been warned of some specific wrongdoing. Otherwise, it would have taken him a few more days to recognize all was not right. As for King John's missing men, Athos assures me that his men rid the woods of any evidence of the bodies.

"But how can you be certain our assemblage here has remained undetected?" I press.

At first I think he won't deign to answer, but then he sighs, a long weary sigh like my father does when I badger him. "Miss Davenport, all I can tell you is that I have been doing this type of…work…for some time now and I am quite confident at the secrecy of this operation."

Athos relays that he has sent scouts to liaise with Prince Harold, whose men have just made it to the outlying area and are preparing camp for the night. The scouts will convey to the Prince that both Liam and I are safe. They will then explain our plans to aid him with our surprise attack from the rear, which will give us access inside the castle walls. He has yet to detail the exact nature of these plans to Liam and me.

"Miss Davenport, I understand that you are a pupil of your father's tutelage on castle defenses. You see this narrow gate, guarded from above, situated precisely so that a sneak attack on it would be almost impossible. How do you think we should gain entry?"

For a moment, I am surprised he addresses this question to me. Is he just ridiculing me? No. The keen expression in his eyes shows he tests me. And I want to pass this test!

I sit back against a tree, quiet my mind, and focus on all the factors of this particular gate plus all the information my father and I have discussed over the years. Aloud, I work through it in my mind. "Well, let's see, to get in the back gate, first you would need to get rid of the sentry in a manner that would attract no attention. Especially considering the castle is full of armed mercenaries expecting an attack. The most helpful information to know would be what time the sentries are changed so we would not come across two of them at once." Here, I glance at Athos. "Which you already know, don't you?"

He merely nods in assent, as if this fact is a trivial detail. Athos knows the answer already and he just waits for me to puzzle it out. I concentrate, trying to put all the pieces together when the simple answer dawns on me.

"A delivery," I say, my voice half-surprised at the simplicity of it. Athos beams and Liam nods, impressed.

"But you would have to know when one was coming and…" I trail off, then say to Athos, "You know when there is to be one, don't you?"

Naturally he does.

"A regular delivery is due within the next day or two containing spices, fabrics, and other such sundries from the Mainland." How he knows this, he does not bother to explain.

"One of my men stationed at the incoming port put in a few generous bribes to make sure that this shipment will arrive here at six o'clock tomorrow morning. I have a squadron of men waiting downriver to commandeer the supply barge. These men will then pilot it up to the gate, gain entry, and dispose of both the door guard and the sentry above. They will then assume these positions, signal to us to cross the river, and await my signal to open the back door. Once inside, we will cause a distraction big enough to draw attention away from the main gate."

When he concludes, Athos glares at us challengingly, as if ready to defend any criticisms we may have of this plan. But Liam and I merely stand there with our jaws agape.

"It's a brilliant plan, but even brilliant plans are not foolproof," I say. A quote my father taught me.

"Yes, yes, there are a thousand things that could go wrong at any point." Athos concedes more graciously than I would have thought.

"But I can't think of a more solid plan. You truly are amazing, Athos. I am glad you are on our side. Were you a military man once?" I ask, hoping to get some small glimpse into his past.

"You say 'amazing'. Most people, your fathers included, would say 'cunning'. In the end, I am sure they will begrudge any help I do supply," Athos says dryly. "And what I was or was not once has no bearing on what I am now. In fact, with the price on my head, Prince Harold's army is as likely to run me in as work with me."

"Not if I have anything to say about it," Liam booms defiantly. "Your actions toward Olivia and I alone should be enough to grant you a pardon."

"Ah, yes, *should be*—dangerous and deceiving words. There are many *should be*'s in life. Whether or not they come to actuality is a different matter entirely," Athos says and snorts with more than a touch of bitterness.

Whatever his story is, he has no intention of sharing it with us. When a scout materializes out of the trees, Athos strides over to him and begins to whisper.

Liam takes the opportunity to sit next to me. We rest our backs against a large alder tree. Its nearly bare limbs stretch high into the sky. With his head cocked, he studies me.

"You are pretty amazing yourself, Olivia. Thinking of a delivery. Very impressive."

"Impressive or a little disturbing that I think the same way as an outlaw," I joke, absently brushing dust off my breeches.

He inches closer and puts his arm around me. My heart starts to race. With his free hand, he lifts my chin. "No, you thought like a soldier. Your father will be so proud."

I smile, but cannot form a reply. My ears pound. My head swims. Our eyes are locked. I feel the warmth of his breath on my face. This is the second time we are in this same position, and each time it has been initiated by him, so he must feel something for me. Surely, it must be more than just the novelty of the situation. He just compared me to a soldier, yet I am still not brave enough to ask a simple question. But if he kisses me wouldn't that be an answer to my unspoken question? Or will it just make everything more confusing?

"Ahem…" Liam and I jump to find Athos standing over us.

The moment is broken. Again. Our faces fall away from each other, but he keeps his arm around me. Athos pulls a small silver flask from his belt and takes a long sip. Neither Liam nor I speaks. We know Athos' penchant for assessing all angles when receiving new information.

"Good news," he finally says, "your brother is grateful for our help. He thinks our accessing the castle grounds will be pivotal for him to gain the upper hand. We have also confirmed from men who were in the King's original escort that only His Majesty and Sir Jack are being held captive. As of now, they are both still alive."

Relief floods through my whole body like a waterfall. We are not too late.

"One more thing. Prince Harold personally sends word that he is most thankful you both are safe. And he orders you to find a safe haven for waiting out the battle."

Our mouths open in protest, but we are cut off.

"Since we all know *that* is not going to happen, I will leave you two to get some rest before we have to get into formation." Athos winks and disappears into the trees.

The sun sets and a chilly evening air spreads over us. Lighting a fire is out of the question given the secrecy of our mission. Liam and I pull some food out of our bags and eat a simple dinner of meat jerky and dried fruit. When we finish, Liam sits close to me again and lays his cloak over our legs for some extra warmth.

After a moment of silence, Liam lets out a long, frustrated sigh. "It is just so typical that Harold thinks I should sit out the battle. My family is always trying to protect me and treating me like I can't take care of myself. I'm surprised he didn't just send a bodyguard over to hold my hand the whole time."

I know the feeling, understand how much it hurts. He is quiet, but I know no words of mine will lessen the sting. It's funny to think that only three days ago I had been so sure of Liam's sense of arrogance and entitlement. In reality, his life contains the same restrictions and powerlessness that mine does.

When Liam speaks again, I feel as if he has plucked the thoughts right out of my head. "You know, I have enjoyed the past few days so much. Obviously I would not have wanted for either of our fathers to be in danger, but I feel like these last few days I have finally discovered what it is like to genuinely *live.*"

Yes, I agree with that sentiment wholeheartedly. These last three days have been more exhilarating and interesting than all my life's previous days combined.

"It's killing me to know that somehow, some way this adventure will end and things will have to go back to the way they were; every moment of every day dictated and monitored," he adds despondently.

Yes, that will be hard. But harder for me is the knowledge that we will never be with each other again. Not like this. The thought hits me hard. A cold, bare pit forms in my stomach. I will go from a girl who can sit right next to him with his arm around me, to a girl who does not even merit personal access to him. Maybe the palace will make an exception for me since Liam and I have shared this adventure together. But what good would that do? Then I could watch as a parade of "suitable" girls is brought in to win his hand in marriage.

For the first time I understand why women become mistresses. Prior to now, I had always wondered how a woman could settle for being second best all the time. But, if it is the only way I can be with Liam, wouldn't I consider it?

No.

It would be unbearable to have to watch him with his real wife. Better to move as far away from Adelina as possible. Maybe Prince Arthur can arrange a match for me in Prescott. The emptiness of a life with no Liam pounds over me like a giant wave that crashes in and sweeps away all light and hope. How will I be able to forget Liam the man when he has to go back to being Liam the Prince?

Liam, who has been lost in his own thoughts, half chuckles and says, "Maybe Athos will just let us join his band. Problem solved."

"Yes, if only we could—that would be an ideal solution."

We both sigh wistfully.

I must doze for a bit, my head resting comfortably on Liam's shoulder. His woodsy scent and steady breaths calm me. The nip in the air cannot overcome the warmth I feel just being close to him. Whether Liam sleeps or sits in contemplation, I do not know. Some while later, Athos sends a man back to fetch us, and we follow him to the tree line.

The band is assembled at the edge of the woods. We squat among a ramshackle border of scraggly pines. A needle-strewn ground muffles our footfalls, and their sharp scent permeates the air with every movement. I hover under one tree's low-lying branches, my hand resting on its sticky, rough trunk. All around me men crouch in the concealment of the trees. We are like ghosts in a graveyard who lurk behind the tombstones waiting to strike. A heavy silence hangs in the air; the combined force of our anticipation is almost a physical presence.

We await sight of the commandeered supply barge. I wonder how we will ascertain Athos' men indeed have control of the vessel, but trust Athos and his men have this covered. It is just before sunrise and a brightening stain smears the eastern edge of the sky. An expectant hush fills the air around us as every eye strains upriver.

Gradually, the outline of a barge appears on the horizon, so tiny at first it could be overlooked. It approaches, and we hold our collective breaths. The forest itself seems suspended in anticipation as the boat steadily makes its way toward us. Silhouettes of one man poling the boat along and another man sitting in the front among the boxes and barrels of goods come into focus. When it passes just in front of our position, I hear the poler whistle a soft tune, his head cocked ever so slightly toward our shore. All the men exhale at the signal.

The poler guides the craft to the dock. Once there, he easily ties it up while the other man jumps onto the dock. The sentry above the wall yells down curtly, "Password?"

My heart stops. There is a *password?*

"T-t-tarragon," the boatman stutters out.

"You're not Smitty," the sentry's angry voice booms. "He is our usual deliveryman. Where is he?"

"I am sorry…sir," the boatman answers in a nervous stammer, "but there is a pestilence in our village and Smitty has come down with it. Please sir, I am only doing what I was told." He removes his hat, wrings it in his hands with his head bowed. His flustered mannerisms are quite convincing.

After a moment's deliberation, the sentry says, "If that be the case, and Smitty sent you, then tell me the color of his eyes."

"Well my lord, blue. At least the *one* he's got left is blue," the boatman states matter-of-factly.

A long moment of silence passes; again the tension in the forest around me is palpable. At length, the sentry yells down the words we pray to hear.

"Open the gate."

Our men, Dag and Hez, need to take care of the sentries and gain control of the gate. Then one will signal that we can use the barge to move across the river. It is either that or they will be discovered, and the plan will fail in its earliest stage. If Dag and Hez are captured alive and questioned, they are to pretend to be Prince Harold s men, so as not to give our company away. This way we can proceed with Plan B.

Unfortunately, there is no Plan B.

All eyes on the far side of the river stare intently at the gate, willing themselves to see what transpires behind the walls. I strain for any sound of struggle or combat, but all I hear is the murmur of the river and the last of this year's crickets chirping somewhere off in the distance. Nature still carries on her way, unconcerned with the mere battles of men.

We wait for what in truth must be only a few moments. They seem like an eternity.

At last, the gate opens, and two pairs of men emerge. Each duo contains one man who is being supported by the other. The two incapacitated figures are dropped onto the barge in a heap, then the other two men reenter the gate. A few faint notes are whistled just as the gate closes. Athos trills three soft notes of his own. Quick as lightning, four men steal out of the woods and silently enter the river. They swim to the barge and proceed with the arduous task of leading it to our shore. Here the current is not nearly as strong as it was at the makeshift bridge we crossed, but the undertow drags the swimmers some yards down before they make it to shore.

Additional men creep down to assist, and among them all the boat and its contents are pulled up onto land. The motionless sentries' limp bodies are borne off into the woods.

"Are they dead?" I manage to rasp out in a hoarse whisper.

"Not likely. Killing might leave blood behind, which would need explaining. They are unconscious from a blow on the head. We just need to keep them bound, gagged, and out of our way," Athos says.

"Better to keep them alive," Liam responds. "We may need them for questioning."

I can't help but notice that the entire contents of the shipping vessel—barrels, crates, and trunks—have all been carried off into the woods as well. No doubt they will be deposited into Athos' already impressive cache for his own personal use, or as valuable trading commodities.

The rest of the band maintains position by Athos. There are only about fifty of us altogether, by no means a great host of men, but hopefully enough for a surprise group whose main occupation will be to cause chaos and distraction. A few moments later, the bandits who secreted both humans and goods in the forest rejoin us. Liam stands next to me, his presence a reassurance. Every once in a while we share a meaningful look and nod with confidence at the other. Technically, I should be more scared that I am about to risk my life. And though there is a part of me that is frightened, it is not the dominant part. The larger part of me is eager to put all my training to use, to feel like part of a unit working toward the same goal. Once we are in the thick of things and blood is flowing, maybe I will lose my nerve and run. My father always said that all the training in the world is useless if one's fear gets the better of him. He has seen soldiers, ones he felt had great potential, fold under the horrors of battle. If I feel myself faltering, I will remember that it is my father who inspires me to attain my potential.

The rosy light of dawn breaks over the horizon while we wait for the intended time to cross the river. Every face is hardened and alert, every muscle set as tense as a drawn bow string. Prince Harold is to marshal his force at the front gate and demand the return of the prisoners. If that request is denied, he will request to enter and see the prisoners to confirm they are still alive. Presumably, then King John's men will open the front gate.

Meanwhile, Athos is to lead the men across the river and have them amass just outside this back gate. Once the front gate has been opened for Prince Harold, his trumpeter will blow the notes that routinely announce his entry anywhere. This will be our signal that the gate has indeed been opened. Athos will then lead his men through the river gate and come at King John's forces from behind. Hopefully, this will cause enough of a diversion for Prince Harold's men to storm the front gate and gain a foothold inside.

It is a risky plan, where more things could go wrong than I can count. My father always says that daring plans like these largely come down to three things—planning, courage, and luck; the first and the second are within your control, but unfortunately in the end, there isn't much you can do but pray for luck. I pray hard now that King John's men open the front gate because without this, our plan has no legs.

Earlier, when we had discussed this tactic, I asked Athos what we would do if King John refused to open the gate because he expects a trap. He replied we would then need to meet back up with Prince Harold to strategize another course of action. Granted, a day or so more time should bring the large host of Prince Arthur's men from Prescott, which would increase our options for attack, but it also may increase the possibility that King William and my father would be harmed.

Truly though, King John must see how precarious his position will become if he blockades himself in the castle, knowing that reinforcements must be coming our way. He would do better to negotiate sooner rather than later. But as his motive for this kidnapping in the first place is beyond my grasp, who knows what line of reasoning he will follow.

At last, the time arrives to cross the river. The first group slinks down to shore. Most place their weapons aboard the barge and hold the side while they swim across, leading the vessel as they go. This method will move the men more swiftly across than if they all weighed down the vessel. A few men stay aboard to watch that the arms do not accidentally fall off and wash away in the river. Their movements are swift and graceful, the small dock reached in no time. They slither onto it like a pack of vipers except for the two who guide the craft back to our shore.

While I wait, I ponder the one part of the plan that has me terribly worried. If King John agrees to show the prisoners, he will bring them out into the courtyard where they will be at best unarmed and at worst in restraints. But if fighting then breaks out all around them, they will be defenseless. King William would then essentially be a sitting duck. In such a situation, my father would do everything possible to protect the King, thereby placing himself in a completely vulnerable position. I consider mentioning this to Liam, but decide he either has already thought of it himself or is better off kept unaware for the moment. My main goal is to seek out my father and arm him as quickly as possible once the fighting breaks out.

Athos taps my shoulder. Only a few of us remain, and Luke, the plan's mastermind, is poling the now-empty boat back to our shore. We steal out of the cover of the trees, slog through a couple of muddy steps of icy water, and hop onto the barge. The men on the other side huddle both on the narrow bank that runs just outside the wall, and on the dock.

Liam is as white as a sheet. Athos claps him on the back and whispers cheekily, "Don't worry, Your Highness, I won't be letting you drown just now when there will be so many more valiant ways to die today."

As the barge pushes off toward the dock, I have the profound sense there is no going back. The current is rough, rocking and bobbing the barge on our short journey. My stomach drops for a brief moment with an overwhelming urge to jump into the river and swim to the safety of the abandoned shore. But then, from somewhere deep inside me, my resolve steels itself. An awareness fills me that all the training I have done in the past has prepared me for exactly this type of situation. I realize that not only can I handle this battle, but it is what I have been preparing for my whole life, despite being a girl—or because of it.

We are halfway across the river when I hear faint trumpet notes carry on the wind. At the front gate, Prince Harold must be delivering his demands to the enemy. The barge pulls up to the dock where it is moored by Luke, and the last of Athos' men step onto the castle side of the river. Slowly, Athos inches open the unlocked river gate and the men start to file inside. I clutch my sword and march forward with determination. Liam clasps my free hand; his face has changed from pale, frightened boy to hardened warrior.

He leans and whispers, "Promise me whatever happens you will stay with me. That we will not be separated." His eyes communicate his worry.

"I promise."

We are herded into a small holding area where merchandise can be held while it awaits shipping or sorting. It is a long narrow space that bursts with products, its width no more than a few feet. Crates and barrels are stacked neatly around. Rolled-up carpets and bolts of cloth lean against the wall. Accommodating fifty plus men is a tight squeeze. Liam and I are jammed into a small space next to a large ebony-colored wooden trunk, ornately carved and decorated with inlays of smooth white stone. Ivory, maybe? The smell emanating from it is as exotic as the trunk itself, and I wish I had some time to examine it more closely.

Directly across from us in the far wall, a set of large double doors leads into the castle grounds. Overhead, upon the parapet bridging the front and back wall of the small storeroom, is a sentry position. From this vantage point, one can overlook both the river gate and the doors. Dag now mans this location, his gaze frozen out onto the river. He never once so much as glanced down while we all filed in underneath him.

The doors are held shut by a sturdy lock, which fortunately for us, has the key sitting right in it. Athos removes it and tosses it aside. Presumably there is a similar lock on the other side of the door as well. Hez's job was to take care of this gatekeeper and leave us the key. He was then to dispose of whoever opened the lock on the other side.

Athos approaches the gate and softly whistles a few notes. Hez answers them with his own. He has done his job. Now we wait for Prince Harold's signal to enter the main castle grounds. Some of the men regulate their breaths after the exertion crossing the river. Others shift from leg to leg to keep limber. It reminds me of the horses in a stable after they have been for a run. The exchange between Prince Harold and the castle guards is more discernible from this spot.

"If King John wishes to negotiate with me, he needs to prove my father and Sir Jack are unharmed," Prince Harold's voice booms.

"We will show you the man but not the King," a harsh voice calls back.

My father is still alive! Relief sweeps through me, my knees almost giving out.

"How am I to know the King is still alive then?" Prince Harold demands. This is dangerous ground. We did not plan a contingency for where one man is shown and the other is not.

"We will bring his man. Ask him. He will confirm it for you."

A long time passes. My heart beats right in my throat. It is like swallowing over a peach pit. That is, if I had any saliva—my mouth has gone bone-dry. Liam squeezes my hand. What is taking them so long? Is it only a bluff? Is my father already dead? Horrifying visions of his torture and death crowd through my brain. Finally, we hear the distinct click and hum of the portcullis being raised. Then, the groan of the drawbridge being lowered.

"May I approach him?" Prince Harold asks.

He must be referring to my father, who must have been marched out as a prisoner and stands unarmed in the midst of all these mercenary soldiers. I pray that Prince Harold has a viable plan for keeping him safe when the fighting breaks out. Although I am grateful he is alive, my blood simply boils at how vulnerable he is.

"You may, but only to the gate and no further," the man orders.

A few seconds later, the trumpeter's high-pitched notes echo through the air. The signal has been sounded.

Instantly, the double doors fly open, and we pour quickly into the castle grounds. We find ourselves in a dark, dank alley that runs behind a number of small buildings that ring the courtyard in front of the castle. This is the route the newly imported merchandise takes to its destination. The lane lies heavily in the shadow of the castle wall, the ground moist and mossy underfoot. Back doors of various businesses and shops open out onto it. Refuse is piled in crates outside each one. Flies teem around the area, unfazed by the rancid aroma. In such tight quarters, it is almost unbearable.

The space allows us only to proceed two by two. Athos leads the men and, I must say, appears to be heartily enjoying the action. Liam and I are about halfway back, side by side, in the thick of all the men. Our swords are drawn, though so far, we have not encountered any resistance. A shopkeeper emptying trash quickly retreats inside at the sight of us, far more concerned with his own well-being than the safety of the city. My foot catches on a loose stone and I stumble, knocking some errant flies off my shoulder in the process. There is nowhere to fall, a hair's breadth separates me from the bandit I follow, and I regain my balance in time to notice there is light ahead.

Quite abruptly, the passageway ends and opens into the main courtyard. We disperse into space, the entrance to the front gate ahead of us on the right. The few people in the courtyard all stand with their backs to us, straining to see what transpires at the front gate. There are only about twenty armed men at various intervals in the rather sparse crowd. None of them are alert to their surroundings, and we fan out behind them unnoticed. I desperately try to locate my father, but the crowd blocks our view.

Not far in front of us, a little boy, no more than four, hangs on his mother's skirt. All of her attention is focused on the action. The boy catches sight of us. His eyes grow wide with excitement. For a brief moment I think of Lydia, the boy's expression is so reminiscent of her face when she is excited.

"Mommy, look," he says amazed as he tugs on her skirt and points, "you were wrong, the enemy army *is* inside the grounds!"

His mother turns distractedly, ready to shush her child for making her miss all the real excitement. Then she spots us. A brief second of confusion passes over her face before she lets out an ungodly scream. She snatches up her boy and runs off. The boy, meanwhile, bursts out crying, more in shock over his mother's reaction than anything.

This outburst draws attention to us—which is, after all, the plan. The castle folk panic and run in all directions. Shouts of "Breach! Breach!" and "From behind!" can be heard from the sentries on the wall. Citizens scatter out of sight, leaving only the few armed men among them to face us. They draw their weapons and cluster together, ready for the fight. More soldiers run from the gate to their aid. Just what we were counting on.

With the crowd out of the way, we can see the main gate where the commotion is unfolding. Soldiers now scramble to cover the breach at their rear. The element of surprise worked brilliantly. Our enemy does not know our numbers and sends many more men than are needed. This causes the needed weakening of the defenses at the front. Prince Harold's men now break forward and charge full force through the compromised opening. Cries of "Attack! Attack at the front gate!" ring out through the courtyard.

The fighting erupts in earnest. A surge of enemy men bears down in our direction.

"Take care you two, mercenaries fight ugly," Athos warns over his shoulder. Then he exuberantly calls out the charge to his men. I am just about to be swept up in the tidal wave of bodies when Liam grabs me and pulls me to the side.

"We must find our fathers. Let the soldiers fight," he yells over the roar of men.

"My father is in front of the gate and he is unarmed," I scream back, hoping my voice is not drowned out by the cacophony all around us.

Liam nods. We skirt the edge of the fighting and make our way in the direction of the gate. A random fighter engages me in a volley of swords. When Liam steps in to help, the fighter, sensing he is outnumbered, backs off from us and wades deeper into the scrum of men. Everywhere steel thunders against steel. Men grunt as bodies collide and engage in an indescribable confusion of limbs and blades. I recognize the metallic smell of blood. The hair on my neck stands on end. Casualties. Hopefully theirs and not ours.

Gradually, we power our way to the area in front of the main gate. I see my father, bleeding from his mouth and nose, trying to fight off an armed man with only his fists. He punches the man in his jaw and blood spurts out in crimson drops. But my father staggers back from exertion. The mercenary is clearly gaining the upper hand as my father tires. I clutch Liam's arm and point as we thrash our way through the sea of combat toward them. We are almost there, when my father catches his foot on a discarded helmet and stumbles to one knee. The mercenary raises his sword to strike.

"Father!" My frantic shriek reverberates off the very stone of the castle.

Startled, both Father and the mercenary jerk their heads in my direction.

"Sir Jack," Liam yells, tossing his own sword to my father.

In one lightning fast move, my father catches the sword and springs back up onto his feet. His opponent reacts with equal speed, and they begin furiously striking weapons. As my father attacks, the enemy, who had held the edge against an unarmed man, soon learns that as an armed one, this opponent is lethal. The scales of victory tip swiftly in Father's direction.

My attention on them is broken by a hard shove from Liam. It sends me reeling, and I stagger to regain my balance. Liam is locked in battle with an enemy soldier. Now swordless, he has pulled a large knife from his belt. Although the soldier is not a big man, his sword gives him a distinct advantage. The Prince's moves are to defend himself rather than to actually disarm or wound.

In a flash, my sword is drawn and I leap to Liam's side. Liam blocks an oncoming thrust, but the enemy cunningly grabs Liam's wrist and wrests the knife out of his hand. It falls to the ground with a loud clatter. The mercenary kicks it out of Liam's reach and for good measure kicks Liam hard in the side. He doubles over in pain. The air around me stills. My focus, honed by years of training, reduces to a singular goal. Defeat of this enemy becomes my sole objective. I charge him with sword drawn. A seasoned warrior, he sees me out of the corner of his eye. He spins to meet my blow, and our swords connect with a force that vibrates me from fingertips to toes. If my mind could comprehend the danger I had just thrown myself into, this fight would soon be lost. But my mind has no input here, indeed there is no time for thinking, my body simply acts instinctively, every movement in perfect unison and with such purpose. Every thrust, parry, and lunge, every step, every feint, unfolds out of me as natural as walking, easily matching my opponent's.

"Humph, not bad for a squire," my adversary snorts out with breath that stinks of sour ale, "but I think you are in over your head, son."

The mercenary unleashes an unrelenting barrage of hits that propel me backward and down, his entire strength unleashed against me. I counter with such exertion that I cannot catch my breath. My chest begins to constrict in pain. He will overpower me. There is nothing I can do. His strength is just too great. I fight for breath and try to block the onslaught, but my arms feel like lead. It is over. Suddenly, the man screams in agony and stumbles to his knees. Liam lies behind him, his recovered knife buried in the enemy's calf. He had crawled to retrieve it despite his obvious pain. Not ready to give up, the mercenary continues flailing his sword around, but I am able to knock it out of his hand. My foe now kneels at my mercy.

Time completely stops.

In a split second a thousand thoughts run through my head. Will I be able to live with myself if I kill an unarmed man? Wouldn't a judicious person spare him and merely take him prisoner? How many loved ones are awaiting his return? Can I stand the thought of leaving a wife a widow? And any children fatherless? Had he known that his life hung in such a balance, one that was tipping toward sparing him, he may not have tried his next move. He grabs the knife that is wrenched deep in his calf muscle, yanks it out with a groan, then makes to thrust it into my chest. Before my mind can make a conscious decision, my arm runs him through with my sword. I pull it back out and watch him crumple to the ground. Liam leans forward and takes the knife from the dead man's hand just to be sure.

"Are you all right?" I cry, rushing to his side and dropping to my knees. The enemy's blood pools out all around us, a scarlet flood of death. Absently, I note how warm it feels on my legs as my breeches soak it up.

"Yes. But I think I have a few broken ribs." He winces. He puts his arm protectively against the side that was kicked. The bulk of the fighting has moved off in the direction of the castle entrance, leaving us pretty much alone but for the dead and wounded strewn around here and there.

"You saved my life," I say, throwing my arms around him, but jerk back as he moans in pain. He makes the excruciating ascent to his feet, doubled over by the ache in his ribs. I lend him my arm for support.

"Yes. A stab in the calf. It's a move I learned from an accomplished soldier," he says, even manages a teasing smirk through his pain. Our eyes meet and, as always, a world of thoughts and feelings pass silently between us.

"Come on, you two. This way," a voice orders.

I hurl my arms around a familiar neck. After all my worry for his safety, my father had needed only a sword and half a chance to rescue himself. If he is surprised to see his daughter and the man who was supposed to have escorted her home three days ago standing in the middle of the conflict, he doesn't show it.

"Here," he says gruffly, shoving Liam's sword back to him.

My father knows the battlefield is a place of singular focus. If you let your mind start to concentrate on anything else, you won't be around long enough to finish concentrating on it. In that spirit, he leads us toward the castle. The combat is thicker here, and he slashes his way forward, shouting for a few specific men to follow him. Before wading into the thick of the fighting, he yells to Liam, "His Highness is being held in King John's private quarters."

We hammer our way up the steps to the castle entrance. Surprisingly, there are no guards outside, and we cross through without incident. Upon entering the castle, the recesses of my mind register a harsh, acrid smell. The smell of something burning. I do not have time to process the thought fully. Several armed guards spring out into our path from behind the columns lining the entryway. There are not many of them, and my father's men fend them off.

My father points down a corridor to the left and says to Liam, "Make haste that way. Go to the end of this hall and make the first right. Follow the long hall straight to a set of double doors. That is where King William is being held." Then he jumps into the skirmish.

"Let's go." Liam pulls me by the arm.

Sprinting off down the hallway, Liam puts up a hand to slow me as we near its end. Drawing our swords again, we slowly approach the intersection and turn right. No one is there to block our path. This lengthy hall is lined on each side with many rooms. We tiptoe past large salons, comfortable parlors, and exquisite dance halls, expecting resistance at each one, but not encountering any. The acrid smell starts to become overpowering, and I am on the verge of saying something to Liam, when we pass by a large room on our left.

And that is when we see the smoke.

Whatever burns, it is on one of the floors above us. Smoke billows from a stairway at the far end of the salon, winding slowly toward the hallway. Liam and I exchange a look of surprise, but do not slow down. If anything, our task is now more urgent than ever.

We pass through a stone archway leading into an atrium. Straight ahead are two large mahogany doors, each ornately carved with a giant linden tree. Their exquisite design leaves no question that we have arrived at the personal chambers of King John. A long spear crosses the two handles, trapping any occupants inside. Judging by the silence, however, no one tries to escape.

Liam dashes to the door and hurls the spear onto the flagstones, its crash reverberating throughout the atrium. Behind us, smoke coils like a venomous snake down the hallway. Its caustic scent singes my nose when I inhale. Our time to find the King and bring him to safety becomes more limited by the moment.

Liam throws the doors open, and we rush into an open airy space. There is a regal chair set with jewels upon a dais against the left-hand wall. A large damask burgundy curtain frames the chair from behind, folding away in elegant drapes. At the back end of the room, a long table flanked by a number of high-backed chairs sits before several sets of French doors. This is the personal reception room of King John, where he can conduct his business and entertain the requests and pleas from the people of his kingdom. Tiny as Lindenwood is, it still operates with all the pomp and protocol that is the signature of the larger courts.

In a flash, we are across this room, our attention on the door that leads to the King's private chambers. Liam races in with me hot on his tail. I catch my breath at the sight of the magnificent chamber. Light pours in from French doors, illuminating the splendor. The bed alone is breathtaking in its scale and detail. Each of the four posts is carved in the likeness of a linden tree, with the silk canopy seeming to mimic the soft-green forest leaves overhead. Its headboard and footboard show scenes of woodlands and a fox hunt presided over by an imposing man on a great steed. Bedding crafted from the richest silks, satins, and velvets I have ever seen envelops a plump mattress with numerous pillows arranged atop it, like so many sumptuous jewels. Every other inch of the room is just as finely furnished and appointed, the ostentation from the outer room seeming to increase exponentially in this space.

As beautiful as the room is, it is also empty of any persons whatsoever.

"Father, are you here?" Liam yells out from across the room.

"King William?" I inspect the room for any possible clues to his whereabouts.

For a second I think I hear a muffled noise from a wall behind me. But at that moment, several armed men burst in from the French doors in front of where Liam stands and immediately engage him in battle.

Leaping over a delicate bench, I charge to his side, my sword drawn. Smoke arrives with our combatants. It streams in through the open doors, and a haze starts to fill the room. Liam and I hold our ground, but the smoke makes it increasingly hard to breathe. I am tiring faster than normal. Loud noises across the room announce the arrival of my father and several other men. The fighting becomes fiercer and more desperate when the mercenaries realize they are outnumbered. Our men gain the upper hand, and I use the opportunity to make my way back to the wall. Did I only imagine a sound coming from behind it?

"King William?" My voice is raspy from the smoke, but I swear I hear banging from somewhere on the other side of the wall.

I approach the spot and call his name again. This time there is no doubt. Someone definitely pounds on the other side of the partition. But how do I get to the other side? The cloud of smoke obscures my vision, so I close my eyes and run my hands along the barrier. Sure enough, my fingers hit a seam—and a couple feet later, another seam. A hidden door. But how does it open? *Think!* Vaguely, I recall a lesson about the many different ways secret doors, drawers, and the like may be opened. An idea comes to mind, and I push inward on the space between the seams. There is a click, and the wall presses in about an inch, then slides to the side, revealing a secret room.

It is a small, round chamber dedicated to the private prayer of King John. The first thing that hits me is an odd, rotting-like smell, even stronger than the burning odor. I feel sickened as I try to get my bearings. Directly across from the door, an altar topped with a dazzling golden cross sits on a plain stone slab. This is fronted by a large rug, its near edge indented with the outline of a prie-dieu or prayer bench, which now sits right in front of the door. Tied to it, wrists and ankles bound and mouth gagged, is King William. He dragged himself and the prie-dieu to the door so that he could alert any rescuers to his presence. His forehead is covered with a sheen of sweat, and his chest shudders with labored breaths.

"Your Majesty!" I exclaim and pull out my knife to quickly cut the gag from his mouth.

"Thank you, young man," his normally robust voice manages weakly.

In an effort to reassure him that his rescue is imminent, I start to say, "Liam…" but then bite my tongue in horror. I knew addressing Liam so informally would make me slip! "Um…Prince Liam is right outside with my father," I say, cutting off the binds on his wrists and ankles. With a now-free hand, King William lifts my chin and stares into my eyes. I am certain he is about to reprimand me for using Liam's Christian name so informally.

Instead, in a half-shocked voice he rasps out, "Miss Davenport?"

"Um…yes it's me, Your Majesty," I admit and drop into a swift curtsey.

For a brief moment, the trace of a smile shows on his face. Then it vanishes and he immediately takes in his surroundings, his brow furrowed. As he regains his wherewithal, I hear a faint cracking sound from above, but it is quickly drowned out by the battle taking place outside.

"So my men are fighting just out there? With your father? And what is the smoke from? Is something on fire?" The monarch attempts to rise, but his feet, which have been bound for goodness knows how long, are not yet ready to comply. He needs to lean on the prie-dieu to remain standing at all. All his royal robes have been removed, leaving him in plain leggings and a tunic. His disheveled hair and stubble show he was not kept in accommodations befitting his station. I marvel at how absolutely ordinary he appears, stripped of his finery. It is easy to forget that underneath all the trappings one's King is, in the end, only a man like the rest of us.

"Sire, our men are prevailing, at least they were a moment ago. My father and the Prince are leading them. As for the smoke, some part of the castle is on fire, but where and to what extent I have no idea."

How he can smell smoke over the sickly odor of this room is beyond me. I hold my shirt up to my nose. There is a popping sound, like wood splitting, but much louder and more menacing this time. A large beam breaks off the ceiling and drops down with a loud thud, landing right in front of the doorway of the tiny room. Flames lick off of it angrily. Our exit is cut off.

"Olivia? Are you in there?" my father's voice booms from the other side of the door.

"Yes, Father, I am here with His Majesty. We are both fine, but the beam blocks our way out," I yell back. Even as I answer, more burning wood crackles from above. The stone and beams over the doorway sag precariously.

"Don't worry. We will get you out." Now it is Liam's voice. I am not sure how he plans to help us, but I know time is running out. Scanning the sparsely furnished room, I try to find anything that may be of some help. There is not much to pick from, but an idea seizes me.

"Your Majesty, let us pick up the rug and try to smother the flames on the fallen beam," I suggest, hoping that a young girl and a weakened man will be able to accomplish this without setting the rug on fire too.

"Excellent idea, child."

We move to take hold of the rug when a thunderous, splintering crack fills the space. The whole ceiling above the doorway collapses. Beams and masonry crash to the floor in an avalanche, swallowing up the small room with flaming debris and choking dust. I hear my name shouted in desperation, but whether by my father or Liam, I cannot tell. Gripping each other for support, the King and I stumble backward onto the rug. And that is when the floor falls away under our feet.

22

For a brief second, there is the sensation of falling. Then I hit the ground. Hard. My shoulder jams into the floor, the wind completely knocked out of me. Dazed, I stare at the hole above us. It is a perfect rectangle. Fuzziness dances in my brain, but I sense the King on the ground nearby. Gathering my wits, I lean on my elbow to sit up, and a sharp pain jolts through my shoulder. At my quick intake of breath, the decaying stench hits my nostrils, so acute now it is almost unbearable.

King William struggles onto his knees facing me. He takes one look over my shoulder, and then he freezes. "Dear God, preserve us!" he prays.

Slowly, I follow the King's gaze. There on a bier covered with satin and amidst fine drapery is a corpse. It can only be King John. His body, surrounded by incense and unlit candles, is bedecked in all regal splendor, the vibrant silks and sparkling jewels a ghastly contrast to his rotting flesh. I am no expert in death, but judging by its state, this is the remains of someone who has been dead for at least a week. It is the most grisly sight I have ever beheld, even worse than the mercenaries Adam killed in the forest. They were at least fresh with death and resembled a person. King John's body barely resembles anything that was ever human. My King and I sit immobile in stunned silence. We must make quite a picture, the three of us—one frozen in death and the other two in horror.

At length, I put my sleeve up to cover my nose and mouth. I remember my father's voice instructing me, *In danger, Livy, always keep your head, constantly remain focused, and assess your surroundings.*

Closer examination of the ceiling shows the rug had covered a trap door, which now dangles down on broken hinges. It had given way when the King and I staggered back onto it. We are now in an underground room with dirt walls interspersed with some rudimentary wooden supports. A secret chamber under King John's personal prayer room for the comings and goings of people the King did not want to be seen in public. There is a ladder on the back wall; however, climbing back up into a fire-engulfed room is not an option. But if this room is a hidden way into the prayer room, there must be another way into and out of it. My eyes scan the entire perimeter, but nothing jumps out at me as an obvious exit. King William still has not spoken. I glance over to find him standing by King John, his head bent in silent prayer. Respectfully, I rise and stand in silence by his side. A small plume of smoke wafts down from the prayer room above. We need to move. Fast. The King finally crosses himself.

"Sire, I am certain there is another way out of this chamber. We must find it."

He evaluates the room with a sweeping gaze. "Yes, that would seem most likely for a secret chamber, but with this body being hidden down here, there is every chance it has been sealed off to avoid discovery."

Good point, although the stench certainly would be a good tip off to someone that something was amiss.

"It is times like this that your father is useful," he muses. "But from what I understand, he has taught you like a son. And your lessons were clearly well learned. What do you recommend?"

Humbled to be thus acknowledged by the King, I bow my head. Now I need to prove that all of my father's teaching and training was not in vain. Crossing to the wall opposite the bier, I carefully examine it. Lit by a handful of sconces, this is the brightest part of the room. From top to bottom I note its hardness and its texture, but find nothing unusual. The two side walls provide no answer either. The only wall left is behind the departed King.

I squeeze into the narrow space between the drapery and the wall, my sore shoulder barking in protest, and grope along the length of the wall in darkness. I encounter nothing remarkable. Its feel and texture are the same as its three counterparts. Just as I am about to give up, I feel it. A gap. It is not wide, only big enough to edge through sideways, but an exit nonetheless.

"King William, over here."

Emerging from behind the curtains, I am alarmed by how quickly our chamber fills with smoke. The King takes two large candles off the makeshift bier and lights them with one of the sconces. He hands me one, and the opening is illuminated.

"Well done, Miss Davenport," he says.

We slip through the gap into the middle of a long, dark passageway, the precise thing my father instructs me on at home right now: the castle's escape tunnel. It runs out of sight in both directions. Heading right will lead away from the castle, which seems our best bet given the fire above. The tunnel, dank and cold with a distinct peat-like smell, is no wider than the span of my arms. Several rats squeak out in indignation at our candlelight before scurrying away in the opposite direction. Up ahead, a faint light dimly glows. When we arrive at the source, we find another hidden doorway in the wall. A small torch sits in a sconce just inside a dirt chamber much like the one we just left. Another secret exit into the escape tunnel—one that was recently used.

"Lord Otto, I would bet. He is behind all of this. He took me hostage, though his motives remained unclear. He was angling for some end that he would not name. And now that his plan has failed, it seems he is trying to escape," King William says.

He inspects the room, but all it contains is a ladder propped up to the door above. We reenter the tunnel and pick up our pace.

"Do you think once he realized the grounds were breached, he set the castle on fire to cover his escape?"

"I would say that is a most likely scenario. Let us hope he is long gone and we don't encounter him down here. He is surely armed," King William says gravely. I reach for my belt to check that my little knife still hangs there. It does, but how much use it would be is questionable. Then I ask the question that most troubles my mind, "Sire, did Lord Otto kill King John?"

"No, I don't believe so. From what little information I was able to get out of the woman who brought me food, King John had been deteriorating for some time, a sickness from within. Lord Otto decided to come and usurp his half-brother's power at the end, when John was much too weak to do anything about it."

"Well, that only makes him immoral, not a murderer, but deserting his men makes him a coward; a coward who deserves some reckoning," I muse.

"I couldn't agree more, child."

On and on we creep with no end. After many monotonous minutes, we pass through one area stacked with stone from floor to ceiling and reinforced on the top, almost a tunnel within a tunnel.

"We must be passing under the river," I murmur to myself.

"Good point," says King William, his eyes narrowing. "Keen of you to notice that, young lady."

On the other side, the way becomes dark, musty, and cramped. It is so narrow our arms scrape the walls. This new ground is soft and springy under my feet. A deep earthy smell, one normally found in a newly plowed field, hangs thickly in the air. Our candles' faint light barely penetrates the darkness ahead and behind us falls rapidly into blackness. The only sound is our breathing, which seems magnified by the tunnel's confinements. I feel entirely claustrophobic. How long will we go on and on like this? My chest tightens at the thought of never being able to find our way out.

Focus and assess, I hear my father's voice command, and I snap back to attention. If Otto had come this way then that is a hopeful sign he knew an exit existed sooner or later. But it is only a guess that Lord Otto came this way, founded on seeing a burning torch in a doorway. Perhaps he had left it there earlier in case he needed to make for the escape tunnel. It does not necessarily mean he had ever come down here. *Think*. There must be a way to confirm whether he has recently been here or not.

Suddenly, it hits me. "Sire, please stop."

He halts, and I squeeze past him a few steps. Kneeling down, I dip the candle close to the ground. And sure enough, there they are—footprints, and better than that, fresh footprints. They run on ahead of us out of sight. So Otto, or someone, has been here, and by the looks of it, not too long ago. Another important point—there is only one set of footprints. Whoever came down here was alone.

King William's face, illuminated in the candlelight, is full of admiration. "We must proceed cautiously lest we find him cornered like a treed animal. Here," he says, motioning for me to get behind him once again, "let me take the lead."

We resume our progression, step after excruciating step. The stifling air feels as if it fights against us. A monotony of dirt walls pass for what seem like hours. But time is a trickster when anxiety is high, appearing to move as slowly as possible to drag out the agony of the sufferer.

Quite abruptly, we come into a wide circle with higher ceilings than the rest of the tunnel. In front of us the circle splits into three different paths; one runs straight, one slightly to the right, and the final slightly to the left. At first glance, there is nothing remarkable about any of them. They seem identical. It is not uncommon to have such intersections in an escape tunnel. If it is your castle's getaway route, you would know where all three paths lead, whereas anyone pursuing you would be left to guess. Most often one tunnel led to the actual escape while the other two either doubled back to the castle or resulted in dead ends. Or...

King William follows the path with the footprints. Lighting the way with his candle, he races headlong into the left tunnel.

"Wait!" I yell. "The wrong passages are often booby trapped!"

I am too late. King William activates a trigger. Two large iron gates crash down, one in front and one behind him. He lunges back, but is not quick enough to stop them from falling into place. He shakes the bars, tries to make the gate move in any direction. It does not budge.

"Old fool," he scowls at himself.

Again, my years of lessons kick in. This trap was set to catch a person, not harm him. A captured enemy could prove to be a valuable prisoner. Therefore, there must be some way to extract said prisoner from this pen.

With deep concentration, I study the small circular space for any indication of how to raise the gates. The floor shows nothing out of the ordinary except that there are footprints leading down the right tunnel as well. At least we know which way Otto has gone.

"He went down the right tunnel," I inform the King while I continue to search. He stands with his arms hanging between the bars, holding his candle up in an attempt to give me more light.

"Otto was clever enough to put his footprints down this tunnel hoping to trap someone. I see here the trip wire. How glad he would be to know that I fell for it. I would tell you to go down the right tunnel to safety, only I question if it would be safe. Oh, curse me for acting so rashly!" he exclaims. Pulling his arms through the bars, he slumps down.

As he sits, his circle of candlelight passes over a spot on the left-hand wall next to the entrance of the left tunnel. In that briefest of seconds, a glint catches my eye. Dashing over I hold my flame close. The dirt on this part of the wall is smudged, as though it had been recently disturbed. Peeking out is the smallest hint of a stone. I rub the dirt away and find a pile of stones stacked from about my knees to my stomach embedded in the wall. There does not seem to be any mortar between them, so I use my knife to scrape around the top one and finally manage to pull it free. Once it is removed the rest fall to the ground with little effort.

I bend and examine inside. There is a rope wrapped around a turning wheel, a winch. This rope runs up a hollow in the wall into the ceiling out of sight, where it must attach to the gate on this side of the tunnel. A trip wire undid a locking mechanism, sending the gates crashing down. Now it is just a matter of spinning the wheel backward to coil up the rope and raise the gate.

What seems easy, though, is a harder proposition than I thought. The winch handle is rusty and difficult to grip and even exerting all my force against it, will not move a whit. My tender shoulder does not help. King William, who was silent at my discovery, now stands in his prison watching me with desperation. No doubt he rues the fact I am not a strong, broad-backed man.

I grab the handle and lean with all my might. Shards of metal and rust dig into my palm. The wheel gears are so tight I am afraid the handle will simply break off. That would be disastrous. If only I had a lubricant that could get the process started.

But wait...I do! Holding my candle inside the opening I let some wax drip onto the notched wheel. I rub it around with my fingers, working its warm smoothness into the gears. Then, with a deep breath, I try to turn the handle again. Almost unbelievably, it moves one tiny gear notch. Again I drip in some wax, and again it moves a notch or two.

"Amazing ingenuity," the King says. He can now slip a finger under the gate.

At last, the wheel begins to rotate in earnest. It is slow going, but the gate lifts inch by inch until King William is able to crawl out from under it. He is free.

Exhausted, I let the wheel go, and the gate crashes back down, empty air its only captive now. Better to leave it that way on the outside chance someone comes down the tunnel searching for us. My mind travels to my father and Liam, whom I last saw in a burning castle fighting off the enemy. I pray they have both made it out to safety.

"Well done, Miss Davenport," the King praises.

We sit shoulder to shoulder panting while I stretch my sore arm out. I reach for the water cask held in my belt and uncork it. I take a small swig and then, absently, make to hand it to the King.

"Oh, my every pardon, Your Majesty!" I gasp in horror, yanking my hand back as if it was burned. My mother would die a thousand deaths if she ever finds out that I just offered the King my used water cask.

But King William merely chuckles. "Don't put that away, dear, give it here. Kings get thirsty too, and considering the fact that you just saved my hide, I would be honored to share a drink with you."

He takes a long sip. Before I can stop myself I blurt out, "My mother is going to be so embarrassed about all this!"

Again, he chuckles. "Well, that's what mothers are for."

He stands, hands me back my water, and dusts himself off. "This path, yes? Best get on then, before the candles burn down to nothing and we can't see where we are going anymore."

Now that is a circumstance I had not considered. I scramble to my feet and follow the King down the passageway on the right.

We move as fast as the terrain allows, the candles growing smaller with every step. After a good while, the ground rises for a few yards before leveling out again. The passageway widens enough for us to walk abreast and the mustiness dissipates. Inky blackness gives way to a muted darkness full of discernible edges. Finally, the tunnel ends in a small, square dirt room. Above us, the shape of a rectangle glows in the ceiling, whispers of daylight radiating around the edges of a trap door. A ladder propped against the wall leads right to it—the way out.

I place my candle carefully on the floor and sprint up the ladder, my hands scraping against the splintery rungs. The lock swings open, its chain untethered. Eager for a breath of fresh air, I push on the door. It does not budge. Undeterred, I use my good shoulder as leverage and ram it again with all my might. Nothing.

"What is wrong?" asks the King.

"Something large and heavy must be on top of the door outside." I groan in another futile effort to open it.

"Let me go up and give it a try."

I lower myself down, rubbing my sore shoulder. King William hands me his candle and ascends. He shoves on the door, but after several attempts, has no more success than I did. My heart sinks. We are trapped. Defeated, I slump down on the ground.

The King bangs on the door and yells for help. There is nothing but silence in reply. After a few minutes, he climbs back down despondently and eases onto the floor next to me.

"Don't worry. My men will figure out we took the tunnel and send a search party here to rescue us." He pats my leg in a reassuring manner.

Not likely.

How would they even know about the tunnel? The castle was burning. They needed to evacuate. There would have been no time to examine the room that had collapsed around us. And even if they did figure it out, how would they know where the tunnel ended? These woods could be searched for months without finding it. King John and Lord Otto knew the termination point, but with one dead and one on the run, they won't be telling anyone. What can we possibly do?

Focus and assess.

No position will give us good leverage against the door, even if we could find a lever. We could each alternate banging and yelling for help, but unless someone is near, it would be a waste of precious energy. The thought of trying to tunnel through the dirt on the sides of the door frame occurs to me, but is quickly dismissed. For one, it would be difficult to dig while standing atop the ladder, and two, if we disturb the ceiling at all, it may come crashing down and bury us alive.

There is no food and enough water to last for only a day or two. The vast woods could take weeks to search. Conservation of all resources is now paramount. King William's candle burns low, sputtering with its last bit of life. I blow mine out to save for when this one is consumed. When they are both used up, we will be trapped in relative darkness, especially after the sun sets. This will not aid us in our bid to escape. I would suggest we make a fire with the pieces of flint and steel in my utility belt, but the only wood in the room is the ladder.

No ideas surface to heroically save the day. King William had seemed so confident in his talk of a rescue that I can barely bring myself to contradict him. Silence between us drags on, heavy and foreboding. Hard, cold earth cramps my back and rear, but I have no inclination to move. Instead, I stare at the hints of light around the door. They are less vibrant than they were when we first entered this room as the sun starts its descent into the western sky. The likelihood of someone finding us in the dark is all but impossible.

King William breaks the silence. "I know rescue does not seem probable given our circumstances. You have led us this far valiantly. Any thoughts on what we can do to get out of here?"

I want to blurt all the reasons why there is no way to get out of here, but for once I remain silent, tracing little circles in the dirt with my fingers. The situation seems so hopeless that I don't think I can handle hearing it out loud. My head thumps back on the dirt wall, and I shut my eyes. None of my training prepared me to deal with such a bleak situation. The lit candle, burnt down to a stub, flickers out. Hopefully, I can get the other to light with a spark from my stones later. If not, perhaps I can use some scraps of my tunic for kindling and light it that way.

Somewhere above, a birdcall floats faintly through the air. We are so close to the outside world we can hear it. How sad it will be to waste away and die in a hole only a few feet from freedom. Perhaps one day, people will find our remains resting motionless on this dirt floor.

My bones ache with exhaustion, as if my entire body was wrung out like a dishcloth. The will to focus and assess has left me. Too tired to think any more, I start to doze, not caring if I ever wake up again. The bird trills again a bit louder. I imagine it soaring in the clean, beautiful freedom of the sky, its wings spread in the breeze. Suddenly, in that place between consciousness and slumber, a connection materializes in my mind.

I know that birdsong!

King William barely has time to react when I spring up the ladder. Frantically, I pound on the door and scream, "Here! We are here!"

He watches as if I have gone mad—which, given my current behavior, I can hardly fault him for.

But then, there it is—the sound of voices. A commotion overhead and the door lifts open. The light of the late afternoon sun rushes in, momentarily blinding me. I shield my eyes just as an arm reaches down and hauls me out, placing my feet firmly on the ground.

"Well, Miss Davenport, I am happy to find you here. Please say that you are in the company of the King," the familiar voice drawls out.

"She is indeed," King William's regal voice announces, his head appearing out of the door. The arm that pulled me up reaches down again, this time helping the King ascend onto the forest floor.

For a brief second the two men stand eye to eye. Then the rescuer sweeps into a low bow. "My Liege."

The King merely nods in acknowledgement before replying dryly, "Athos."

There is a part of me simply astounded that Athos found us out here. But a larger part of me grants it is in fact no surprise at all. Athos is a master at the completely unexpected.

He stands flanked in a half circle by about six men. More emerge from elsewhere, having heard all the commotion. We are deep in the woods, no trace of civilization apparent. Tall trees stand all around a floor covered in old and rotting leaves with no visible path in sight. A forsaken place for a person making an escape to emerge into the woods unnoticed. There are several large stones lying haphazardly around the opened trap door, the culprits of our imprisonment. Lord Otto wanted to make certain that any pursuers would be stopped in their tracks.

King William and Athos regard each other intently, neither moving, neither blinking. Athos' men stand tensely as well, unsure what type of welcome outlaws will receive from a King who has issued a price on their leader's head. At last King William asks, "To what do I owe the pleasure of such *renowned* company?"

"Well, I must say, it is quite an intriguing story if I do say so myself. So please, take a drink." Men come forward and offer us both a waterskin. "I will regale you with the whole of it on the walk back to your men."

King William and I drink greedily. My throat is parched from the smoke of the fire and the dirt, dust, and dankness of the tunnel. I hand the skin back to the men and can't help but notice my filthy arm. Upon further inspection, I find that every inch of my visible self is caked in soot and dirt. My hands are crusted with dried blood and goodness knows what else. When I reach to my hair, a shower of debris falls onto my shoulders. So much for Claude's clean clothes. King William, however, despite being dirty and disheveled, still emanates an imperial air and carries himself as such.

We walk through the woods with Athos, who proceeds with ease. The landscape is not a mystery to him or his men, who advance with all familiarity. King William and I would be lost without their guidance. Is there any part of this land that Athos does not know perfectly? Judging by the slant of the sun, it is nearing dusk. Many hours have passed since we fell through the floor in the prayer room.

"How far are we from the castle?" I ask, having lost all sense of direction and distance in the tunnel. It is such a relief to be out in the open air again. I am sure nightmares of being trapped in an enclosed space will plague me for some time to come.

"A good two miles and not on any established path," Athos answers. "That exit is meant to be a well-kept secret."

"A secret which you obviously knew all about!" King William interrupts in an accusatory tone.

It is understandable that King William may imagine Athos had some type of dealings with Lord Otto and now implies as much to see how Athos will react. I suspect that once the King finds out how much Athos helped Liam and me, his doubts will be put to rest.

"Yes, well, the life of an outlaw disposes one to an intimate knowledge of the place one calls home. These lands," Athos gestures around with his arm, "hold many secrets that reveal themselves upon investigation."

"Fascinating," the King says, sounding unconvinced. "Please do share with us how you came to be our heroic rescuers."

"I was fighting with the mercenaries in the courtyard when I noticed Lord Otto in one of the turrets above," Athos begins. "He frantically observed the fighting below, stricken that the castle walls had been breached. When he disappeared back into the castle, I wanted to cut him off from escape and raced to intercept him. As I climbed the turret stairs, I saw smoke billowing down from above and realized there was a fire."

The trees become less dense around us. Patches of scrubby bushes and wild grasses fill in the new spaces. Somewhere a woodpecker drills loudly on a trunk, the sound reverberating through the forest. Cool sips of water ease my irritated throat.

"I then spotted Otto running down the stairs toward me, but he quickly ducked through a doorway above. I pursued him down a hallway which was filling with smoke, but he disappeared through a hidden door. Unfortunately, it sealed shut before I could reach it. I made a superficial search for the mechanism that would open it, but was unsuccessful. The smoke rapidly filled the stairwell and I had to retreat. But I had a good idea that Otto made for the escape tunnel and decided to try to cut him off at the end point."

We come to a subtle track of worn ground that winds into the distance. The beginnings of a path, I hope. Athos and the King lead the way, with me a step behind. Athos' men fan out at our sides and rear, forming a perimeter on high alert for any danger; they are as silent as wraiths.

"On my way out, I heard the shouts for help. I found Prince Liam and Sir Jack frantically trying to beat down the fire in a burning room. They told me the two of you were trapped inside and the floor had caved in. It was a lost cause, the fire was too fierce, but they could not be dissuaded."

"Are they all right?" I can barely keep the hysteria out of my voice.

"It was then Prince Harold, having overtaken the mercenaries, raced in with his men. It was all we could do to drag the young Prince and the Master of Arms to safety.

"I had hoped when I heard the floor caved in that you may have fallen into a room that would lead to the tunnel. And you were lucky you did fall below. The room above was entirely engulfed in flames. You never would have made it."

Thank goodness he and Prince Harold were able to get my father and Liam to safety. The thought of losing either of them sits like a dead weight in my stomach.

"I had then made my way outside and gathered my men to make for the tunnel exit. When we finally arrived, we found the trap door piled with stones and heard Miss Davenport's shouts. So it seems Lord Otto was here and we likely did not miss him by much. I sent a few of my men to track him, but we are near the sea now. If Otto had a boat waiting for an instance such as this, he will be sailing safely away long before my men have a chance to overtake him."

King William agrees with this assessment.

"The only piece of the puzzle I cannot provide is the whereabouts of King John," Athos muses, "other than he has not been seen by any of my men in more than three weeks."

King William is silent for a moment but then, convinced Athos is not in collusion with Lord Otto, says, "Unfortunately, that is an answer we can provide. King John is dead. We saw his body, or what was left of it. He had been dead some two weeks, perhaps a little more."

"It is as I feared then. God rest his soul, he was a decent man. All pardons to whatever disagreements may have lain between you, Sire."

"Whatever type of man I thought him, he deserved a better end than he had," the Kings says graciously.

Eventually the path becomes wider and more well worn. Walking a bit in the two men's wake, I hear Athos explain how he encountered and assisted Liam and me in the woods. King William actually expresses gratitude.

The sun sinks almost below the horizon, the sky tinged with rose and gold as the world falls to dusk around us. I try to figure out how far we have walked, but I am so tired and hungry, I have trouble making sense of anything. Becoming hardened to the trance of fatigue and the pangs of an empty stomach is a part of knightly training on which I clearly missed out. But perhaps these are the types of lessons that a soldier can learn only on duty. Puck had shared a handful of stories about nighttime drills my squire class performed (without me, I may add begrudgingly) but had not included any details of such discomfort. When we get home, I will have to ask Puck if they were deprived of sleep and food. That is, if Puck ever speaks to me again.

Rubbing my neck, I bend my head side to side to relieve the stiffness and notice there are fewer men behind me than there were when we began our journey. I decide to pay more attention to them. Sure enough, every few yards one of the men ducks off the path and melts into the woods. One by one they perform this feat without words spoken or gestures made among them; a well-practiced routine that requires no communication. Soon, only King William, Athos, and I remain on the path.

The sound of flowing water fills the air. We have reached the river. A crude wooden bridge arcs over it to the castle side, not a well-traveled overpass judging by the missing planks and rotting supports. Yet the sight of it fills me with relief and anticipation. It means we are almost back to camp.

A step before the bridge, Athos stops abruptly and bows. "And here is where I take my leave, Sire. Your men are camped not one hundred yards away just over that small rise."

King William turns to acknowledge him and then glances around, momentarily surprised by the lack of any other men. Then understanding crosses his face. "You and your men are welcome to enter our camp. You have my word that no hand shall be raised against any of you. I will happily credit you all for the invaluable help you have supplied to me, my family, and our kingdom."

"Many thanks, Your Highness, for your most gracious offer, but my men and I prefer to keep a low profile. No sense muddying the royal waters at your triumphant return."

"As you wish," King William concedes, "but please accept my personal and sincere gratitude for coming to the aid of not only myself, but also my son and this young lady. You have done your kingdom proud with your service. I hereby grant you and your band permission to hunt and kill the King's game for one year's time in tribute for your assistance. Your men are brave and serve a keen and courageous master. Likely in another time and place, we would have functioned as great allies instead of adversaries."

With these words, the King bows and crosses the bridge toward camp.

For a moment, I stand frozen, not ready or willing to admit that I too must take my leave of Athos—a man who changed my perception of many long-held beliefs, who showed me a different meaning for the word *honor*, and who inspired me with his strange blend of ingenuity, acumen, and kindness. I could fool myself by pretending this was not good-bye forever; that there would be another time to join Athos and his men on a new adventure. But, sadly, those thoughts are not grounded in reality.

He must read my despairing thoughts because he walks over and places his hands on my shoulders. His forehead bends to touch mine.

"You are a courageous, feisty, intelligent young woman. A person whom I would have felt lucky to count as one of my men. But instead, I will be content with counting you as one of my friends."

I smile at him as tears fill my eyes.

He reaches into a pocket and pulls out a small grey stone, no larger than a grape, and places it in my hand. Its cold, smooth surface is etched with a black symbol:

"Take this. If you ever have need of me again, this stone will help you gain access to my whereabouts. And if you never have need of me again, please cherish it as a reminder of this adventure and what makes your spirit so unique and alive. Promise me you will never forget that."

I nod, unable to speak, tears now flowing openly down my cheeks. There is no way I will forget one minute of all that has happened on this journey—the good or the bad. Athos will always have a special place in my heart. How can I, in this one brief moment, impress upon him the effect he has had on me? My mouth, so accustomed to blurting things out at will, cannot adequately convey all the feelings in my heart. I wrap my arms around him, hoping the hug will express what words cannot.

"And now, sweet Olivia, you best hurry back to your father and your prince and put their minds at ease," Athos says in a crafty tone. At my puzzlement, he adds, "Since at the moment they still think you are dead."

As I stand digesting this statement, he bows, kisses my hand, and disappears gracefully into the forest.

It takes me a moment to process *they think you are dead,* but then, of course, it makes perfect sense. After watching the whole prayer room collapse, what else could they possibly think? How devastated they must be: the Princes for their father, my father for his daughter, and the soldiers for their King. With all haste, I cross the bridge and rush to catch up with King William. Out of deference, I decide to walk a few steps behind him.

"Are you all right, Miss Davenport?"

"Yes, Sire. Just a bit hungry and tired," I answer, downplaying honesty a bit. My legs feel as if they are made out of lead, my feet are numb, my throat still burns, and my stomach pangs are so intense I almost feel nauseous from them.

"Yes, I am 'a bit hungry and tired' as well. Come, a good meal and a soft bed await on the other side of this hill." He motions for me to join him and puts a fatherly arm around me.

Heartened by the thought of these comforts, we pick up our pace and mount the rise. At the top, we see the army is indeed camped below — in fact, quite a few more men than I would have thought. Yet for such a large group, they are eerily silent. The castle, sitting off to the right, is gutted and charred in the dim light; only daybreak will reveal to me the full extent of the damage. The smell of ash is heavy in the air, and a dark cloud hangs over the site. A large piece of debris falls from one of the upper stories. It crashes onto the smoldering pile below, the impact echoing through the forest.

We pass through the outskirts of the camp, unnoticed at first. Soon, individuals on the fringe start to murmur and one of the closest drops to his knees in homage. More soldiers follow this example, some crossing themselves, some shouting out blessings or cheers. The buzz of the crowd grows louder and there is much murmuring and finger pointing. All along our path, men sink to their knees to praise both God and their King.

There is a loud commotion in front of us, and the crowd separates as Prince Harold and Prince Liam barrel through at a run. I am sure that protocol dictates a formal bow from them, but I am equally sure that King William does not mind when the bow is omitted for a giant bear hug by both sons. Cries and cheers of joy ring out from all sides.

After a moment, Prince Liam pulls back from his embrace and says something to the King, who glances around seeking something in the crowd. His eyes fall on me, nearly swallowed up by a sea of bodies, and he beckons to me. The mass of people again parts as I step forward. Liam's and my eyes meet, and his face is flooded with relief. My heart simply dances at the sight of him, all fatigue and hunger swept away in an instant.

"You're alive!" he says, almost disbelievingly. I nod and give a slight curtsey, acutely aware that many witness this scene.

Liam grasps both my hands and pulls me toward him. Is he going to hug me right here in front of all the men? My cheeks flush at the thought. But another man has elbowed his way through the crowd to get to me. My father bursts in between us, embracing me in such a tight hug that my feet come off the ground and I fear my rib cage will shatter. He is saying something, but I cannot hear anything now except the roar of the celebration. One glance in my father's eyes, however, shows me how happy he is to hold me in the flesh, safe and sound.

We are jostled toward the center of the camp. The throng of men has become a human current and there is no choice but to follow its flow. An ebullient atmosphere spreads through the camp. Soldiers break into music and dancing as word spreads of the King's "resurrection."

My eyes meet Liam's frequently over shoulders and heads during the course of the evening, but there is no way for us to speak alone amidst all these onlookers. The disappointment of not being able to connect with him stings deeply. But did I honestly expect that he would whisk me up in front of everyone and declare his undying love for me to the cheers of the crowd and the blessing of his father—and mine?

Well, yes actually. A part of me wanted this to happen against all odds, foolish as it sounds. I was hoping for the storybook ending. But here I sit with my father, his arm clamped down across my shoulders as if he will never let me go again. And though I am glad to see him, disappointment runs through my veins that it is not someone else's arm around me.

My brooding is interrupted when a man comes to shake my father's hand. Prince Stephan, the King's nephew from Prescott, greets us. He and his men arrived a short time ago as reinforcements, only to find the mercenaries on the run, the castle in ruins, and King William pronounced dead. Shock is apparent in his eyes after systematically facing one astounding development after another, and he seems to be made rather speechless by it all. A squat and toad-like little man, he is quite a contrast to his handsome cousins. The Prince also does not seem as caught up in the celebrating as the rest of the men, but they are known to be more stoic in the south.

A joyous mood sweeps over the camp. Two deer roast over fires to accompany berries and nuts collected from the forest. Barrels of ale have been recovered from the wreckage of the castle's stores, and mugs are dealt out like playing cards. There are songs and shouts from all corners in what will be a long evening of merrymaking. I, however, can barely keep to my feet. Father pulls me away from the gathering and takes me to a quiet area lined with tents. He stops in front of one.

"Go inside. There is a basin of water to refresh yourself and some light food to eat. Then take some rest, sweetheart." He kisses my forehead. I make to protest, but he puts a finger to my lips. "There will be plenty of time to catch up with each other tomorrow. We will need to spend a day assessing the area and preparing to leave. For now, Livy dear, please sleep. You look too much like a walking ghost for my taste."

Inside the tent, I wonder how he can possibly expect me to rest with the racket outside. I wash the grime and soot off my face and hands, but am too tired to deal with the cakes of black under my nails. An apple, a small wedge of cheese, and some walnuts should fill my stomach enough to settle it. While I nibble them, a swirl of emotions hits me full force.

Liam.

It was torture to be just feet away from him and not be able to speak to him. Is this how it will be from now on?

With so much still left unsaid between us? There simply must be a way to talk to him. I would sell my soul for five minutes alone with him. But, if I had it, would I be brave enough to tell him my feelings for him? Would they even matter in the end?

Settling onto a blanket spread out on the floor, I resolve not to rest until I devise a plan of action. My exhausted body, however, has other ideas. I am asleep the second my head hits the ground.

The sound of birds announces the advent of the dawn. I roll over and see my father asleep, wrapped in his cloak a few feet away from me. My muscles complain stiffly as I stretch and rotate out my sore shoulder. Something musty and sour hits my nose, and I am disgusted to realize it is me. Clearly I need to wash up, but the thought of putting my stained, sooty clothes back on is less than appealing. When I quietly stand and head toward the exit of the tent, a pile in the corner catches my eye. Upon examination I find it to be a small tunic and breeches, both deliciously clean, along with a bar of soap. Father knew what my first priority would be and had conscripted these items in anticipation. His thought and consideration bring a warm rush of relief. He is not so furious with me that he will make me ride home in my filthy clothes.

I poke my head out of the tent flap. We are on a flat, treeless field just outside the Lindenwood Castle walls. No sun appears on the horizon; only the pinkish orange sky to the east indicates its imminent arrival. The early fall air is crisp and refreshing but for the faint trace of the smoldering embers of the castle. It stands ruined and defeated inside its broken walls.

Two figures who are seated just outside the tent arise when I step out. Sir Michael and David, one of my squire classmates, approach me. Sir Michael gestures stiffly to the pile I am holding. "We are to escort you to the stream and then guard the area to protect your privacy while you bathe," he snaps. Apparently, there will be no fond greeting or amity from him.

Unsure how to respond, I simply nod my assent. Sir Michael leads the way down a narrow overgrown path, with me and David falling in behind him. I wonder how David feels about my adventure. Would he hold it in the same seeming disdain as Sir Michael? Will all the knights and squires be resentful of my escapade?

I sneak a sideways glance at him only to find him doing the same. Our eyes meet and his face breaks out into a huge grin; and then, clandestinely, to avoid Sir Michael's notice, he pats me on the shoulder as if to say "good job." My smile back conveys my deepest thanks, relieved that at least a few people appreciate my adventure.

Sir Michael abruptly halts and points down a small hill to a serene, babbling stream below. "We will remain here," he says, standing with his back to the water. He glares at David and sharply adds, "About face, boy." David obeys and stands by Sir Michael's side, but not before giving me a surreptitious wink when I pass.

Anyone who has ever been enveloped in coatings of filth for days on end can imagine the sheer bliss I feel upon entering this stream. Layers of muck, grime, and soot wash away, revealing my forgotten white skin. Leaves, soot, and small rocks are rooted carefully out of my hair. I will definitely have a new appreciation for bathing from now on. Once clean, I float on my back luxuriating in the feel of the cool water lapping over me.

The sun has risen, bathing the stream in pale light, which glows off the trees all around. Leaves are just beginning to change to vibrant yellows and oranges with the onset of the cooler weather. Birds and butterflies flit around the banks basking in the new day. It is all so tranquil and lovely, I do not want to leave and face all the agonizing consequences with both my family and my broken heart. Try as I might, I can think of no reasonable plan to see Prince Liam alone.

When my skin gets pruny, I worry Sir Michael may be angry at my dallying. I climb out and don the fresh clothing. Standing on the shore I take in several deep breaths and enjoy the freshness of the air here, which must be upwind of the burning castle.

Voices carry down from the top of the hill. No doubt the two men are deciding whether to tell me to hurry up or not. I can only imagine Sir Michael's indignation at having to wait for a mere girl to bathe, which I must admit, I find amusing. Sir Michael probably never thought he would be troubled with issues such as these. The pleasure of causing him annoyance makes me put no effort into hurrying.

When Sir Michael yells down, "Miss Davenport, are you decent? Are you dressed?" I suppose I have made them wait for long enough.

"Yes, I am ready. I will be right there."

I gather up my old clothes, which should probably just be burned, and make to head up the hill. To my great surprise, Liam strides down toward me. The light from the sun falls on him, brings out warm highlights in his hair. He too is clean and freshly shaven and, naturally, looks amazing. My entire being warms at the sight of him and tingles buzz in my fingers and toes.

All the agonizing and fretting over how I could get to see him again, over what possible excuse I could find just to be able to talk to him, and now here he is—coming to *me*. I had rehearsed a few imaginary scenarios in my head for when we were alone. They promptly vanish without a trace, leaving me with some hazy fragments of how much the last few days have meant to me, and how I will treasure forever the memories. Nothing that does my true feelings any justice.

Likely, he is coming to tell me that he has to go back to being Prince Liam now, and that I should not misconstrue the friend-like status we had developed during our time together. I best make it clear I do not expect anything from him and let him off the hook easy. Better than completely humiliating myself, right? It's not as if I will be the only one to ever suffer a broken heart.

"Hi," I say, staring down at my toes. I lay the dirty pile in my arms down on a rock.

"How are you today?" he asks softly.

"Fine," I whisper. Who knows how much of this Sir Michael and David are able to hear? Automatically, my eyes drift up the hill to see if I can spot them.

"I sent them away. I wanted to see you in private."

Here it comes—the "let me down easy" part. I must be strong in front of him, I can cry my eyes out later, but no point in making a spectacle here. Can I possibly keep it together in front of him? My insides feel as though they are being torn apart.

He takes a while to speak, no doubt trying to think of the most delicate way to tell me I have no place in his life. Breathing steadily, I brace myself while waiting for the inevitable. But instead, I hear his strangled voice, "I thought you were dead."

His tone more than anything catches my attention. My eyes lock on his—and in them I see how wrong I am. They reflect back to me all the same feelings that I have for him. It is not that he doesn't want to be with me, he simply knows this would never be allowed due to his rank. The choice is not his to make.

"I was worried about…"

You too. I was going to say "You too," but before those words get out of my mouth he takes my face in his hands, pulls me to him, and kisses me. My body responds with the most natural ease, as if we have already done this a million times. His touch, his taste, his feel are so familiar, as if our souls remember this from some other time in the past. Our bodies mold together like two halves of the same whole. Time stops, our mouths the only things left in the universe.

Finally we part and stand silently facing each other. He gazes down at me, but my mind, which has been desperately trying to catch up with the situation, has me in a daze. His brow furrows. "Was I too forward? Have I offended you?"

"No! It's just…" I stammer at first and then in true fashion I blurt it all out. "I mean I am so happy to have this between us. It is all so perfect and magical in a way I never thought existed. And the time we have spent together has been amazing. But that is what makes it so sad at the same time." At his puzzled face I continue, "Because even if you really do feel for me everything I feel for you, we can never be together."

He considers this a moment, then asks shyly, "And how *do* you feel about me?"

"I love you. I mean, I think I love you. I have never actually been in love before so I have nothing to compare it to. But I do know that I think about you all the time and I want to be with you all the time and I want to know everything about who you are, where you've been and what you want for the future. And all that sounds like how people describe love, so that is what I am calling it. But now, none of that matters because we have to go home and I won't ever see you like this again, or get to talk to you like this again, or kiss you again and…"

He puts a finger up to my lips to silence me, which is a good thing since I am now pretty much just babbling. Not to mention, I am running out of breath.

Once I am silent, he cocks his head and regards me for a moment. "Well, if you are worried about never kissing me again I can fix that now."

He bends and kisses me for a long dizzying moment. How can people in love even function? My legs are jelly, my heart races, and I never, ever want to let go of him. We could just stand here in this exact spot for the rest of our lives and that would be fine with me.

"And as for all the other things you said, I have to disagree. I plan on seeing as much of you as possible when we get home. "

"How? Your family would never agree to a match between us."

"You know, these past few days have taught me to not worry so much about what I am supposed to do and made me realize that sometimes I need to stand up for what I want out of life. And I want to be with you."

It all sounds so simple and logical that I truly want to believe it. Surely in history there have been instances of royalty marrying below rank. I must make sure to investigate that when we get home. Perhaps the fact that I aided the King will elevate me in the eyes of the kingdom. But, judging by the vicious catfight for Prince Harold's hand, I doubt some major players at court will step aside to make way for the likes of me. Besides, Liam has never had a say in any aspect of his life before. Why should now be different?

"Come, let me walk you back to camp before we are missed." We can hear my father's voice calling my name even as he says this. Skepticism must cloud my face, so Liam adds reassuringly, "Don't worry. I will figure something out. In the meantime, let's just concentrate on getting home."

We can hear my father coming closer. I desperately want to believe him.

"Do you trust me?" he asks.

"Yes, of course."

"Then don't worry."

I realize that we are holding hands. It had happened so instinctively between us that I had not noticed until Liam gently lets my hand drop just as my father appears on the path ahead.

"Ah, there you are," he says, relieved. Then, spying Liam, he drops into a small bow. "Your Highness."

"Good morning, Sir Jack. I hope today finds you well. I am just escorting our girl here back to camp."

Our girl? What will my father make of that? Nothing good. Of all people, he will realize the impossibility of a match between us and all the trouble any suggestion of it will stir up. But suffice to say that my heart leaps at the reference.

All business, though, my father says, "Yes, I can see that. Thank you for your service, Prince Liam. I will take over her escorting from here."

"As you wish," Liam says and gives me a furtive wink before striding off back toward camp. I notice how he slightly favors the side where he was kicked yesterday.

My father and I are finally able to speak for the first time since he thought he had sent me home; yet, here we stand in silence. I can feel the intense purpose in his gaze. Will he admonish me for being found in an inappropriate situation with Liam? Will he issue uncounted reasons why a relationship between Liam and me is out of the question? Will my hopes, just starting to rise to unfettered heights at Liam's promise, now come crashing back down at the sober realities my father will present?

"Olivia, you could have *died*."

Taken off guard, I can manage no response but bewildered silence.

"By not going back home when I sent you, by insisting on continuing back to Lindenwood. And then teaming up with outlaws, for crying out loud! And to drag poor Prince Liam into all of this—forced to go along with your disobedience! Do you realize what might have happened to you on any number of occasions during this jaunt? Death…or worse!"

And here I mutely stand, expecting to be yelled at for one thing—in fact the only thing I can actually think about now—and my father is angry for a whole different reason. A reason which, though unspoken, resonates in his eyes. He was afraid he had lost me.

"I am sorry, Father." I wrap my arms around him. He hugs me back so tightly I can barely breathe.

In a shaky voice he says, "Never, never do anything like that to me again. I could not bear to lose you, my Livy."

"I promise." My eyes well with emotion.

"No promise is necessary since I intend to lock you permanently in your room when we get home." We stare at each other a moment before laughing. Slowly, hand in hand, we walk back to camp.

"You and Prince Liam have become fast friends."

"Um…yes." I agree cautiously, worried he is setting the stage for his "this can't happen" lecture.

"Well, that does tend to happen when people are in battle together. And who knows, maybe someday it will be advantageous to have a friend in such a high place."

Inwardly, I smile. My father is oblivious to my feelings for Liam and his for me. Funny, because I think it is so obvious; certainly written on our faces when he found us and certainly oozing out of every pore in my body at this moment. In the end, I guess my father's own theory is true: people see what they want to see.

"The most important thing is that you are safe…although that is debatable. Goodness only knows what your mother will do to you when we get home."

"You must tell her what a brave and true soldier I was," I tease.

"Well indeed, that is King William's account of the matter. Perhaps that will please Miriam enough to not harm you," he jokes.

Then he stops and becomes serious, taking me by the shoulders. "And I am proud of you, Livy. Your actions were heroic and admirable—more than I ever hoped for, even from a son."

It is the highest praise my father could ever bestow upon me. What a morning—love confessions and recognition of my skills after I expected a broken heart and lectures. The world seems fairer, the sun brighter. I stand on my toes and kiss Father on the cheek.

We arrive back at the busy camp. Some men prepare to investigate what is left of the castle, some pack up, others saddle up to take messages back to Adelina. The army is numerous when you count Prince Stephan's contingent. There are easily four hundred all together and I the only woman among them. What types of stories are spreading throughout the camp about me? Gossip has a way of festering and mutating into extraordinary tales that people are only too willing to believe. And repeat.

"Thankfully, Lindenwood will now be back under the control of King William. Though the castle area is uninhabitable now, I am certain we can think of a good use for it in time. And the mining villages should continue on relatively undisturbed by the change in rule," my father says contentedly.

The mention of the castle grounds, whose ashy remnants begin to sting my nostrils, brings a question to mind that has been nagging me.

"It seemed strange that Lord Otto would have gone through all the trouble of usurping King John's throne and then luring King William to the north. King John had no successor so why did Lord Otto not try diplomacy to have himself named heir? He would have seemed a logical choice."

"Perhaps he did try diplomacy at first, and when that did not work, he resorted to poisoning or some other sinister method. Although our intelligence suggests that King John did not die suddenly, but had been ill for some time. In the end, all Lord Otto probably needed to do was wait for the inevitable."

"But why ask for King William to come up? He had control of the castle. Why bring unnecessary notice and begin a fight that would be impossible to win?" I press.

"Ah Livy, my keen girl," my father sighs, "I have been asking myself these same questions. And I have come to no conclusion other than men like Lord Otto only know how to fight and they are usually fighting at long odds. Perhaps he thought any show of power would help bolster his credibility as the new ruler. Or perhaps he was conspiring with someone from the Mainland who agreed to supply him endless troops in order to gain a foothold in Stewartsland. As he chose to retreat like a coward and desert his men, we are not able to ask him his motives. In the end, what matters the most is that he is gone and King William and, thankfully, you, are safe."

We reach our tent, which one of my father's men is in the process of dismantling. With a kiss on the head, Father tells me to prepare my things for the journey, adding that we would discuss Lord Otto's motives more thoroughly when we got home. Then he strides away to ensure that the rest of the area is being properly and swiftly decamped.

My future. What could it hold? I pray that Liam can convince his parents that Love should trump Rank in the game of life. But have I thought about what would happen if they agree? Am I prepared for life in a royal fishbowl where every move, gesture, and comment are dissected and analyzed? That would be hard for me. Attention is not something I normally crave. And the thought of having to put so much effort into my appearance and behavior quite frankly scares me. But not as much as the thought of a life without Liam.

Just a week ago, I had been perfectly content with the thought of marrying Puck even though I knew I was in truth marrying for "like" and not for "love." A mere week ago that difference had not seemed consequential enough to factor into the decision. But now that I had a taste of love, I realize that nothing can make up for it—not all the comforts or riches in the world. Without Liam's love, my life would only be half a life, a life lived in the shadows forever yearning for the sun.

"Hey, Olivia." The sound of my name startles me. It is Seth, one of my fellow squires who dismantles my tent with our comrade Francis. "I heard everything you did and I just wanted to say, well done."

"It's fair to warn you though, some squires, including me to be honest, are pretty angry at the stunt you pulled to get on the trip. It wasn't fair to Puck," Francis says.

"But I think she more than made up for it by rescuing the King," Seth counters. He has always been one of my more reckless classmates, a very "ends justify the means" type of person.

"Well, thanks, Seth," I say. "And Francis, I truly am sorry for hurting Puck." He nods, but the look in his eyes belies his agreement.

I guess I am in for some possible tension at the next sparring session, and not just from Puck. Ah, things to look forward to. That is assuming I can talk my father, and more importantly Mother, into continuing the training at all.

"Personally, the part I enjoyed most," Seth adds with a mischievous lifting of his eyebrow, "was the expression on Sir Michael's face when he discovered you."

"Yes, that was priceless!" Francis agrees.

"Made it entirely worth it if you ask me!" Seth says. We all laugh over that recollection.

Most of the army sets off around midmorning. With favorable weather and a good pace, we can make it home by the dusk of the next day. The standard bearers go first, followed by King William and his entourage. Prince Liam hangs back a bit, though, and makes sure to ride next to me, a little to the right of my father. A few soldiers remain behind in Lindenwood to account for any citizens and secure the area.

I could say that the sun shone brightly, the birds sang gaily, and the winds blew gently, but I do not notice any of this. All my senses are focused on Liam, how he sits so relaxed and yet in control in the saddle, how one lock of hair keeps blowing haphazardly across his forehead, how he sneaks glances at me every so often.

My mind warns me to downplay any reactions to him, to not give any impression that would alert anyone to my true feelings. But how does one hide such strong emotions? I see those emotions reflected back in Liam's gaze. We never so much as speak a word that is not the most cursory remark, or so much as touch one another's little fingers together, yet the connection between us is so strong, the energy so raw and potent, that I truly think every living creature in the forest is aware of it.

We make camp rather late in the evening and eat a hurried meal. There is barely time for anyone to speak, let alone for us to find a stolen moment together. All too soon, my father and I lie on blankets alone in our tent.

Just after he blows out the candle, he says, "Ah, tomorrow you will be home in your own bed, my dear. I am sure you cannot wait. Only one more day of riding with this army and its lack of comfort. It is so good of Prince Liam to keep you company. It must make the time pass quicker, which is nice."

This is said with such innocence of our true feelings that I laugh to myself.

"Yes, Father, it is nice."

I wonder if he would still use the word "nice" if he accurately understood the situation. Somehow I doubt it.

Home. Clean clothes, fresh sheets, and the promise of three hearty meals a day beckon me. Yet when we arrive I will have to face the fact that it is over—this journey holding Liam and me under its spell.

Last night I tossed and turned, a troubling thought preying on my mind. Once Liam is restored to his life of ease and privilege, will he decide that he had not actually been in love with me at all, but with the adventure itself? Extraordinary situations can elicit feelings that quickly disappear when one is back in familiar surroundings. For my part, I know there is no possibility of this happening. But can the same be said for him? Yet every time I meet Liam's eyes, the silent message to trust him is too apparent to miss.

On this last day, we start out early and stop only briefly for a midday meal. We don't even sit, just stand in groups while the horses drink from a stream. Father cheerily talks about how much he plans to eat for dinner, but I barely hear a word. My eyes drift over to Liam, who stands deferentially listening to the old priest. Once again, all attempts for any private conversation between us are thwarted. Disappointment is all I taste, the food settling like a lump in my stomach. All too soon we are ready to continue.

Liam holds the reins of my horse as I mount. My head dips down slightly toward him as I fling my leg over the far side of the saddle. His hand squeezes mine and he whispers, "Still trusting me, I hope!"

With an army watching, all I can do is give him a hidden smile of affirmation. The pain in my gut eases, my doubts chased away for now. When we near the city, a herald sprints ahead to announce the arrival of the King. Adelina's walls rise over the horizon, a strong and secure presence. At first sight of them, I feel a deep sense of gratitude and comfort. I have always been so determined to leave, always took for granted my city would be there waiting for me. Now, I understand more fully the perils of war and the possibility of leaving to never come home again. My home, my family, and everything mundane and ordinary about my life are more important than I ever realized.

Fields bursting with unharvested wheat and vegetables line the outlying lanes that cross the main road. Handfuls of citizens stand at these crossroads to welcome their King home. Dressed in their finest clothes, they resemble bright patches of blossoms waiting to be plucked. The roads closer to the city, including the one that leads to my home, are empty, their inhabitants joining the festivities in the main courtyard of the palace.

The sun is just beginning to set, illuminating the flat grassland just in front of the gate into a blur of color, like a living rainbow. At the sight of our party, the sound of the waiting citizens grows from a drone to a jubilant din. Some cheer, waving bright banners, others throw petals into our path when we pass. Children shout from shoulder tops. Now we are close enough to make out the guards standing in the gatehouse towers. We cross the last expanse of road before the gate, the King's trumpeters ringing out the call. A sizeable crowd spills out the edges of the opening, the great courtyard not large enough to accommodate the assembly amassed inside.

Nerves seize me, my hands trembling against the reins. Surely, word of my insane antic has spread far and wide, so besides the reaction of my family and Puck—poor, dear Puck—I will be subjected to the curiosity of every gossipmonger and busybody the city has to offer. Hopefully, today they will be too enthralled with the King to worry about me.

Our horses, sensing the proximity to the familiar comfort of their stables, trot with renewed vigor. The royal party waits at the gate, the Queen herself coming down to meet us, a testament to the close call her husband has suffered. My father falls back a bit from the King, the Princes, and the advisors, and he motions me to do likewise. I steal one quick glance at Liam, who nods ever so slightly, then withdraw.

King William rides though the gate to resounding cheers. The people in the crowd crane their heads to see where the Queen awaits. He dismounts and kneels before her, raising her hand to his lips. Her eyes glisten with tears, the love they share evident in the glow. When he stands, she throws her arms around him. The audience applauds with delight at this most unroyal gesture. Next, each of her sons and her nephew come forward and bow to her in turn.

Most of the army has remained outside the gate with the exception of the royal family, the royal entourage, my father and his most senior knights, and me. Stable boys, squires, and any other able lads gather our horses to bring them to the paddock. While the animals are led off and the royal family climbs the castle steps, the throng of people folds in on itself. Some people search out their loved ones while others just try to congratulate those of us who have returned. In the confusion, I am separated from my father as the mass jostles me to and fro.

My thoughts, which should be focused on not getting trampled, are completely preoccupied with Liam. Has the royal family simply gone inside the palace to celebrate privately? Will I not even be able to get a glimpse of him again today? If not, how on earth can he possibly contrive for us to meet again anytime soon? I am in such a "Liam fog" that I hardly notice people patting me on the back.

"Livy, child!"

My thoughts are broken by the familiar voice of Lucy. Before I even see her, she has me wrapped in a smothering bear hug, her ample bosom pressing into my stomach and her unruly curls tickling my nose.

"Hi, Lucy," my muffled voice replies.

"Don't you *ever* scare me like that again! Do you hear me Missy! When I think of all the things that could have happened to you—" her voice cracks and tears begin to flow, "—alone in the woods! At the mercy of the elements!"

I am going to tell her that there was no point when I was ever alone, but given her exaggerated hysterics, I figure it won't make a difference.

"And losing Grace's best berry pail on me in the process…"

"Um…your pail?" I half laugh, but the distress on her face is so genuine.

Grace has quite specific uses for each and every item in her kitchen. She likely thinks we will never be able to pick berries ever again and Lucy will feel to blame since she was the person who gave it to me.

"It isn't lost. I know just where it is," I reassure her, amazed that this is the first conversation I am having with someone.

"That's wonderful, child!" She grabs me again, crushing me against her, which leaves me to wonder just how much trouble could this missing pail have caused? Its finding appears more important than mine.

"Now let me take you to your family."

She puts her arm tightly around my shoulder, and we weave our way through the horde. Somehow I sense reuniting with my mother will not go as easily as it did with Lucy. We edge around the outskirts of the people, alongside a road that leads to the stables. A helmet falls out of the hands of one of the boys scrambling by to tend to the horses. It lands with a thud and rolls to a stop at my feet.

Stooping down in midstep, I grab it and rise to hand it back to its owner and find myself face to face with Puck. The sight of my dear friend startles me. I want to throw my arms around him, but halt at the anger and hatred written all over his face.

"Oh Puck, I am so sorry!" I want to add more, to add the magic words that will make the hurt disappear from his face, change him back into my Puck. But he just fiercely yanks the helmet out of my hands and, spinning purposefully on his heels, stomps away.

"Puck, wait…" I plead after him to no avail.

It hits me then. No matter what, things will never be the same now. His whole image of who I am has been altered. He trusted me, and I betrayed him. And my ensuing adventure transformed my whole idea of life and what I want out of it. Puck's and my halcyon days of youth have passed and can never be duplicated, the last precious moments slipping by without ceremony. Cruel that no one was there to warn us what we were about to lose, so we may have savored the last of it. Though the crowd buzzes all around, I stand alone, crushed at this realization.

"There, there, Miss Livy," Lucy comforts. She strokes my hand, not comprehending the depth of awareness I have just experienced. "Give him time. Some wounds take longer to heal than others."

"What if it never heals?" I ask meekly.

Lucy starts to say something, but then thinks better of it. She simply defaults to her "time heals all wounds" adage, and she pulls me along to find my family.

Lydia sees me first, her little golden head darting in and out of legs in the moving sea of people. Screaming my name, she runs at me so fast she nearly knocks me flying when we collide. I bend, and she showers me with hugs and kisses all over my face. Then she proudly points, "Look! We even brought Midnight!"

And there is Ellen, wearing a smirk, holding the obviously displeased cat in her arms.

"He missed you ever so much!" Lydia avers.

"Oh yes, *ever so* much," Ellen chimes in sarcastically as the cat squirms and claws at her. "Now that he has seen Livy, let's have him go home." She moves to the edge of the crowd to release him. He races off more or less in the direction of our house. We laugh and Ellen throws her arms around me, sweetly whispering how much she missed me.

My mother and older sisters wait just behind them. Stony glares and haughty postures are my only greeting. I approach my mother and embrace her, but I receive a mere cool, quick hug in response.

"How are you, Olivia?" Her tone could transform a puddle to ice.

"Fine, Mother."

I brace myself for a reprimand, but she surprisingly says nothing more.

I notice Jayne, who stands next to her husband, Lord Davis. There is stark pity in her eyes. When we part after an awkward embrace, she just shakes her head as if at a total loss for words. Her husband regards me with outright contempt, which is not totally out of character for him. Ever since he found out that I trained with the squires, he treats me like I am a disgusting type of bug. Although they both clearly have negative opinions of my actions, they choose not to voice them at present.

Anne, however, who shudders like a volcano about to erupt, does voice hers.

"Mother, why don't you enlighten Olivia on the embarrassment and shame she has brought on Father and the rest of the family?"

And by this she surely means herself.

"Why don't you tell her how ridiculous her little stunt was? And for goodness sake look at her—hair chopped off, filthy with travel. Her behavior is despicable and disrespectful and…"

"That will do, Anne!" my mother snaps. "This is not the time or the place for such a discussion. Certainly the Davenports have more dignity than to air our dirty laundry in public for the fodder of all."

So that explains my mother's lack of reaction; she is saving it for the privacy of home.

Anne harrumphs loudly, but walks in step with the crowd, which now filters back into the center of the courtyard. Jayne and Lord Davis follow. My mother calls to Ellen, Lydia, and me, "Keep pace with me so we are not separated. We don't want to be late for the banquet."

"Banquet?"

Ellen fills in the blanks for me. "There is to be feasting in the entire city tonight. And the Queen is hosting a special banquet at the palace for some of the men and their families."

She goes on to say that my father is to be a guest of honor and some other such information, but my mind seizes on one thing: I *will* get to see Liam again tonight. Relief floods through every molecule of my body. Well, relief mixed with anxiety. At a celebration full of courtiers, how will I even get near him? My brow furrows.

Ellen and Lydia flank me, each taking a hand. "Are you sure you are all right?" Ellen asks, her quiet voice heavy with worry.

"Yes. I have a lot of fun stories to tell you," I whisper reassuringly to her. Lydia squeezes my hand in excitement. But we all know not to do or say anything that will incur the wrath of my mother, who has done an admirable job thus far stifling her anger, so we continue on in silence.

Suddenly, I feel rather conspicuous. Everyone else is dressed rather elegantly. I think of my chopped-off hair and travel-worn clothes. Not exactly banquet attire. It likely bothers Anne that somehow my embarrassing state will be a poor reflection on her. She, of course, is stunning, chestnut hair aglow around a gown of midnight blue. All the other single ladies in attendance will be just as eye-catching. And, they will all be fawning and preening for Liam's attention. We have only just returned, and already I will not be able to compete with the lovely ladies of the court in grace or style.

Will Liam come to his senses around all this beauty and figure out I am not what he wants after all?

I will soon find out, I suppose. We reach the main entrance to the palace just as dusk falls. For a moment, I contemplate telling my mother that I feel unwell and fatigued and would like to go home. But my urge to get just a glimpse of Liam outweighs my urge to run away. I clasp Ellen's and Lydia's hands tightly and proceed up the staircase.

We walk through the main entry hall, ceiling vaulting out of sight. A footman directs us through an arched doorway to a large, private courtyard. The aroma of fresh roasting meat saturates the air. Candles glimmer on tables and in wall sconces, their flames casting a luminous glow. Large tuns of ale are tapped, and mugs are passed out generously. Musicians and singers perform on small stages with happy revelers dancing around them. Jesters juggle and acrobats tumble on the steps of a grand staircase that leads up to a beautiful, canopied dais. There sits the royal family in a row behind a large table laden with numerous platters.

Liam sits next to his mother, holding her hand. Every few moments, he bends in to share a private word with her. Next to the Queen, the King sits front and center, enjoying his food and surveying the whole festival contentedly. He leans back and touches Queen Helen's arm affectionately.

Prince Harold sits next to his father, with his betrothed, the Lady Emily, at his side. She is practically in his lap and alternates between feeding him bits of food and clinging to his arm as if her life depended on it. For a second, I think she appears every bit the fool. That is, until I realize how thoroughly and completely envious I am of her. I want to be sitting next to Liam right now so much I can taste it. The sad truth, however, is that if I even tried to approach the table I would be stopped by the ever-present royal guards, and the ensuing scene would likely send my mother to an early grave.

My father finds us and leads us to a table in an enclosed area near the royal dais. The preferment of this seating arrangement, coupled with being reunited with my father, placates my mother. For now, she has something better to concentrate her attentions on than her anger at me. While my family eats and talks, I sit quietly on the end staring at Liam, but naturally, try to seem as though I am not staring at him. Amid these hundreds of people, I feel empty and alone.

Lydia comes over and lays a glass of warm mead in front of me. "Here, Livy, this is for you. You must be thirsty from your journey, so drink."

I force myself to smile at her, but Lydia, even at her tender age, can tell when something is wrong. "What is the matter, Livy? Aren't you glad to be home again?"

What can I possibly say that can make her, or anyone for that matter, understand? Now that my heart has chosen to love someone who will be forever out of my reach, home is now an ever-present reminder of what I can never have—or more accurately, what I had for the briefest of moments, the slightest of sips, only to have it wrenched away. And now I have to go on living with the knowledge of what I am missing every moment of every day until my last breath.

"Didn't you miss me?" Lydia asks, confused.

"Of course I did." I hug her quickly and bury my face in her golden curls, so no one can see the tears forming in my eyes.

A trumpeter's blare quiets the crowd. King William stands and addresses all assembled. "My dear citizens, thank you for joining us to celebrate this evening. I am thankful to tell you that all is well. You need not worry about an uprising in the North. Lindenwood has been defeated and will now be reinstated to the rule of Stewartsland."

Rousing applause and cheers ring out, echoing off the building. Lydia holds her ears against the deafening roar. King William raises his hands, and the clamor gradually fades to attentive silence.

"As some of you may have heard, I was taken captive and my life was threatened." Knowing how juicy news spreads like wildfire, I am sure that most have heard some version of this story already.

"I would like to take this opportunity to thank Sir Jack, who refused to leave my side and insisted on being held along with me. I am forever in his debt. My thanks to my men as well, who conducted themselves admirably and in accordance with their training. And to Prince Harold and Prince Stephan for the swift mobilization of soldiers they each brought to my aid. The army deserves much credit for their bravery and speed."

He raises his goblet to each; they nod back before taking a drink.

"Finally I have two people in particular I would like to personally thank. To Prince Liam—" he again raises his goblet to Liam, who is genuinely surprised at the acknowledgement, "—who came to my aid with an unexpected band of friends. He showed both true courage and savvy battle intelligence."

Of course, King William would never name Athos directly, but I wonder how many people already know to whom he refers. That would have been a most salacious item of gossip. The King drinks in salute with Liam.

"And last but most certainly not least, I would like to thank Miss Olivia Davenport." His eyes search my family's table and, finding me, he raises his glass.

My mother audibly gasps. Ellen nudges me to stand, which I do, conscious that all eyes are now focused in my direction. Boy, I wish I had been allowed a moment to make myself presentable.

"It is largely due to her bravery, her cunning, and her composure under difficult circumstances that I am here, alive and well with all of you today. Miss Davenport, you are a credit to your father and your family, and I intend to reward you in kind."

Ellen thrusts the mead into my hand and I curtsey to the King before taking a small sip. Someone starts clapping. It is Liam, and the whole crowd joins in applauding and cheering my name. Blushing, I curtsey again in thanks.

My mother appears as if she is about to faint dead away. Jayne, Lord Davis, and Anne all stare at me stupefied, mouths agape. But Ellen and Lydia clap loudly with broad smiles lighting their faces. And my father, beaming with pride, stands beside me and puts his arm around my shoulder. Despite my embarrassment at being singled out, my heart swells with pleasure at my part in the rescue being recognized.

"Now please, enjoy the rest of your evening and may God bless Stewartsland now and forever!" King William holds up his goblet one more time to the people, who shout out the sentiment again amid many cheers.

We settle back down at our table, where there is now a stunned silence. Apparently, my mother and sisters had expected my trip to have been the ultimate disaster, which my father would be dealing with for some months to come.

The fact that I had actually proved useful enough to have the King mention me was not a circumstance they were prepared for. And oddly, though I sense genuine pride from my father, Ellen, and Lydia, the impression I get from my mother and the rest is more one of annoyance that my misbehavior has been so rewarded.

Servants soon lay the table with all sorts of tantalizing foods, the smells of which are so overpowering, my head swims. Hot meat so juicy it falls off the bone. Soft, fresh-baked breads warm out of the oven, bursting with plump raisins and dates. Hard, aged cheese tasting both tangy and nutty accompanies grapes and berries. Sweet cakes and pies, all still steaming, served with fresh, sweet cream. After several days of not eating this quantity and quality of food, I am soon sated and quite drowsy. So much so, that I am having trouble maintaining my constant covert surveillance of Liam.

"Looks like we need to get you home after your big adventure, my sweet girl," my father whispers in my ear. My head lolls onto his shoulder like a rag doll's. I nod in agreement, a large yawn escaping from my mouth. Lydia is curled up with her head in his lap, finally spent with the day's excitement.

"Come now, let's be off," he orders to the table.

Everyone rises and gathers up their belongings. Courtesy dictates that before we can leave, we must say good-night to the royal party. When we step onto the greeting platform in front of the dais, Liam is not there. It feels like a knife has been twisted in my gut. All night, I tried to watch his every move, but my attention was diverted when we were making to depart. Why did he have to go missing at this of all moments?

"Good night, dear friends," Queen Helen says warmly to our bows and curtseys.

Whether it is my extreme fatigue or the crushing fact of Liam's absence, I am not sure, but I am suddenly overwhelmed with the desire to just lie down right here on the platform and sob. Lydia must sense my despair for she takes my hand in her small, steady one and gives it a squeeze. The expression on her tiny face tells me that she wishes she could make me feel better, but she doesn't know how. And there honestly is nothing she can do or say that will change the way things are. But I love her even more dearly for wanting to try.

We descend the staircase and backtrack through the palace, the festive atmosphere replaced by the stately silence of the royal hall. It takes my eyes a moment to adjust to the dimness. Lydia still clings to my hand, but she is so sleepy, it is like dragging a deadweight along with me. Anne, Jayne, and Lord Davis whisper amongst themselves, careful to avoid any contact with me.

Just as we arrive at the exit into the main city courtyard, a familiar figure steps out of the shadows into our path. My heart nearly stops beating at the sight of him.

Liam.

"Sir Jack," he says, extending his hand, "thank you again for your service to my family and your unwavering will in the protection of my father." My father bows, assuring Liam it is his most honored duty.

Liam then faces my startled mother, who manages the semblance of a curtsey. He raises her hand to his lips.

"And thanks to you, Mrs. Davenport, for abiding your husband's service to my father and my family. And also, if I may be so bold, may I compliment your daughter Olivia on

not only her bravery but her beauty—both inside and out."
He steps over and raises my hand for a kiss, with his sly
smile peeking through his lashes. My insides melt into liquid
warmth. Maybe it is time to stop doubting him.

My poor mother is doubly flustered. For one, Prince
Liam has acknowledged her, and for two, he bestowed
compliments on her daughter—the one daughter she feels is
more deserving of criticisms than compliments. She teeters
to my side, awkwardly pats my back, and stammers,
"Yes…yes…Olivia has always been…" Here words fail her.

"An amazing girl," Ellen pipes in.

"Yes, the most amazing!" Lydia agrees.

My mother nods, not in agreement, but because she is
so out of sorts. Jayne, Lord Davis, and Anne all watch in
disbelief, not uttering a word.

Liam, who still has not released my hand, says, "Well,
good night to you all. My sincere thanks again. I look
forward to the reward my father has planned for you, Olivia,
and don't forget *my* promise as well."

We share a knowing smile while the others stand
bewildered. Our eyes are locked as we each try to absorb
every last millisecond we can squeeze out of this moment.
Then, he is gone, and my family heads out of the castle
grounds and through the main city gate toward home.

The drowsiness I felt only a few minutes ago is now
replaced by a sense of weightlessness like walking on the
clouds. No one has spoken yet, which lengthens the
enchantment I am under. Father, clearly satisfied with how
everything has worked out, strolls contentedly. My mother
and her cohorts, struck silent by our royal encounter, walk
as if in a daze.

And then there is my precious Lydia. The meeting with the Prince invigorates her, and she dances and spins in delight up the path ahead of us. Suddenly, she stops and gasps as a thought enters her mind.

"Livy, I have the best idea. *You* should marry Prince Liam and then you can be a princess." She runs back to me to grab both my hands and jumps up and down with enthusiasm. "And then you could live happily ever after! Wouldn't that be wonderful?"

Wonderful? Yes.

And ironic, too. But even possible? I would not have thought so even up to a few moments ago, but now, after our encounter with Liam, it all seems perfectly tangible and attainable.

I gaze down into her expectant eyes. "Yes, Lydia, that would be wonderful."

She bounces away with a cry of delight and sings, "Princess Livy, Princess Livy..." while she twirls the rest of the way home.

"Did you see how good I am at riding? Even on the big horse? I think he liked me because he ate all my sugar cubes. I want to ride him again the next time."

Liam smiles at me over Lydia's endless chatter. After a morning of riding, we head over to the maze, a crisp autumn breeze gusting through at intervals. Trees are in full color now, bright pops of color painted against the clear, blue sky. They only add to the general splendor of the gardens. The ground is a carpet of vibrant leaves crunching underfoot. Large pumpkins, carved into the shapes of various animals and ghosts, decorate the walkways.

"How big is the maze? Have you ever found the center? How long does it take?"

"I can't tell you all the secrets. It will take the fun out of it," Liam replies.

Lydia scampers ahead, exploring every crevice of the royal grounds she can find, determined not to miss a thing. She hardly survived the three days' wait after the invitation arrived. Then again, I had trouble surviving them myself. All I could think of was Liam. I was worried his feelings may have waned, uncertain they were real.

One look in his eyes this morning showed me all fretting was needless. Without a spoken word, I understood the intensity and commitment in them. Good thing, because we have barely been able to get a word in edgewise with Lydia around.

"Thank you so much for this, Liam."

"Well, I did promise her. Remember?" He links his arm in mine. I watch the wind make the curls on his brow dance.

"Yes. I remember and she certainly did. I appreciate you keeping your word."

At the time he had promised, I did not have much hope this would ever come to pass. But I have come to know Liam is more than I ever expected.

We watch as Lydia hops on the rim of a koi pond, her blond curls bouncing like springs. She squeals when bright orange fish bob to the surface hoping for food. As always, Lydia finds pure delight in everything new she encounters.

"You will find I am good at keeping my word." His statement carries undertones about our future—a subject I have been fastidiously avoiding since it has my stomach in knots.

"She was extremely excited." I try to shift the subject back to Lydia. "She woke us all up at four this morning."

"Well, I hope she was not the only one excited," he hints.

"No, I was…quite looking forward to it as well," I manage, though I hear the strain in my voice.

"Well, that does not sound most convincing. What's wrong? Change your mind about me?" His carefree tone belies the concern in his eyes.

"No! Of course not. It just seems unlikely your parents will be as untroubled as you think," I mutter to the ground.

I do not equal his rank. I am not a suitable match. I would make a terrible princess and everyone knows it. These thoughts have been eating away at me ever since we returned from Lindenwood.

He takes my shoulders, pulls up my chin. "I have already made my intentions known to them, not that I was overly interested in what they had to say about this matter. I am happy to say, though, that they have agreed to let us pursue our relationship and will speak with your parents about it shortly."

"But what if they change…"

My protest is cut off by his kiss, a soft, lingering, melting kiss, which chases all doubts away. Liam can be most convincing.

We pull apart dizzily, smiling at each other, then glance over to find Lydia staring at us, her mouth agape. She is finally rendered speechless, for now at least. I am a bit speechless myself after Liam's news. It was beyond what I had ever hoped for.

"Look, the maze entrance is right there." Liam points a short distance ahead. Lydia comes out of her trance and sprints to the opening amidst the high hedgerows. The perfectly manicured bushes tower over her tiny form. She alternates between taking a few tentative steps inside and running back out, a golden blur against the evergreens.

"It is going to be next to impossible to keep her from blabbing about us kissing," I warn.

"So what? People better start getting used to the idea. Starting with you. By the way, have your parents decided if you can continue your training?"

I am deeply touched that he would ask me about this. "Actually, my father and I had some discussion about creating a new position for me where I will act as his assistant and help with the training of the younger boys. It is not everything I wanted, but I am determined to use the opportunity to prove to them I can be a full-fledged knight."

"Oh, I have no doubt that you will prove it exceedingly," he teases with a lopsided smile.

Before I can reply, Lydia races back to us and grabs Liam's hand. "C'mon. Hurry. You must show me the way to the center."

We quicken our pace to the entrance. Lydia has spent many hours imagining the moment she would be set loose in this labyrinth. She has conjured up all sorts of ideas about what lies within, from fairies to dragons. Hopefully, the reality will match up with her fantasy.

And, I realize, this is what I am wishing for as well. I hope the reality of falling in love with an actual prince will somehow compare to the mythical tales of love we all have heard a million times. It is an idea I would never have thought possible until Liam. Knowing he is so resolute about us calms me. After all, he knows his parents better than I. If he is so certain they will not disapprove, who am I to argue, and once they consent, my parents will have to agree. A wave of relief surges through me, my worries floating off on the breeze like the falling leaves. I feel as if I can finally concentrate on my future—my future with Liam.

"Lydia, let's play a game," Liam suggests. "Why don't I give you a one-minute head start to go in? Then Olivia and I will try to find you. Like hide-and-seek."

"Betcha I won't be so easy to catch." She plunges in, mischief in her eyes.

Liam wraps me in his arms. "I would never expect anything less from a Davenport girl."

"Oh, I think we can safely say you have caught one," I murmur, nuzzling his chin.

"And I plan on never letting go," he promises, leaning in for a kiss.

We share one more lingering moment. Then joining hands, we walk into the maze together.

About the Author

Jane McGarry cannot remember a time she did not love reading and this progressed into a passion for writing. She lives in New Jersey in a house full of boys including one over-indulged cat. In her rare quiet moments, she can be found curled up with said cat and a good book.

You can visit her online at janemcgarrybooks com

Also from Clean Reads:

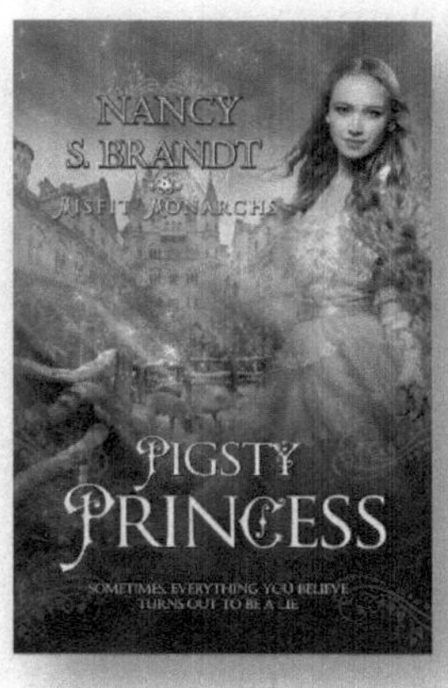

Chapter One

Progenna Mariana, fourth child of Queen Alexandria and King Jonathan of Valborough, watched the couples twirling around the dance floor. Beneath their feet, colored mosaics representing the eight magical elements danced as well, the patterns changing in time with the music.

The annual ball in celebration of the Queen's birthday was in full swing.

Mariana watched in delight as her brother, Cognate Prince Ramone, Heir Presumptive, danced with his wife, who would be delivering their first child within the next month. The white sash draped from Grand Sahdess Victoria's right shoulder to her left hip indicated Air Sensitivity and explained how she could be so light on her feet even with such an advanced pregnancy.

Mariana idly ran her fingertips along the fold of her own black satin sash, narrower than any the rest of the royal family wore. Traditionally, black was for children whose Sensitivities haven't manifested yet, or the rare Insensitive Commoner invited to royal celebrations.

The color of her sash shouldn't have bothered her anymore. Everyone in the kingdom knew Mariana had no Sensitivities. In fact, even her title, "Progenna," had been created especially for her. The title identified her as a daughter of the King and Queen, but also made it clear she had no magical abilities and, therefore, no place in the line of succession. She was, officially, a royal nobody.

The music from the quartet of stringed instruments stopped, and the couples paired up in two lines in the center of the floor for the next dance, a lively reel.

Mariana moved along the tapestry-covered walls toward the three sets of double doors that led to the balcony.

She had to find Darius, son and Heir Presumptive of Clarence, the Margrave of Sasoin. As Mariana surveyed the dance floor, she couldn't see Darius, who was known as the Rieravo of Sasoin, a title he inherited when his father's landholdings increased and the older man was given the higher title.

As one of the few still-unmarried Heir Presumptives of a high-ranking noble in the court, Darius had a partner for every dance of the evening. Mariana assumed he had to be out on the balcony getting some fresh air after all the dancing he'd done.

She and Darius had been an unofficial couple for some time now, and one more dance would make it official. Then, her father couldn't keep them from announcing their intent to wed. After all, a third dance at such an event was practically an engagement announcement all by itself.

As she passed by, guests bowed their heads and muttered greetings. However, she ignored them all, as she was only interested in finding Darius.

Suddenly, she was halted by a black wooden cane thrust horizontally in front of her. Its bearer was a short bald man with one eye, who smiled so wide at her his yellow chipped teeth were visible.

"Pir Leo," Mariana said, making a small curtsy of respect to the Sahdeer of Valentine, advisor to the King. "How nice to see you this evening."

"My dear Progenna Mariana, I have been hoping to dance with you." He grabbed her gloved hand and kissed it. As always, he lingered longer than was appropriate before releasing her. Marianna suppressed a shudder.

Pir Leo had been a figure in her life since she was a child. Because he was an expert in diplomacy and foreign relations, he was a frequent visitor to the palace and even at family gatherings. He had always frightened her.

The wealthy Fauna and Flora Sensitive, who was old enough to be her grandfather and not as tall as she was, had a puckered scar running from above his right ear, across his empty eye socket, nose, and left cheek, and down his neck to below the collar of his shirt.

"Thank you, Pir Leo," Mariana said with another small curtsy, "but this dance is promised to Darius Sasoin." He couldn't know she was stretching the truth a bit.

The lopsided smile on the elderly man's face disappeared, and she took an involuntary step back from the angry glint that sprang into his good eye.

"I didn't realize the King had given permission for your relationship with the Rieravo of Sasoin to become public at the Queen's birthday celebration."

Mariana scowled and interrupted him. "I was not aware that your counsel with my father had extended to family matters. Who I dance with and how often is none of your business. Now, if you will excuse me, I believe our conversation is at an end."

"Of course, Progenna." The man bowed as protocol demanded, but he never took his eye off her face, giving her the sensation someone had slipped ice down the back of her gown.

She spun away from him, and unfortunately, the path to the balcony as well. She decided to slip into the ladies' dressing room to give herself a chance to calm down.

The first time Mariana saw the Sahdeer, she was about four years old, and his appearance had terrified her. She'd run into the butler's pantry and hidden behind a barrel of apples until her mother found her at bedtime.

Years later, when Mariana was ten, the Queen had explained he'd gotten the injury when his whiskey distillery had exploded and four employees had been killed. It wasn't until Mariana was sixteen that she discovered the accident had been his fault for using inferior materials and working his employees for days without a break.

In retaliation for that accident, the father of two boys who'd died confronted Valentine in an alley near the distillery and cut off the Sahdeer's left hand, leaving a stump that was now covered by a custom-made velvet and lace cap.

The dressing room was empty when Mariana entered, so she splashed some water on her face and adjusted the jewels in her hair. Those small routine behaviors returned her to a sense of normalcy. She left the dressing room with her head held high and all thoughts of Pir Leo dismissed from her mind.

"Progenna?" A tall, slender man with skin the color of the rich chocolate her mother imported from her home country of Poole stepped in front of her before she got halfway across the ballroom, blocking her view of the balcony.

"Fredrick." Mariana curtsied. "I'm afraid I'm in a bit of a hurry."

Fredrick, the Margrave of Mindenwall, was her brother's head of household. His father, the Sahdeer of Mindenwall, was an important member of the House of Pirs, a branch of the government that oversaw legal matters of landownership and inheritance. As such, he often came to the palace, and Frederick and his brother and sister practically grew up with the royal children. In many ways, Frederick was more like an annoying older brother to Mariana than one of her brother's servants.

He sighed. "I assume you're looking for Darius. Do you think a third dance with him would be wise this evening? I'm sure you don't want to take the spotlight from the Queen."

"Have you been watching who I dance with, Margrave?" The use of his formal title, and hiding her smile behind her fan was the kind of flirtatious act her sister Ursula would employ to take a man's mind off an unpleasant subject. "I had no idea of your interest."

Frederick straightened his spine. He stood about half a hand taller than she was, but his proud manner made her feel much smaller.

His brown eyes grew darker as they met hers. "Mariana, you are like a sister to me, and I don't want to see you get hurt. Perhaps it would be better for you to find a different dance partner." He studied the crowd. "I'm sure Vishah Purchon would be happy to dance the next set with you."

Marian bit back a growl. "Vishah Purchon? He owns no land and from what I hear has many gambling debts. Why is it better that I dance with someone with no prospects than with the son of a Margrave?"

Frederick raised a single eyebrow. "It's only a dance, Progenna. Purchon may have little money and no land, but from what I hear, he can be an amusing dance partner. I'm sure your parents would like to see you enjoying yourself on the dance floor."

"Why does everyone in the kingdom think they can dictate who I dance with?" She tried to push by him, but he stopped her with a gentle hand on her shoulder.

"Someday, your brother will be King, and who you spend time with in public will be of extreme importance. You would do well to choose more wisely."

She glared at him, wishing she didn't have to tilt her head up to do so.

"Darius is the eldest son and Heir Presumptive of a Margrave," Mariana said. "He is entirely suitable as a husband, especially since I will never be in line for the throne. Of course, he hasn't officially asked for my hand yet." She added the last bit for the benefit of anyone eavesdropping. The ballroom was filled with Air Sensitives, who could, potentially, listen in to the slightest whispers even from the other side of the room.

"There is more to suitability than birth status," Fredrick said. He took her arm as the music changed again to a waltz. "If you are not interested in dancing with Purchon, perhaps you would do me the honor?"

Mariana wrenched her arm out of his hand. "No. I have no intention of dancing with you. Don't you have some woman more suitable to court?"

"I am not considering marriage to anyone at the moment. I serve at the pleasure of the Cognate Prince, and right now, I am trying to keep you from making a mistake that could cause embarrassment to the throne."

"What kind of embarrassment?" Mariana narrowed her eyes. "Surely, you don't believe the court gossip about what the unmarried Presumptives do when they go into town."

Frederick blinked in surprise, and Mariana raised her eyebrows.

"You didn't think I'd heard it?" She shook her head. "I am not a child anymore, Frederick, but you would be surprised at how many people forget that. Apparently, it is easy to ignore an Insensitive. People talk much more freely around me than perhaps they should."

"What have you heard?"

With a sigh, Mariana took a glass of champagne from a passing waiter. "Just disgusting speculation about what Darius and his friends do at the taverns at night. Dice, card games, and lots of drinking." She shrugged. "I don't see how any of this affects me."

His eyes flicked to the people around them, and she followed his gaze. Several of the lesser nobles of the court had stopped their own conversations and were not hiding their interest in Mariana and Frederick's.

"Let's continue this somewhere a little more private," Frederick said and took her arm.

She pulled away. "No, let's not. I understand you are concerned but I questioned Darius...the Rieravo." She met the eyes of the eavesdroppers. As she expected, most had the good sense to look chagrined and turn back to their companions.

"What did he tell you?" Frederick asked.

"He said some of the other Presumptives and younger sons enjoyed spending time with serving wenches and other women who...ply their trade at night."

"And does the Rieravo of Mindenwall take part...I mean, approve of this?"

She shrugged. He hadn't answered her when she asked that question, but she couldn't tell that to Frederick.

"He doesn't do that sort of thing." Mariana couldn't meet his eyes, so she found a spot of lace on her sleeve hem that needed her attention.

Frederick shook his head. "He's out on the balcony, Progenna, but he's not alone. There are two women with him. He may not be interested in shop clerks or tavern wenches, but there are commoners at court as well."

Mariana's heart began to beat so loudly she wondered, briefly, if Air or even Water Sensitives would hear it. "Only maids or those in the kitchen. Surely you don't believe he would dally with the likes of them when he is practically promised to a daughter of the King?" She raised her head proudly.

"Promised, Progenna? Has there been an understanding?"

Everyone knew there hadn't been one. Mariana clenched her jaw. Why was she letting him get to her like this? He might be Ramone's Head of Household, but he had no say over her life.

"I am going to the balcony to get some fresh air," she said, dropping into a curtsy. "It has suddenly become quite stuffy in here."

Frederick did not bow, meaning he did not consider their conversation finished. "Progenna, I am only thinking of your welfare. The women with Darius are both daughters of minor nobles, with weak Sensitivities. I heard their laughter and some of their conversation. I promise you, you do not want to go out there. I would hate to see you humiliated."

She bit back any response, for to answer him would mean he had the upper hand in this situation. She excused herself and brushed past him toward the curtained glass doors that led to the balcony.

Once outside, the chill night air drifted through Mariana's light gown, and she shivered. No one else seemed to be out here, and she sighed in relief. Frederick was wrong. If Darius had been here, with or without companionship, he had probably gone back to the party through a different door.

As she turned to leave, she heard a deep chuckle coming from behind a row of tall potted rose bushes, heavy with enormous blooms. The male laughter was followed by a high feminine giggle.

Curious, Mariana followed the sound and stepped through the natural, fragrant, spicy curtain of Alexandria lilies, named for her mother.

The sight that greeted her caused her thoughts to freeze, and suddenly, her feet seemed glued to the spot.

Darius was, indeed, on the balcony, and, as Fredrick had said, he wasn't alone. He sat on a stone bench with a woman on either side of him.

The woman on his left was Nicoletta, one of the Royal Princess's ladies-in-waiting. Her blonde hair, which had been carefully arranged by Liliana's own maid, was in disarray. That state was probably because Darius had his hand in her hair and had pulled her head toward his. Their lips were firmly pressed together. The second woman had her head on his shoulder.

"Darius?" Mariana's voice sounded calmer than she expected, given her heart was racing.

The man in question lifted his head from Nicoletta's mouth to look at the Progenna, but other than that, he didn't move.

Both women, however, gasped and tried to compose themselves.

"Mariana," Darius said, scowling. "What are you doing here?"

"I…what's going on?"

"It's none of your business," he said. "Why don't you go back inside and dance with some foppish penniless fool who will be content to sit near you without touching?"

"What does that mean?" She stared at Nicoletta. "Will you compose yourself? At least for the time being, you still serve the Royal Princess."

The woman bit her lip and spoke to Darius. "I should go. I cannot afford to lose this position."

He shook his head slightly. "Don't worry about it, Nico. She won't fire you."

"You dare to speak for my sister?" Mariana said, looking at him.

He nudged his other companion off the bench. She rushed to the balcony railing, avoiding Mariana's eyes and refastening her bodice buttons.

"Why would the Royal Princess fire Nicoletta?" Darius asked, putting his arm around the distressed lady-in-waiting. "Are you going to tell your sister that she was kissing me?"

"I should." The ground seemed to sway beneath Mariana's feet, and she grasped a nearby column for support. Something in his voice caused her to tremble. He'd never spoken to her so coldly, without a trace of the affection he'd shown her in the past.

Darius continued, "Will you also tell the Queen and Royal Princess I need to kiss other women because you're afraid to let me touch you?"

"I'm not afraid." Mariana straightened her back and lifted her chin, wishing she were taller. "It just isn't proper to engage in…those kinds of activities before we're officially engaged."

To her chagrin, he burst into laughter. "I'm sorry, Mari, but can you be that naïve? 'Those kinds of activities,' as you call them, are part of an adult relationship. You need to wake up and accept this."

She swallowed. "Then come back to the ballroom and dance with me again."

He shook his head. "I like you, Mari, but I'm not going to marry you. I can't afford to bond with a commoner."

"Commoner? What are you talking about?"

"Mari, you can stop pretending. Everyone in the kingdom knows you're not the King's daughter by blood. How else do you explain your Insensitivity?"

Mariana felt as though her bones had liquefied. With great effort, she stayed upright until she found a nearby bench and dropped to it. The two other women rushed away, giving her sidelong glances as they passed. "Why would you say these things to me? I thought you had feelings for me. Real feelings."

"I did. " He sat next to her and took her hand. "I was young. I thought your deficiencies wouldn't matter, but I'm a Metal Sensitive, and I need to wed someone who can complement my Abilities. I have to think about my inheritance."

He stared into the night on the other side of the balcony railing. Mariana wondered what he was seeing.

"I can use my abilities to strengthen the defenses of Sasoin. Maybe one day, I can add to our holdings. My sisters will need property to take to their own marriages, unless they wed above their stations."

"My father will give me property." Her argument was weak, for while Liliana had gotten a large estate, she was the Royal Princess and second in line for the throne until Grand Duchess Victoria delivered her child. Liliana's husband, Nigel, had been of high noble blood, his father an Amar, a cousin of her grandfather.

Darius shook his head. "I cannot count on that, and there is still the issue of the Bonding. Face it, Mariana, I need to do better."

Clean Reads
GREAT STORIES. NO GUILT.
www.cleanreads.com

www.ingramcontent.com/pod-product-compliance
Lightning Source LLC
Chambersburg PA
CBHW061656190726
48289CB00006B/1893